MURDER ON A MIDNIGHT CLEAR

MURDER ON A MIDNIGHT CLEAR

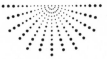

SARA ROSETT

MURDER ON A MIDNIGHT CLEAR

A 1920s Christmas Mystery

Book Six in the High Society Lady Detective series

Published by McGuffin Ink

ISBN: 978-1-950054-35-0

Copyright © 2020 by Sara Rosett

Book cover design by ebooklaunch.com

Editing: Historical Editorial

❀ Created with Vellum

CHAPTER ONE

21 DECEMBER 1923

*D*espite the gray clouds hanging low over London, the city sparkled with Christmas cheer. Boughs of evergreen, glittering tinsel, and sprigs of holly decorated the storefronts as I made my way along the pavement in the bustle of holiday shoppers. The aroma of roasting chestnuts wafted through the air as I waited for a gap in the traffic before crossing the street, my breath making little white puffs that the sharp wind whisked away.

My mood didn't quite match the jolly atmosphere. I was frustrated with a case. I'd been on the hunt for information for days, but I'd discovered absolutely nothing. The Baroque edifice of Harrods came into view, and I made an effort to shake off my irritation. I was meeting my cousin Gwen for afternoon tea and Christmas shopping. I'd seen her so rarely since her engagement that I didn't want my crossness to set the tone for our time together.

I passed a row of children with their noses pressed to the glass outside the store. Harrods' elaborate window display was set up to look like a fashionable drawing room, complete with a fully decorated Christmas tree and Saint Nick emerging from the fireplace, his bag of toys on his back.

I was early, so I threaded through the shoppers to the Food Hall with its colorful tile roundels. Peacocks, fruit trees, and medieval hunting scenes decorated the ceiling and walls. The array of food was rather dizzying, especially considering that I'd passed a soup kitchen on my walk to the department store. Stacks of fruit and vegetables were arranged in brightly colored pyramids. Rows of fresh bread dusted with flour sent out a warm yeasty aroma. Meat, cheeses, eggs, and chocolate all had their own areas and tempted me with elaborate displays. A few months before, I wouldn't have been able to afford more than a few buns. Today I had funds in my bank account, but I couldn't bring myself to buy anything but essentials since I was already splurging on afternoon tea with Gwen. I ordered tins of Earl Grey and Darjeeling at the tea counter and arranged to pick them up later.

"Olive!"

I spotted Gwen moving through the throng, her blonde curls peeping from under the brim of her pale blue cloche. "It's wonderful to see you," she said as we brushed cheeks. "I've missed you. I have so much to tell you."

"I can't wait to hear it."

"But I'm famished. Tea first?"

"I couldn't agree more."

We went up to the Georgian, and once we were seated

and had ordered, I said, "First, I want to hear all about your visit with Inspector Longley's parents."

"You must call him Lucas, you know," Gwen said.

"It will be difficult, but I'll try." I'd met Longley during a murder investigation at Archly Manor. It was hard for me to think of him as anything but an inspector. His Christian name seemed to lodge in my throat, but surely with practice it would become natural to refer to him as Lucas. "How was the visit with *Lucas'* parents?"

"It went quite well. They're charming and were very welcoming."

"I'm so glad, but I expected nothing less." Gwen was one of the sweetest people I knew. She had a warm disposition, and I couldn't imagine someone being disappointed with her as a daughter-in-law. "And Mr. and Mrs. Longley will be at Parkview for Christmas?"

"Yes, and you really must come up before Christmas Eve."

"Oh, no. I don't think so. Your families are still becoming acquainted. The visit is a time for Mr. and Mrs. Longley to get to know Aunt Caroline and Uncle Leo. I don't want to intrude on that."

"You're not intruding. You're family."

"That's kind of you, and I do appreciate it, but I still have a few things to take care of here. And I'm quite happy in my little flat. It's wonderful to have a space of my own." As much as I'd liked my former landlady at the boarding house, having my own space was splendid. "I'll arrive at Parkview on Christmas Eve, just as we planned."

"Have you heard from your father?" Gwen asked as our tea arrived. "It's definite he and Sonia won't be back before Christmas?"

"I had a letter from Sonia. They arrived and are settled

into their *pensione*. It's cooler there than they expected but much drier than Nether Woodsmoor, so they're quite happy with the arrangement."

"How long do they expect to stay?"

"At least until after the New Year. Sonia isn't one to take chances with Father's health."

"It's a shame they won't have an English Christmas, but I suppose the arrangement is for the best."

"When it comes to Father's health, I completely defer to Sonia, even though I will miss them." My father had had a bad health scare a while back, and Sonia had nursed him through it. When he developed a cough a few weeks ago at the beginning of December, Sonia had declared she didn't like the sound of his rattly breathing. She'd decided they had to depart for a warmer, drier climate, and she'd packed and made arrangements to leave immediately.

"I don't see why you won't come down to Parkview earlier. What's holding you here in London? You don't have a case, do you?"

I hesitated, and Gwen, who had been choosing between the smoked salmon sandwich and the watercress, looked up and studied my face. "You *do* have a case."

"Only one of my own making."

Gwen selected the smoked salmon and tilted her head. "What does that mean?"

"Well . . . it's something that I'm curious about, so I'm looking into it."

Gwen paused, the sandwich suspended in midair. "You're not still chasing about after Jasper, are you?"

It was no use dissembling to someone you had known since you were in a pram. "Yes, in fact I am."

Gwen placed her sandwich on her plate with great

care. "I don't think it's a good idea, following Jasper. I'm sure he's just doing his normal things."

"What do you mean?"

"Oh, you know." Gwen waved a hand. "Attending art shows, going to his club, and making up numbers at dinner parties—that sort of thing."

I gave my attention to stirring another lump of sugar into my tea. I couldn't reply because that was exactly what Jasper had been doing. Except for repeatedly using the Gloucester Road tube station, I couldn't detect anything unusual in his actions. But I wasn't about to give up.

My face must have given away my intentions because Gwen said, "Olive, if Jasper is 'up to something,' as you call it, he'll tell you about it . . . eventually."

"Will he?" The teaspoon jangled against the saucer as I put it down. "When has he shared details of his little trips out of London?"

"He told Essie about the hunt he attended. She wrote it up in her column."

"But those were only a few tidbits about what other guests were doing. Jasper doesn't share what *he* does in any detail."

"Have you asked him where he goes when he disappears?"

"Yes. And he always makes some vague comment or changes the subject."

"He's a private person."

"He's being secretive."

"Jasper has always been one to play his cards close to the vest."

"Yes, but after the Winter Ball, I thought—" I stopped, unable to put into words what I'd hoped. Jasper and I had shared a delightful kiss. In fact, it had been more than delightful. It had changed everything between us. At least, I thought it had. We were sweethearts now. I thought that would mean he'd share more with me, but my questions and queries had been left unanswered.

"Lucas doesn't tell me everything about his cases."

"Yes, but that's his work. He can't share all the details about his investigations with you. And I'm sure he does take you into his confidence, at least in a general way."

"That's true. He says I give him a different perspective." Gwen's expression softened as it always did when she spoke about her fiancé.

I floated an idea that had been in the back of my mind for a while. "Perhaps it's the same with Jasper."

Gwen's eyebrows came together in a frown. "What do you mean?"

"Perhaps the situation with Jasper is that he can't speak about what he does."

Gwen burst out laughing. A dowager at a nearby table slowly turned her head and scowled at us. Gwen cleared her throat and sat up straighter. "Whatever can you mean? Jasper doesn't *do* anything."

The waiter arrived with a fresh pot of tea, and I bit back my response. Jasper didn't go into an office each day, but several small details had made me question if he had some sort of . . . unusual employment. His constant disappearances and the lack of details about his trips out of London were two factors that had prompted the idea. He'd been quite valuable to me over the last few months when my cases had become complicated by murders. He'd put his knowledge down to his love of crime fiction, but I wondered if there were something else there. Everyone seemed to think he did nothing but lounge about his club all day and attend high society events, but I knew he was clever—much cleverer than he let on.

The waiter refreshed our tea, and Gwen reached for a scone. "Well, I know better than to try to dissuade you. You'll press on with your own agenda as you always do. Just don't complain to me if he finds out what you've been doing, and he's angry with you."

CHAPTER TWO

*T*he strains of "When Hearts Were Young" filled the air of the Blue Moon Club as I circled the dance floor in Jasper's arms. "Enjoying yourself tonight, old bean?" Jasper asked as he swept us into a turn.

"I'm having a lovely time." Jasper was an excellent dancer. We floated along, swirling through the throng.

"Your Christmas shopping expedition was successful?"

"Very. Gwen and I spent hours in Harrods. My shopping is done. How was your day?"

"Nothing nearly as pleasant as that. The same as usual."

Since I'd spent the morning following him, I knew he was speaking the truth. Before I met Gwen at Harrods, I'd shadowed Jasper as he went to his tailor, then his club. A guilty feeling curled through me, but I pushed it down. I merely wanted to know if Jasper was keeping something from me. Surely a girl had a right to know that about her sweetheart? "What are your plans for Christmas?" I asked. "Will you go up to Haverhill?"

"Yes, I'll look in on the *pater* on my way to Parkview."

"And have you found a gift for him?"

"No. Father prefers not to indulge in festivities."

"What do you mean?"

"We don't exchange gifts."

I was so surprised that I forgot to move with the music and came to a halt. "No presents?"

Jasper swung us back into the dance. "No. And no tree or Christmas dinner."

"Whyever not?"

He focused his gaze across the dance floor. "No idea. Father has always been like that. He sees no need for it, he says."

"No need to celebrate one of the most important Christian holidays of the year?"

Jasper lifted a shoulder. "He's not one to have his edicts questioned." He smiled suddenly. "You can imagine how wonderful my first Christmas at Parkview was. Quite a revelation for a small boy."

"One's mind truly boggles." Being the daughter of a former vicar, my life had been steeped in religious holidays as well as all the secular trappings, including everything from Christmas trees to crackers.

"It was like a storybook come to life—and not one of those horrible dark fairy tales. This story was full of mulled wine, caroling, sledding, and presents."

"As the holidays should be." A spark of anger flared inside me at Jasper's father. Why deprive a boy of the joys of Christmas? "I'm awfully glad Peter invited you to spend the school holidays with him at Parkview."

"I am too." His gaze locked with mine, and that spark of anger shifted, blooming into a warm feeling toward Jasper. He pulled me closer and rested his chin against my hair. We didn't say anything else for the rest of the dance.

The music ended, and we pulled apart reluctantly. As I

led the way through the couples leaving the dance floor, a petite woman with dark hair rushed up to me. "Olive!"

"Gigi, I didn't know you were in town."

"Christmas shopping, darling. Only here for a day. Hello, Jasper. Topping to see you." She linked her arm through mine and walked with us back to our tiny linen-draped table at the edge of the dance floor. "You must come and see Bascomb Hall. I'm being frightfully domestic there—actually supervising the renovations. I'm leaving at a horribly uncivilized hour tomorrow morning —the first train, if you can believe it—because I must be there to direct the new workmen who are arriving to see to the plumbing."

Jasper signaled for another chair. "And how are the renovations going?"

"Swimmingly. I know, I'm shocked too. Who would have thought I'd enjoy it? It's simply fascinating to tear things out. You never know what you'll find."

"Are you doing any of this removal?" I asked.

"Don't be silly. I'm supervising, darling. But the wallpaper! Layers and layers of it. Some of it's so ghastly that I find it rather fascinating. Anyway, do say you'll come see it, Olive. I suppose you're going to Parkview for Christmas?" She didn't give me time to answer. "Do drop in on your way there. Stop by and have tea. It's on your way— well, practically. You can see Mr. Quigley's new home. The conservatory is the single place in the whole house that doesn't require a renovation. He's quite enjoying it."

"I'd love to."

"Brilliant." She glanced over my shoulder. "I must fly. Cheerio, darlings."

The waiter arrived with another chair, but Jasper waved him off. "No need now. Sorry, old chap."

I took a seat as Jasper held my chair. "Gigi always is a whirlwind."

"More like a typhoon. Well, old bean, what's it to be? Another drink? Another club? Or are you ready to toddle on home?"

"It's been a lovely evening, but I still have quite a few things to do tomorrow. I'm ready to return to my little flat."

In the taxi, Jasper ran his arm along the back of the seat behind my shoulders. "Perhaps we should have tea tomorrow at the Savoy for a change?"

I snuggled into his shoulder, inhaling his citrus aftershave. "I look forward to it."

At South Regent Mansions, he told the driver to wait while he escorted me inside. We paused under the lobby's crystal chandelier. He kissed my hand and gave me a look that said he would like to do more but wouldn't since the hall porter sat at his desk in the little alcove watching us.

I took the lift to my flat and let myself in. I drew the curtains over the big window in the sitting room, lit the fire, and made a cup of tea. I changed into a dressing gown, then settled into the club chair in the sitting room, kicked off my shoes, and tucked my feet up under me.

I picked up a book I'd purchased at Harrods, but I couldn't get lost in the story. My thoughts kept wandering back to what Jasper had said about his father's attitude toward Christmas. Jasper hardly ever spoke of his family.

I only knew that his father had been a civil servant in India. Jasper had been born there, and his mother had died when he was young. He'd been sent back to England for school, and Jasper had never returned to India. His father had stayed there until his retirement, then he'd returned to England and now lived at Haverhill Hall.

Jasper visited his father occasionally, but he was always extremely reticent on the subject. He'd told me tonight more than he ever had, small amount that it was. I could practically hear Gwen's voice in my head counseling patience. Perhaps she was right. If I waited, Jasper would eventually share more with me.

I finished my tea and prepared for bed, resolved to be less nosy and more patient.

$\sim$

22 DECEMBER 1923

Habit is a hard beast to shake. I awoke the next morning, prepared for the day, then left my flat, and my feet moved automatically to the tea shop that had been my recent morning haunt. It wasn't that far from South Regent Mansions, and it afforded an excellent view of the building where Jasper had rooms. On the first frigid December morning I'd decided to watch Jasper, I'd taken up my vigil outside his building, but my fingers and toes were numb within a quarter-hour. I'd taken refuge inside the tea shop and discovered they served a delicious Chelsea bun.

I'd just popped the last warm bite of the bread dotted with currants, sprinkled with cinnamon, and layered in a light glaze into my mouth when Jasper emerged from his building and trotted down the stairs. I swallowed the bite and checked my watch. This was the earliest I'd ever seen him appear. Instead of turning right at the foot of the stairs, which was his usual routine, he turned left and came toward me. I ducked my head as if I were reading the folded newspaper that lay on the table, open to an article about two lawn tennis stars who were engaged. Out of the corner of my eye, I saw Jasper pass the tea shop, his pace a notch faster than his usual leisurely stroll.

He moved out of my sight, and I sat for a moment, my finger tapping away on the rim of my teacup. *Patience*, I mentally lectured myself. *Wait and see.*

I made it another half a minute, then I couldn't stand it any longer. Patience had never been a virtue I excelled in. I put coins down on the table and hurried out the door.

A chilly wind whipped along the street. The day was sparkling bright, the sunlight glinting on windowpanes and highlighting every bare tree branch that danced in the wind. I pulled the lapels of my coat closer and angled my head down as I paced into the breeze, glad I'd used two hatpins to anchor my cloche today. I stayed well back. Jasper's tall form with his wavy fair hair showing under his fedora was easy to keep in sight.

When he paused at a street corner and glanced around as he waited, I became immersed in studying the wares at a grocer's stand. I hoped I looked like a woman who was debating which potatoes were the best to select. I was wearing my warmest coat along with the plainest hat I owned. It was a drab brown color, and I'd contemplated handing it over to the rag and bone man, but my days of scrimping to make ends meet weren't that far in the past. I couldn't bring myself to give away a useful item, no matter how unfashionable. I hoped my unremarkable ensemble meant that Jasper's gaze would pass over me without stopping.

I dodged along after him in fits and starts, skirting around Hyde Park to South Kensington. Finally, Jasper crossed the street and disappeared into the Gloucester Road tube station. This was the third time he'd gone to this particular tube station. Each time I'd followed him, he'd taken a different route through London's streets, but every time he'd gone to the station at Gloucester Road.

Two women, probably housewives intent on completing their holiday shopping, were heading for the entrance. I fell into step behind them. When I reached the platform, I stayed near the women, making sure they were between Jasper and me. As before, Jasper waited at the far end of the platform. He looked out across the tracks, one hand braced on his silver-topped walking stick.

A draft of air stirred his heavy gray overcoat as the train swept into the station. I went up on my tiptoes so I could see over the women's hats. The doors opened, and people flooded onto the platform. A man who was familiar to me from my other jaunts of trailing along after Jasper left the train. He wore a black overcoat and trilby and had a fan-shaped mustache. He paused beside Jasper, seemingly caught up in the bottleneck as the two currents of people, one moving out of the train and the other moving into it, met and swirled together, then separated.

I couldn't be sure, but it didn't look as if the two men spoke to each other. Just as they'd done during the previous times, Jasper shifted with the throng on the plat-form and merged with the group heading for the tube's exit. The other times I'd followed Jasper, he'd always left the station and taken a meandering route back across London to his flat. This time I kept an eye on the man with the mustache. He walked along the platform and reboarded the train.

I made a snap decision and stepped into the compart-ment moments before it departed. I moved away from the man to the opposite end of the carriage. He'd taken out a newspaper. The image of the slender, golden-haired actress Bebe Ravenna smiled out from the page. The photographer had caught her as she waved to the crowd before entering a London theater. I wondered if Jasper knew she was in town. In the past, he'd often been her escort, and I'd seen plenty of gossip column photos of the two of them together.

The carriage swayed, and I reached out to steady myself as the tube eased to a halt at the next station. The man with the mustache left the train. I hung back and let several people exit before I followed him. I kept his trilby in sight as he moved out to South Kensington. I thought he was headed for the Victoria and Albert or the Natural History Museum, but he turned and made his way up Cromwell Road.

I tucked my chin and trudged along after him. If we kept walking in this direction, we'd arrive back at the Gloucester Road station. Was the man simply moving in a circle? If he were out for a stroll—a mad idea on such a cold, windy day—then I might as well leave off and return home. But then he jogged up the stairs and went inside a building with a black door and no nameplate.

As I lingered, the cold air surging around me, another man approached the black door. Dressed in a tailored wool overcoat and bowler hat, he appeared to be a businessman. He used his walking stick as he climbed the steps more slowly, then he went inside without using a key. So it must be a business of some sort. I gave the man a lead of a few minutes, then followed.

The door opened into a small empty foyer. A staircase with a worn runner faced the door. A metal plate with slots for businesses to insert cards bearing their names was fastened to the wall by the stairs. Most of the slots were empty. Those that had paper were of such an antique look that I decided the board probably wasn't an accurate reflection of the current tenants. It was a rather large building. I couldn't knock at every door asking if a gentleman with a mustache who wore a black trilby was employed there. And what would I say if I should track him down? *Why have you been on the train platform at the same time as Jasper Rimington on several occasions?* I sighed and left.

I arrived back at South Regent Mansions weighted down with wrapping paper and ribbon. I'd decided to finish my last Christmas errands on my way back to my flat. The hall porter took my packages and handed me an envelope. "This arrived for you a half-hour ago, Miss Belgrave."

"Thank you." I recognized Jasper's neat handwriting. Upstairs in my flat, I had the porter deposit my shopping on the sofa. As soon as he'd left, I tore open the letter.

Dear Olive,

I'm terribly sorry, but I won't be able to escort you to the Savoy for tea today. An urgent matter has come up, and I must depart London immediately.

I hope to have it sorted quickly. I look forward to seeing you at Parkview on Christmas Eve—where I hope Gwen has decked the halls with an abundance of mistletoe. Until then . . .

Very sincerely yours,
Jasper

CHAPTER THREE

I stripped off my gloves but didn't bother to take off my coat or hat. I went directly to my desk and rang up Jasper.

"Hello?"

I hesitated because a woman answered. The operator must have crossed the lines. "I'm sorry. I was trying to reach the residence of Jasper Rimington."

"This is Mr. Rimington's. May I take a message?"

"Oh—" I wasn't sure what to say. When I'd telephoned in the past, Jasper or his manservant, Grigsby, had answered the telephone at his flat.

The woman must have sensed my confusion because she said, "I clean for him. Twice a week I come in."

"I see. I was hoping to speak to Mr. Rimington, but it sounds as if he's not in?"

"That's right. You just missed him. He and Mr. Grigsby lit out of here so quick that Mr. Rimington hardly had time to say hello to me. And he always takes time to talk with me and ask after my family. He's a proper gentleman."

SARA ROSETT

"I suppose he's gone up to Haverhill earlier than expected." My uncharitable thoughts about Jasper's father popped into my head. "I hope it wasn't bad news from his family that's caused him to leave so abruptly."

"Oh no, miss. He didn't go to Haverhill. It was another place—what was it? Oh yes, Holly Hill Lodge. I liked the name of it. Musical, it was."

"I see," I murmured, although I was far from understanding why Jasper had left so suddenly. I supposed it was a country estate, but I'd never heard of it.

"Is there a message, miss?"

"No. No message." I thanked her and rang off.

I put down the phone and reached for my gloves. I needed a map.

∼

AN HOUR AND A HALF LATER, I was motoring out of London. I'd made a quick trip to a nearby book shop that stocked a nice selection of reference books and maps. I'd discovered that Holly Hill Lodge was located only an hour's drive from London. I was even more delighted to see it was a few miles away from Gigi's new home, Bascomb Hall.

After my visit to the book shop, I'd returned to my flat and made two telephone calls. I'd confirmed that Gigi had indeed returned to her new home that morning. She was thrilled with the idea of me dropping by to see the progress of the renovations that very afternoon. "I just arrived in from London," she'd said. "And yes, do come for luncheon. The house seems rather quiet after town, and we didn't have the opportunity to chat at all."

I'd made a second telephone call to the garage where I

20

stored my dear little Morris Cowley and asked them to have it brought around to South Regent Mansions. I packed my case with my Christmas finery and had the porter stow it along with the presents and wrapping paper in the motor. I'd purchased gifts for Aunt Caroline, Uncle Leo, and my cousins, as well as Father and Sonia. I'd leave the presents for Father and Sonia at Tate House so they'd find them when they arrived back from Italy.

I headed out of London bundled in my coat, gloves, two scarves, and my warmest boots. The day was still clear, but I was driving north, directly toward a bank of dark clouds on the horizon that indicated the weather might change. There were only a few hours of daylight left, but I knew I could make it to Bascomb Hall before one o'clock. My plan was to visit with Gigi, drop by Holly Hill Lodge, then spend the night at an inn in the area before departing in the morning for Nether Woodsmoor. The map in the book shop had shown a fairly large town near Bascomb Hall, Chipping Bascomb. I should be able to find lodging there that night. I'd stay at Tate House for one evening so as not to disturb Gwen and her new in-laws, then I'd arrive at Parkview Hall on Christmas Eve.

Gigi had given me detailed instructions on how to find her new home, and surprisingly, I found the correct lane and didn't have to backtrack at all. From the outside, Bascomb Hall was a delightful Georgian block set on a ridge that gave a view of the wooded rolling hills. Inside was a different story.

"It looks like complete madness, I know," Gigi said as she escorted me through room after room with scratched and warped floors, great patches of damp on the walls, and piles of debris in every corner.

"It—um—has nice large rooms with wonderful views."

Gigi laughed. "Yes, that's about all one can say for it at the moment. The architects assure me it will be a showplace . . . eventually. Come into the conservatory. It's the only truly livable space right now." The rooms of Bascomb Hall had been freezing cold, but when she threw open a pair of double doors, a wave of humid air engulfed us. I'd been holding my arms close to my sides in an effort to stay as warm as possible, but now my arms and shoulders relaxed. Humidity on the glass walls and ceilings blurred the view of the sky and trees into an Impressionist landscape.

"Come in, and I'll see if I can draw Mr. Quigley down from his perch. His favorite place is the tall palm tree over there." Gigi whistled, and the African gray parrot came wafting down and landed on her shoulder. She tilted her chin. "There's a good boy." He rubbed the top of his head against her cheek and made a trilling noise.

"Well, he looks very content," I said. "And what a lovely setting for him. It's perfect."

"Yes, it is, isn't it? I spend most of my time in here too. It's so lovely and warm and pleasant with all the greenery. Let me show you my little retreat." She set off through the banks of flowering plants and went down a set of steps with Mr. Quigley perched on her shoulder.

A wicker table in the center of the room was laid for luncheon. A maid brought in soup and sandwiches. "The kitchen is also being renovated," Gigi said, "so our meals are simple." Mr. Quigley flew over and settled on the back of one of the empty wicker chairs while we ate. Once we'd finished our meal, Gigi passed me a plate of gingerbread cookies. "You must have one. Cook managed to make these despite the work being done in the kitchen."

"And will you have plum pudding?"

"Of course. It wouldn't be Christmas without it." She waited until the maid brought a fresh pot of tea, then said, "I do wish I could offer you a place to stay, but I'm afraid we don't have a room suitable for a guest."

"I hadn't intended to stay. I'm on my way to Parkview, but I'm glad I was able to drop in to see you and Mr. Quigley." I didn't explain any more or give the detail that I planned to stop over in the nearby village. If she knew, Gigi would insist I stay. Mr. Quigley tilted his head, then let out a squawk that echoed up to the palm fronds above us. "Have you taught him any new sayings?"

"A few." Gigi sat forward. "What do we have, Mr. Quigley?"

He whistled, then announced, "Ain't we got fun?"

We both laughed, then Gigi fed him a scrap from her plate. He flapped away and settled on a banana tree branch. "He hasn't lost his old ways, though," Gigi said. "He's constantly reminding me to be a good girl. Now, tell me, how is everything with you and Jasper? Will you see him at Christmas?"

"Yes, he'll be at Parkview." I didn't want to go into detail about my complicated feelings about Jasper, so I asked, "How is life away from London? Have you met your neighbors?"

"A few. Several houses are closed up for the winter, and one is on the market, so there's not much socializing. Fortunately, the renovations keep me busy."

"What about Holly Hill Lodge? I saw a signpost for it on the way here."

"That's the home of Frank and Julia Searsby. Mrs. Searsby had me over for dinner recently. Delightful people. A bit older than me, so I don't know that I'll see them that often. Very hospitable, though. Mrs. Searsby is one of those people who is forever collecting lame ducks —of the human and animal variety. Her husband teased her about it when I was there. In fact, I believe they have a house full of guests right now. Mrs. Searsby said she wanted to show them a proper English Christmas."

A workman appeared. "Begging your pardon, ma'am, but it's the wall in the picture gallery you want taken down, isn't it?"

"Good gracious, no. It's in the next room over." Gigi jumped up. "I'll show you."

"And I best get on."

Gigi paused, her glance going to the glass ceiling. As we'd visited, the line of steely colored clouds had moved in, casting a gray tone over the conservatory. "It looks grim outside—like snow will come down in torrents at any moment. Perhaps you *should* stay the night. We could make a pallet—"

"Thank you, but no. Don't worry about me. The forecast on the radio this morning was for clear skies turning cloudy, but no snow. I'm sure it will be fine."

～

I LEFT BASCOMB HALL, drove back to the village of Chipping Bascomb, then turned at the signpost for Holly Hill Lodge. The air had a frosty edge, and the gray clouds were hurrying sunset along. A few stray snowflakes twirled down, but they melted on contact with the windscreen or the ground.

It would be dark by teatime, so I had an hour or so to give Holly Hill Lodge a look, then I'd return to Chipping Bascomb and stay at the inn I'd spotted as I passed through. I motored along the deserted road through the rolling wooded hills for about twenty minutes, then the hedgerow on one side of the road dropped away and was replaced with a brick wall. When a pair of gates came into sight, I slowed the motor and crept along. The gates, wrought iron topped with gold-tipped spikes, were enormous and closed tight.

I inched along, peering down the dim tree-shaded drive, but it twisted to the right and disappeared into a stand of chestnut trees. The sole visible building was a gatehouse set a short distance away. No smoke came from the chimney, and shutters were closed and latched. I imagined the position of gatekeeper was probably a casualty of the Great War. Even the grandest houses had found it necessary to cut back on staff.

I put the Morris in gear, drove about a quarter of a mile farther down the road, then pulled onto the berm. With my breath making clouds of white around me, I climbed out and went to examine the brick wall. It was at least seven feet high, but this section was covered with a layer of ivy. I pushed back the ivy's leaves and smiled. The vines were thick, most of them at least the circumference of my fingers. I gripped the vines and tugged. They didn't give an inch. I inserted one booted foot into the ivy, found a toehold, and boosted myself up. The trees on the other side of the wall were dense, and I couldn't see anything but thick branches and underbrush.

I hopped down and moved a few feet along the wall until I could see gray clouds in the sky instead of trees on the other side of the wall. I hoisted myself up again, and this time a Tudor-style manor house came into view through the break in the woods.

The name "Holly Hill Lodge" didn't sound pretentious, but the building was an imposing three-story brick manor. Smoke drifted from several of the chimneys, and a warm glow shined from the mullioned windows as the meager gray daylight faded to twilight. I watched the house for a few moments, but I was too far away to see any details.

I jumped down, my heels pounding onto the hard ground. I had just the thing that would help me get a better look. I hurried back to the motor, glad that I hadn't had time to wrap my Christmas presents before I left. I opened the box that contained the gift for Father, a set of binoculars.

I'd found them at Harrods and decided they were the perfect gift for someone who didn't really want any sort of present at all. Father spent time outdoors in the spring and summer while Sonia worked in the garden, and I thought the binoculars might encourage him to take up bird watching. I knew Sonia would approve because it would get Father out of his study and into the sunlight more often. I removed the binoculars from the leather case and hung the strap around my neck.

I returned to the wall and climbed up again. With my legs locked and my elbows resting in the ivy leaves that covered the top of the wall, I leaned forward. I adjusted the binoculars until the tall, thin chimneys with their crisscross brick pattern jumped into focus. I panned down to the steeply sloping roof, then to the rows of bright windows, then farther down to the peaked stone arches over the front door.

I swept the binoculars back and forth. The grounds were immaculate. Not a single stray dead leaf marred the wide gravel sweep. I didn't see any people either. It was a cold winter afternoon, and everyone was probably staying inside. I surveyed the house's windows again. A few dim figures moved back and forth, but I couldn't make out any details.

I watched Holly Hill Lodge for a few moments, then blew out a sigh. Well, a lot of good that had done. What a foolish errand, thinking I could trail Jasper to a country house and find out what he was doing. I wasn't about to jump the wall to get a closer look. Just because there was no gatekeeper didn't mean there wasn't a gamekeeper, and I didn't want to risk being chased down by him—or any dogs he might have.

Unless I was going to fake a breakdown . . . No. I cringed at the thought of the machinations involved in that ploy. I wouldn't resort to that sort of behavior. A view from a distance was all the information I could gather about Holly Hill Lodge. Clambering up walls and using binoculars was scandalous enough. Thank goodness the road was not well-traveled. Not a single motor had driven by, so no one had seen me or my very improper behavior. At least the day hadn't been completely wasted. I'd seen Gigi's new home.

I ran the binoculars over the mansion in one last sweep, and a woman's laughter rang out like the chime of a silvery bell. I swiveled the binoculars in the direction of the sound. The trees and grass were brown, and the day was gray-tinged, so when a white blur filled the lenses, it startled me.

The clip-clop of horses' hooves sounded as I jerked the binoculars away. Not more than twenty feet away, a beautiful white horse emerged from a glade of trees. It was so much like something out of a fairy tale that I blinked and remained frozen in place.

The woman who rode the horse looked as elegant as any princess in a fairy story except that she wore a modern black riding habit, jodhpurs, and boots. She was twisted around, speaking over her shoulder to her companion. Her riding helmet hid most of her hair, except for some platinum curls visible at the base of her neck. When she turned back, she was close enough that I could see it was Bebe Ravenna. Her companion, who rode a sorrel horse, trotted out of the trees into the little glade.

"Well, I never—!" I muttered under my breath as Jasper pulled on the reins of the sorrel and halted his horse beside hers. They were angled with their backs to me as they looked at the house, and they were too far away for me to hear what they were saying. Bebe nodded and set off at a gallop. Jasper followed, his body tucked low over his horse's neck.

The hooves thundered away, and I released the vines, scrambling down from the wall. "Well!" It was the only ladylike thing I could say. I brushed my gloves against my coat and marched back to the Morris, the binoculars on the strap swaying back and forth across my chest.

I put them away with jerky motions, partly because my fingers were so cold, but also because I was fuming. Urgent matter, indeed! I took out some of my anger on the crank as I started the Morris, then I slammed into the seat and bumped from the verge back onto the road.

As I approached a bridge, I realized I was moving at a good clip and eased off the accelerator so the motor that was already on the narrow bridge coming toward me could cross it before I reached it. I nudged the Morris closer to the brick wall that ran along the side of the road. Both of our motors could probably pass on the bridge, but it would be with a hand-width to spare, and I didn't want to risk scratching the Morris despite the anger fizzing through me.

The other motor, a dark saloon, crested the rise. As it came down the other side, its tires slewed, sending it directly at me. I jerked the wheel of the Morris, turning away from the bright headlamps of the approaching saloon, but there was nowhere to go.

I stepped on the brake as the ivy-covered brick wall rushed at me.

CHAPTER FOUR

$\mathcal{F}$rom what seemed a long distance away, I heard a woman say, "No, wait—I think she's coming around."

A deeper masculine voice answered, "Thank God."

I opened my eyes. I was sprawled across the seat of the Morris. I lifted my head and immediately regretted moving as a queasy sensation swept over me. A young woman with a wide nose and straight eyebrows over dark eyes was leaning in the open door of my motor, her black bob falling forward on each side of her chin. She swiveled around to speak to the man behind her. "I told you it was icy."

"Right. I should have let you drive," he said. "We would have escaped without a scratch."

"We *did* escape without a scratch. *She* didn't. Give me your handkerchief."

"What? Why?"

"She's bleeding."

"Oh, I say—"

"Quickly."

The man unbuttoned his wool coat and reached into the pocket of his suit jacket. I touched my forehead, and bright red rivulets trailed down my fingers to my palm when I pulled my hand away.

The woman grabbed the square of fabric, folded it in half, and pressed it to my hairline. "There you are. Just hold that there. We'll have you out of here straightaway."

"Oh—there's no need . . ."

The woman either didn't hear me or ignored me. She stepped back and said to the man, "You carry her. I'll get the door to the saloon. We'll put her in the back where she can lie down."

"Do you think we should move her?"

"We can't leave her here."

I gripped the steering wheel and pulled myself upright. "I'm fine," I said. "Or—I will be in a moment."

"Nonsense. You've had a good knock on the head. Tommy will carry you."

Before I could protest again, he'd put one arm around my shoulders, the other under my legs, and lifted me out of the Morris. He swung around and headed for the saloon motor, his stride easy and his breathing unchanged. His wool coat scratched against my cheek, and with every step he took, I felt as if an enormous hammer banged away inside my head. I still held the handkerchief pressed to my hairline, and I tilted my head to see around it and look up into his face.

"Well, hello there," he said. "You gave us quite a fright back there."

"You gave me one coming toward me in your motor."

"I do apologize. Even though I slammed on the brakes,

the blasted thing refused to respond at all—rather like every horse I've ever ridden."

He smiled at me as he said it, and I couldn't help but smile back. He was one of those people who had an infectious grin.

A crisp voice from beside his shoulder said, "Ice."

"Yes, I do realize now that the road is icy." His easy-going tone was a contrast to her sharpness. "Fortunately, Miss . . . ?"

"Belgrave. Olive Belgrave."

"Miss Belgrave looks as if she'll be fine. I'm Tommy. How do you do, Miss Belgrave?"

"How do you do?" It was the correct response, but as soon as the words were out of my mouth, I felt rather absurd, considering he was carrying me in his arms. He paused beside the motor while the woman opened the back door. "We'll run you up to the house. It's not far," he said as he settled me gently on the seat.

"But my motor . . ." I trailed off when he stepped back and I saw the Morris. The bonnet was crumpled against the brick wall, and the front tires were turned at an angle they'd never reach during the normal course of driving. "Oh."

"I'm afraid it will require some repair," the girl said, "which Tommy will pay for." She switched her gaze to him. "Won't you, Tommy?"

"Of course. Of course. The least I can do." Tommy slammed the door, and the sound reverberated inside my head.

The woman took the seat in front of me, then twisted around and handed me my mesh handbag. "This was on the front seat of your motor. I thought you'd want it. We'll take you up to Holly Hill Lodge. That's where we're staying. You can rest there until you're recovered. I'm sure Mrs. Searsby won't mind. In fact, she'll be delighted to have a new house-guest—and an injured one, at that. We'll see to retrieving your motor. I'm Madge, by the way. Madge Lambert."

Even in my befuddled state, the name rang a bell. "The lawn tennis player?"

"That's me," she said, clearly delighted I'd recognized her name. "And the horrible driver is my tennis partner and fiancé, Mr. Tommy Phillips."

Tommy climbed into the driver's seat and swung his door closed with a bang. I shut my eyes for a moment, then opened them wide when the car lunged forward.

Madge looked over the seat. "Goodness. You don't look so good." She hit Tommy on the shoulder. "Slow down."

The car's speed reduced, and I said, "Sorry. I'm a little wobbly at the moment."

"And no wonder," Madge said.

I rested my head against the back of the seat and concentrated on breathing slowly in and out of my nose, my eyes closed against the dim scenery that whipped by the window at what still seemed to be an alarming rate. The roiling sensations inside my body subsided after a few moments. I carefully took the handkerchief away from my forehead, folded it over again, and dabbed at the tender spot.

Only a faint pink line stained the fabric, but I was sure I looked a fright. I could feel the hair above the cut was matted with dried blood. I had the little gun-shaped compact that Jasper had given to me to scare off people—men, specifically—with bad intentions, but I'd need more than powder and lipstick to repair my appearance, and the thought of even lifting my head seemed such a lot of effort.

I stayed as I was, settled against the seat, and let my eyes close again. Madge and Tommy spoke softly. I couldn't hear what they were saying, but I wasn't interested in contributing to the conversation, and I let the faint murmur of their words flow over me.

After a while, Tommy changed gears, and the tempo of the engine shifted, becoming smoother. Madge's low tones became audible now that the engine was quieter.

". . . let's not go back to that again. We *must* stop him. He's got a lot of nerve, poking his ski-slope nose into our business. I don't want him doing it anymore." Her whispered words drew me out of my daze. From the weary note in Madge's voice, it sounded as if she and Tommy had circled back to a familiar argument. I held myself still. I didn't want to intrude into a private moment—that would be embarrassing for all of us.

Tommy didn't bother to keep his voice down. "I know, but I didn't like it—"

Madge cut over his booming tone. "It will come out all right. You have to trust me on this."

Curiosity overcame politeness. I slitted my eyes. Tommy was shaking his head. "I don't know."

"You never do. I'll take care of it—as I always do."

"I hope you're right." Tommy wheeled the motor off the road and stopped in front of the gates at Holly Hill Lodge. He got out, opened them, drove the car through, then closed the gates. He slammed back into the motor, but the sound didn't hurt my head nearly as much as it had earlier. I braced myself as we bumped off down the drive as it curved into the dimness of the dense wood.

The pair in front was quiet, but there was a tension in

the air between them. I didn't feel it was the appropriate time to remind them of my presence, so I stayed silent and unmoving. After a few moments, the ambient light changed, and we came out from under the trees to the gravel sweep in front of the mansion.

CHAPTER FIVE

A footman opened the door, and I followed Madge inside an enormous hall with a wood-beamed ceiling, oak-paneled walls, and a flagstone floor. Suits of armor and other armaments filled one end of the long room. Couches and armchairs were arranged around a large fireplace that filled the wall at the other end of the hall. The top tier of wooden paneling that ran around the room was decorated with rows of faded flags, weaponry, and mounted animal heads. The light wasn't good, but I was able to make out elk, boar, and moose.

Madge unbuttoned her coat and handed it to the footman despite the frigid breeze shifting around our ankles even after the front door was closed. Madge said to me, "Drafty old place, isn't it? It's called the Oak Hall, and it's the only room in the house that isn't heated—thank goodness. Mr. Searsby says that it would be astronomical to heat it. But everywhere else at Holly Hill Lodge is delightfully toasty." She turned back to the footman. "Where is Bankston?"

"He has been unavoidably detained in town."

"Oh." Madge paused. "How unusual."

"I am the senior footman, Ford. How may I assist you, Miss Lambert?"

"Where is Mrs. Searsby at the moment?"

"Madam is presently serving tea in the large drawing room."

Madge nodded and turned to me. "Are you feeling all right?" She'd asked me the same thing before we emerged from the motor. "Would you like to have a seat here while I speak to Mrs. Searsby?"

"I'm feeling much better. Really." And I was. The brief spell of queasiness had passed. "I'll accompany you."

Tommy, who'd been handing off his coat and hat to Ford, joined us. "I don't blame you." He gave me a quick grin as he let his gaze range over the hall. "I wouldn't want to be in here alone either. Quite alarming, all the mangy old fur and glass eyes. Very off-putting."

We passed through an enormous door with iron hardware and nails to a newer section of the house with white wainscoting and silk damask wallcoverings. A blissful warmth floated over us, evidence of a modern heating system.

Madge took us through a series of short corridors that twisted this way and that, then she spoke over her shoulder as she led us up a staircase. "Not nearly as impressive as the main staircase, but this way is much shorter."

Tommy trotted up the stairs behind me. "Madge and I've been here a week, and we can finally make our way around without asking the servants for directions."

Our surroundings became more elegant as we walked, and I was very aware of my disheveled appearance. I wished I'd asked to tidy up before I met the lady of the house. When I'd dabbed at the tender spot on my forehead before I climbed out of the motor, the handkerchief had come away clean, so at least I wasn't bleeding, but I must look dreadful.

We came to a long, impressive gallery with a row of windows along one side. A maid was moving down the gallery, closing the drapes and shutting out the dusky evening view of the woods. A few snowflakes spiraled down. Oil paintings of somber Renaissance ladies and gentlemen lined the wall opposite the windows.

"Ancestors of the Searsbys?" I asked, trying to place the family. I couldn't think of anyone I'd been introduced to in society with that surname.

"Oh no," Tommy said. "Francie told Madge that her father bought everything from the previous owner, a Mr. Quick—paintings, furnishings, books, the whole lot."

"Tommy!" Madge's tone was severe.

Tommy grinned at her. "Oh, don't worry, old girl. Olive won't let on I told her. Will you, Olive?"

Before I could answer, Madge said, "It's Miss Belgrave," and swept into a room filled with people.

Tommy held the door and paused to let me enter the room first. "Don't mind her. She's always cranky when she loses. I beat her fair and square this morning, and she's still smarting over it."

I must have looked confused because he added, "On the indoor lawn tennis court. They have one here, you know. It didn't come with the oil paintings and books and whatnots, though. Mr. Searsby had it built when Francie took up tennis so she could practice no matter what the weather. She's gone off it now—says she wants to run her a business—so the court is open all the time. Madge and I have been able to get in lots of practice."

There wasn't time to respond to him before we stepped into the spacious drawing room. It was decorated in gold, cream, and navy, and was full of people. Several men were in armchairs by the fire, their newspapers deployed. A game of bridge was in progress, and a group of ladies sat on a sofa, their heads bent over embroidery. After a quick survey of the room, a little tension went out of me. Neither Jasper nor Bebe Ravenna was present. At least, I didn't see Miss Ravenna, and if Jasper were one of the men behind the newspapers, I was sure she wouldn't be far away from him.

Madge went across the room and said something to one of the women in the group doing needlework. The woman fastened her needle to the fabric, put her handwork away, and came across the room. She was plump with bobbed sable hair and large, deep-set brown eyes. She wore an amber dress in the latest style with a calf-length skirt. As she reached me, Madge was saying to her, ". . . bit of an accident, and we brought Miss Belgrave back with us. I think she needs someone to look at her head. She was bleeding quite awfully a little while ago."

Madge presented me, and Mrs. Searsby reached for my hand. The sleeves of her elegant dress were covered with tiny white hairs. "Oh, you poor thing," she said, her expression full of sympathy. "You're as white as a bedsheet. And it looks like you have a nasty cut."

"I'm actually feeling fine now. I'm sure I look a fright, though."

"No, of course you don't," Mrs. Searsby said, "but we must have that cut attended to." She looked around, and I saw that her hair wasn't cut in a full bob. It was only her bangs and the curls that framed her face that had been cut short. The hair at the back of her head was wound up into a bun at the nape of her neck. "Mr. Eggers," she said to a man playing cards, "if I recall correctly, you were a medic in the War. Perhaps you could offer assistance?" The other bridge players put down their cards, but the man Mrs. Searsby had spoken to continued to study his.

He pulled his gaze away, glanced at me, and frowned. "I hardly think this young woman compares to the men in the trenches."

"Don't disturb yourself," I said quickly before Mrs. Searsby could insist.

But he had put down his hand of cards, although he was careful to make sure the exact spacing between each one remained in place. His gold pocket-watch chain jangled as he stood and smoothed down his suit coat. A reflection of the fire's light flashed off the lenses of his spectacles as he raised his head to peer at the cut through his bifocals. Because he was not a tall man, I had a close view of his temples where his light brown hair had receded. "It doesn't look serious. It just needs a good wash." He made it sound as if the whole situation had been blown out of proportion.

"But she was bleeding so much," Madge said. "Are you sure she doesn't need stitches?"

"Head wounds always bleed quite a lot," he said to Madge. Then in a more courteous tone, he turned to Mrs. Searsby. "I suggest you summon a doctor for a second opinion." He took his seat at the card table, straightened his cuffs, and picked up his cards. "Now, where were we?"

"We can certainly see to that," Mrs. Searsby said. "We'll call Dr. Harris to make sure."

I began to protest, but she put a hand on my arm.

"It's no trouble at all. Dr. Harris lives a mile or two away, and I'm sure he won't mind dropping in for a few minutes this afternoon. You must come upstairs. It was a motor accident?"

Madge said, "Tommy was driving too fast and hit an icy patch. I'm afraid Miss Belgrave's motor won't be drivable. Tommy will see to the repairs, of course."

Mrs. Searsby turned back to me. "Oh, then you must stay here with us until they're completed."

"I couldn't do that."

"I insist. It will be several days before the repair can be completed, I'm sure—with it being so close to Christmas. As you can see, we're having guests for the holiday. We'd be delighted for you to stay on, at least until you find out about your motor."

"Well—"

"And you *must* see the doctor first." She motioned for us to walk toward the door. "I'd never forgive myself if you set off before you were completely recovered." In the hallway, she spoke to a footman, "Tell Bankston—no, Ford —to summon Dr. Harris for Miss Belgrave. And inform Mrs. Pickering that we have another guest. Miss Belgrave will be in the striped room. Have her things brought from her motor." Mrs. Searsby turned back to me. "We are rather at sixes and sevens. I sent our butler on a last-minute errand, and he's been unfortunately delayed in town. Just up these stairs. They won't be too much for you, will they?" A Jack Russell terrier ran up. Mrs. Searsby gave the dog's ears a rub, and then it skimmed up the stairs ahead of us.

"No, of course not," I said as we climbed a spiral stair-case with a circular window and cupola above it. It was certainly a more impressive set of stairs than the one Madge had directed us to earlier. Swags of evergreen boughs were draped along the handrail and filled the air with a pine scent.

We reached the next floor, and the dog lapped the entire length of the corridor twice in the time it took us to walk it once. "Thank you for allowing me to recover here."

"It's no worry at all, I assure you." She opened a door to a room decorated with white furnishings. Drapes with a pale lemon background and an ivy pattern twinging through white stripes matched the counterpane and the fabric of the fainting couch. "I hope this will do for you. It's rather small compared to some of the other rooms, but it does have a lovely view, and it adjoins the bath."

"It's delightful. Thank you."

"A footman will bring up your case as soon as it's retrieved. You're quite alone? No maid?" I shook my head. "Then Laura will help you. I suggest you change out of your traveling clothes and take a rest. I'll send Dr. Harris to you as soon as he arrives."

~

23 DECEMBER 1923

The next morning, I peered into the mirror in the bathroom as I arranged my hair over the plaster on my forehead. I'd woken with only a tenderness at my hairline. Dr. Harris had agreed with Mr. Eggers that the cut did not require stitches. The doctor had applied antiseptic, then the plaster, and told me to rest. I should contact him if I had any "distressing symptoms."

I hadn't asked what form the distressing symptoms might take because I didn't intend to develop any. I'd had

SARA ROSETT

a tray in my room last evening. By the time the doctor left I would have been late to dinner. My flare of anger and—I had to admit, if only to myself—jealousy at seeing Jasper and Miss Ravenna in the woods had faded. I'd spent a good part of the evening considering what his actions might mean and what I'd say to him when I saw him.

When I opened the door from the adjoining bath to my room, Laura was drawing back the curtains, flooding the room with white light. "Goodness," I said. "I didn't realize it snowed during the night." I went to the window. The snow lay in a thick unmarred blanket over the hills, the tree branches, and the gravel sweep. It had piled up in white tuffs on the bushes that lined the house. "Oh my." Even if the Morris were able to be repaired quickly, the roads would be difficult now, to say the least. I might have to leave the Morris and take the train to Parkview.

"Yes, miss. The boot boy says there are at least three inches of snow. Would you like a tray in your room this morning?"

"No, I'm quite recovered. I'll go down to breakfast."

I found breakfast laid out on the sideboard in the dining room. Jasper wasn't an early riser, so I didn't expect to find him there. The sole occupant of the room was a young man with straw-colored hair slicked across his forehead. "You must be Miss Belgrave. I was in the drawing room yesterday when you arrived. I'm glad to see you looking well." He spoke in an American accent, and his young, unlined face was eager and open. He transferred his plate of eggs and toast to his left hand and extended his right. "Allow me to introduce myself. I'm Theo Culwell."

I shook his hand. "How do you do?"

"Very well. I'm finding Jolly Old England is swell, real swell. In fact, you Brits are the elephant's elbow."

"I'm sorry?"

Before he could reply, a young woman entered the breakfast room and said, "Theo means he thinks we're the bee's knees." She had a deep, rich voice with a hint of huskiness. "I'm Francie Searsby. I'm happy to see you've recovered from your ordeal yesterday."

Even before she spoke, I was sure she was related to Mrs. Searsby. Francie had the same deep-set brown eyes as her mother. Like Mrs. Searsby, she also had brown hair, but Francie's was a lighter shade and had touches of auburn. She wore a white cashmere jersey, a long tweed skirt, and boots. The materials were expensive, but the cut of her garments was serviceable, not stylish.

"I feel completely recovered, Miss Searsby."

"Oh, please call me Francie," she said. "We're very casual."

"Then you must call me Olive," I said. "And I must thank your mother for her hospitality."

"Oh, she'll be along later." Francie motioned for me to make my selections from the breakfast dishes. I filled my plate and went to the table where Culwell held a chair for me. Francie joined us, her plate piled with food. She settled herself before Culwell could assist her with her chair. She shook out her napkin and said to me, "Theo is here on a business trip from America."

"All the way from Kansas City, where Culwell Luggage has its headquarters," he confirmed with a nod.

"He sells luggage."

He stopped buttering his toast. "But not any kind of luggage. Special luggage."

"Of what sort?" I asked.

"Aeroplane cases."

"I'm not familiar with those."

Culwell put down his knife. "That's because they're new. It's a revolutionary design that every traveler will find beneficial." His words sounded like an advert, but he wasn't just repeating a sales pitch. His smooth face was bright with enthusiasm, and I had the sense that he looked at me as a possible convert since I was unfamiliar with the joys of aeroplane cases.

Francie sipped her coffee. "Theo is an inventor."

"I wouldn't say that," he demurred. "More of—um—an entrepreneur."

Francie thwacked the shell of her boiled egg with her knife. "Did you or did you not create something that didn't exist before?"

"Well, yes, I suppose that's true."

"Then you're an inventor."

I asked, "And what is it about your luggage that makes it innovative, Mr. Culwell?"

"Theo, please. *Mr. Culwell* makes me sound all wet. Anyway, the cases are small and lightweight. One can carry them without assistance."

Francie reached for the salt. "No need to find a porter when one travels. I'm sure Miss Windway will be quite taken with the luggage. You might have heard of her? Miss Beatrix—Blix—Windway, the lady traveler?"

"Oh yes. I read an article about her recently."

"She's arriving later today to spend Christmas with us. I'm sure she'll be delighted with your aeroplane cases, Theo. You should get an endorsement from her. That would be quite a coup."

Culwell looked thunderstruck by the idea. "That would be the butterfly's book!"

"I'll suggest she try a case out, shall I?" Francie said, then turned to me. "The luggage has all sorts of ingenious pockets built inside. It's quite cleverly made."

Culwell added, "And the exterior is the finest leather."

Francie sipped her coffee, grimaced, then signaled to the footman who stood near the sideboard. "Bring a fresh pot of coffee, Ford."

"Yes, miss," he said and departed.

Francie sighed and apologized for the lack of hot coffee. "If Bankston were here, he'd have seen to it. One can't expect Ford to step into the role of the butler and carry it off flawlessly, but plenty of hot coffee is certainly a requirement that can't be overlooked."

"Your butler was expected to return yesterday?" I asked.

"Yes. Most bothersome." A wrinkle appeared between her brows. "It's not like Bankston to be unreliable. I do hope he hasn't left without giving notice. So difficult to keep servants nowadays."

Ford returned with the coffee, and once Francie had sipped from her replenished cup, she said, "As I was saying about Culwell Luggage—it's the highest quality. I was quite impressed with it."

I reached for the marmalade. "You sound as if you're sold on the idea."

"Oh, I am." She looked across the table to Culwell as she said, "I intend to convince Father to invest in it."

He stopped chewing for a moment, then swallowed hurriedly. "I—that's—well, wonderful. I mean, I appreciate any assistance you might give."

"It's an excellent business opportunity, and I think Father should invest. And if he's not interested, I have my own resources. It's really very fortunate, Theo, that you happened to be at Lady Dunford's and met Mother."

Culwell reached for his fork and focused on his plate. "It was a happy accident."

Was his voice a little less enthusiastic? I wasn't sure what had happened, but something about his attitude shifted, muting his eager, open manner.

Francie shifted her attention to me. "Mother adores inviting people to stay. It's her hobby, I suppose. Mother said Theo must experience a proper English Christmas. Have you met the other guests?"

"Not everyone. I met Madge and Tommy after the smashup, of course, and then I spoke with Mr. Eggers in the drawing room."

"He's a photographer, you know. The conditions should be especially good here for his work. I doubt we'll see him today with all the snow. Aunt Pru is coming in on the eleven-ten train. And Blix should arrive soon. Mother invited her down for a true old-fashioned Christmas because Blix has been away from England for so long. Speaking of traditions, as soon as we finish here, I planned to scout around for the Yule log. I expect you'll want to come along, Theo?"

Whatever had caused Culwell to lose his enthusiasm had been a momentary thing because he said, "That sounds like the berries to me—as long as your father doesn't want me."

"Father will be busy all morning. He's always closeted with the house steward or his partners before luncheon."

"In that case, it sounds swell."

"Will you join us, Olive?"

I finished my coffee. "I must see about my motor."

"It was towed to the garage in Chipping Bascomb. I

believe Mr. Rimington is going to the village this morning. He's our newest arrival—excepting you, of course. I haven't spoken to him hardly at all, so he's a bit of a mystery."

"You're not the only one who feels that way," I said in an undertone, but Francie didn't hear me.

"He did mention last night at dinner that you two have known each other since childhood," she said.

"Yes, that's true."

"Well, then you don't need me to give you a summary about him. He can show you the way to Chipping Bascomb. There's a path through the woods that's much shorter than the road, and he walked up from the village that way when he arrived."

"That would be ideal."

"I saw him in the book room earlier, the small room near the end of this hall where newer books are kept."

"That's not surprising," I said. If anything could induce Jasper to rise early, it would be books. I wished them luck on their hunt for the Yule log, then went in search of Jasper. I had quite a bit I wanted to discuss with him.

CHAPTER SIX

The book room was a pleasant space filled floor to ceiling with bookshelves, except for an Adam fireplace. Two large tables with hooded reading lights ran down the center of the room, and a fire blazed, its orange and red flames reflecting on the tile hearth. I expected to find Jasper perusing the bookshelves with his hands clasped behind his back, but he was at the opposite end of the long room near the leaded-glass windows. He stood beside Bebe Ravenna. His golden head was bent close to her smooth platinum bob as they studied something on a table. Their voices were low, and I couldn't hear what they were saying, but Miss Ravenna broke off almost as soon as I entered the room.

Jasper was still looking down, but she shifted her arm, pressing her elbow against his. He glanced up, followed the direction of her gaze, and saw me.

"Olive, old bean!" It was his usual greeting, but he didn't sound as delighted to see me as he usually did. "How are you? Mrs. Searsby told us about the accident."

"I feel fine this morning."

"I'm happy to hear it. Let me present Miss Ravenna. I don't believe you've met."

Jasper introduced us, and I said to her, "I enjoyed your performance in 'Any Two Can Play.'"

I'd seen Bebe Ravenna on stage, and I'd also had the quick glimpse of her on horseback, so I knew she was pretty, but now that I was face-to-face with her, it was clear that her attractiveness wasn't a surface prettiness of well-applied makeup, stylish clothes, or a nice figure. Her beauty was arresting in a way that made one want to stare. She had flawless skin, classic bone structure, and eyes the color of whiskey—although at the moment, her eyes were glassy, her cheeks were flushed, and her nose was pink.

"Thank you." Her voice wasn't the smooth alto I remembered from the play. It had a distinctly nasal quality. "That's one of my favorites roles—" She jerked her handkerchief to her nose and sneezed. It was a delicate little sneeze. If a sneeze could be charming, hers was. "I apologize, Miss Belgrave. I'm afraid I'm coming down with a cold."

She and Jasper exchanged a quick look. I couldn't decipher anything about it beyond the fact that they were on terms well enough to communicate through only a glance. "It was delightful to meet you, Miss Belgrave. I hope we can further our acquaintance later when I'm not in danger of infecting you with my cold. If you'll excuse me, I have a letter to finish that must be posted today."

"Of course. I hope so too." Her smile seemed sincere, but she was an actress. Would I be able to tell if her words were insincere? A little voice inside my head said, *that was catty.*

She picked up the paper that she and Jasper had been

examining. I had a fleeting glimpse of it before she tucked it inside a book she held. I was able to see that it was a hand-drawn map, and the building at the center was labeled *Holly Hill Lodge.*

She came around the table. "I'll leave you two alone. I'm sure you have quite a bit to discuss." When she was even with me, she paused. "Don't be too hard on him, Miss Belgrave. He would rather have stayed in London with you." Before she departed, she gave him a little nod— of what? Encouragement? Permission?

When the swish of her skirts had faded, I said, "Holly Hill Lodge is quite a nice place, but I fail to see anything of urgency here—unless it's something to do with the butler."

Jasper had been tidying up the books and newspapers on the table. There was a slight hiccup in the movement of his hands when I said the word *butler.* He shuffled the papers together. "You're seeing mysteries where there are none."

"Am I? There certainly doesn't seem to be anything else here that could be remotely classified as a crisis requiring a hasty departure from London." Jasper opened his mouth and drew breath, but I went on, "I thought something terrible had happened at Haverhill and you'd had to hurry back there. I was quite worried about you."

"I'm sorry. I didn't mean to distress you. That's why I wrote to you."

"Your letter was rather vague."

"Olive, I—" He went to the window and braced his hand on the sill.

"Won't you tell me what's brought you here? The true reason—not some excuse to fob me off."

Jasper remained motionless, his figure a dark silhouette against the leaded windowpanes, which glowed blindingly as the sun reflected off the white world outside. The fire sparked and crackled. I waited, silent and tense, until he finally pivoted. He linked his hands behind his back and faced me. "I'll do you the courtesy of being honest with you, Olive. There's no explanation I can give you."

I moved a few steps to the side. Jasper mirrored my movement and turned slightly. The glare of the light from the window lit his face clearly, and the tense coil of worry inside me eased. I hadn't thought that Jasper had been lying outright to me. Before, I'd felt there was an evasiveness in his manner and that he'd been holding something back. But now I could tell he was being completely honest with me. His face had the same expression as it had years ago when I'd blamed my cousin Peter for ruining my paper dolls, and Jasper had stepped forward to say he'd been the one who spilled ink on them.

I tilted my head. "You can't give me an explanation. It's not that you won't. You *can't*."

"Let's not parse words—"

"I think it was your work that brought you here."

"My work?" A hint of laughter underlined his words, and the tension in his shoulders eased. "You know I don't have a job, Olive."

"Don't you?" I asked, already sure of the answer.

His smile seemed to freeze. "I'm sorry, what?"

"I think you *do* have a job."

"You know I have no need to work. My investments and a nice legacy I received allow me to indulge in the pursuits of a gentleman."

I went on as if he hadn't spoken. "And I have to wonder if your job has brought you here to Holly Hill

Lodge." I picked up a glass paperweight from the table and let its cool heaviness weigh down my hand. "It fits the pattern. You disappear from London for several days—or weeks—then return with only a vague explanation. You never share the slightest detail of any significance about your absences." I put the paperweight down. "I think you're a spy."

Jasper laughed, his features relaxing. It was a genuine eruption of mirth. "I assure you, Olive, I am not a spy."

"You're not?" I'd had hours to cool off from the initial burst of anger I'd felt on seeing Jasper and Miss Ravenna together. I'd spent quite a bit of the night pondering the situation. The longer I thought about it, the less I believed Jasper was indulging in a secret liaison with her. Why would he? If he wanted to be with Miss Ravenna, there was nothing stopping him.

Jasper and I had exchanged some lovely kisses, and I regarded us as sweethearts, but we weren't engaged. If Jasper wanted to be with Miss Ravenna, he could break it off with me. There was no need for him to sneak off to the countryside to see her in secret. I'd known Jasper long enough to know he wouldn't behave in that manner. So if he wasn't at Holly Hill Lodge for some sort of illicit affair, why would he fly out of London at a moment's notice? It wasn't an urgent family matter that required his attention, and he was at leisure to schedule his days as he liked. I could only think of one reason for his abrupt departure— he was a government agent.

I walked around the table so that I was a few inches from him. "I know you well enough to know that you're not simply idling your time away as a man-about-town. There's a purpose behind your activities. You're not as frivolous—or foppish—as people take you to be." The words had come out in a rush, and now I slowed down, emphasizing each word. "If you're not a spy, then what is it that you *do*, Jasper?"

He held my gaze, his face serious but blank, then the tension in his features eased a bit. "My patriotic duty. That's all I can tell you, I swear."

I felt my face break into a smile. "I *knew* it."

"Dash it, Olive. I haven't told you anything."

"You don't have to."

He ran a hand down over his eyes and scrubbed his cheeks.

"Don't worry—your secret is safe with me," I said. "And I won't ask anything else."

"You won't?"

"You say that as if you don't believe me."

"I don't. I know how curious you are."

"Well, yes, I'll be the first to admit that I do always want to *know*. But I know *enough* now. At least, I know enough to know you're here at Holly Hill Lodge for a reason of some importance related to your not-a-job-type work, and I see that I don't need to be jealous of Miss Ravenna." I ended the sentence with a slight upward inflection.

One corner of his mouth turned up, and that gave me my answer before he said, "Of course not."

"Good. So that means you and Miss Ravenna must be working together on something here at Holly Hill Lodge."

"Olive!" His gaze zoomed around the empty room as if checking to see if someone else had quietly slipped in. "You said you wouldn't ask any more questions."

"That wasn't a question. It was a statement. And it must be correct, considering the grave expression on your face as well as Miss Ravenna's when I first came in here.

And she's obviously not feeling well, yet she made the effort to leave her room and speak to you. Yes, it must be serious indeed."

"Olive—"

"Grigsby will be upset with you if you keep raking your fingers through your hair in that manner. It disarranges it quite badly. I don't mind it a bit, though."

"Olive—" he said, his voice filled with a mixture of a groan and a laugh.

"Of course, I understand you can't speak about what you're doing—not in so many words. But obviously Miss Ravenna won't be able to assist you in . . . whatever endeavor you're here to achieve. I do believe it's something to do with Bankston, though."

Jasper sighed, then looked at me out of the corner of his eye. "It *is* a strange turn of events—a butler disappearing when the house is full of guests."

It was the nearest I'd get to a confirmation from him. "In that case, I understand you're going into Chipping Bascomb today . . ."

"I intend to leave shortly." He said his next words slowly as if feeling his way. "Perhaps you'd like to accompany me?"

"Very much so. We can check on my motor and inquire about your missing butler."

CHAPTER SEVEN

Jasper and I stood side by side, looking down at the Morris' crumpled bonnet and mangled wheel.

"Quite a smashup, old bean," Jasper said. "If I'd flattered myself and thought you'd contrived an 'accident' so you could visit Holly Hill Lodge and see me, this would certainly put me straight." I tried to keep my expression completely innocent, but there must have been a trace of guile because he turned to study my face. "Olive? Did you—?"

"Oh, all right. You're partially correct. I stopped in to visit Gigi yesterday for luncheon. I knew Holly Hill Lodge was nearby, so"—I became very interested in the seam on my glove— "I made a little detour." I tucked my hands into the pockets of my coat and turned to face him. "But the wreck was exactly that—an accident. It was quite ghastly, in fact."

"I can see that." Jasper touched my cheek with his gloved hand, and his voice softened. "I'm glad you're all right."

The owner of the garage had been called away when we first arrived, but he rejoined us, and Jasper let his hand fall. The mechanic wiped his hands on a stained rag. "As I was saying, miss, I sent away for the parts, but it will be after Christmas before they arrive, and then with the holiday . . ."

"There will be a delay. I understand."

"But don't worry. We'll get it all fixed up. It'll look as good as new."

"I'm sure you will. I do hate to see my dear little Morris in such a sad state, though."

"It won't be like this for long. I'll send a message to the Lodge when it's ready."

I thanked him, and he touched his flat cap. "Good day to you, miss. Sir. Happy Christmas to you both."

We returned the holiday wishes, then Jasper extended his arm, and I slipped my hand into the crook of his elbow. "There's nothing more to be done for my motor. What now?"

"I believe a visit to the train station is in order."

Chipping Bascomb was an old market town with a wide high street lined with half-timbered Tudor buildings with mullioned windows. Despite the sun, the air was frosty, and we could see our breath as we walked. The snow was only a few inches deep, so walking through the wood and strolling around the town hadn't been a problem.

"It's not quite so bright on the other side," Jasper said, and we crossed through the slushy middle of the street to walk under the icicle-encrusted jetty of the shops, which partially blocked the sunshine that glittered off the snow. The village was busy with shoppers bundled down with packages. Paper chains and holly decorated the shop windows, adding to the jolly atmosphere.

"Why did Bankston go to London?" I asked.

"Mrs. Searsby sent him to a flower shop. They had a broken glass pane in the Lodge's greenhouse. The cold temperatures ruined the flowers that were to decorate the Christmas dinner table."

"Did you meet Bankston?"

We passed the Cenotaph, its plinth draped with swags of evergreen as Jasper said, "No, he'd already departed before I arrived, but I know what he looks like. Tall—as all butlers are."

"Of course. It wouldn't do to have a short butler. No sense of presence."

"Quite. Besides his stature, his distinguishing features include an angular build, thick dark brows, a sloping nose, and black hair going gray. Of course, the station-master would know him on sight."

We crossed the village green and came to the station, where a train had just departed. We waited while the bustle of travelers disembarked. Because of my conversation that morning at breakfast with Culwell and Francie, I noticed that most of the cases people were traveling with were heavy and rather awkward, and the porters were busy hauling them to and from the station.

A plump elderly woman in a long sable coat came out of the station, moving at a measured pace as she leaned on a gold-handled cane. Her hat was tilted forward over one eye at a jaunty angle, and several tall pineapple-yellow feathers fluttered as she swiveled to look up and down the road. A porter followed her, toting an enormous steamer trunk. "Where is the motor from the Lodge?" she asked him. "Julia assured me she would send it—oh, here it is," she said as a blue saloon motor coasted to a stop in front of her.

Mrs. Searsby emerged and embraced the older woman. "Aunt Pru, it's lovely to see you. I'm so glad you can join us this year for Christmas. How was your journey?"

"Terrible. Crowds pushing and shoving. And on the train, there was the constant yapping of one of those silly little dogs that shivers all the time."

Mrs. Searsby patted her hand. "I'm sorry to hear it. Travel is so fatiguing. Come along. We'll soon have you at the Lodge, and you can have a nice rest."

"Don't mind me. I'm a cranky old woman. It's nothing that a whiz-bang won't cure."

"A whiz-bang?"

"A cocktail, my dear. You really shouldn't bury yourself in the country, Julia, with only your dogs and horses. It's so difficult to stay coherent when you never go to town."

"Coherent?"

"Yes." The older woman circled her hand and cast her gaze up to the sky. "You know, up-to-the-minute. *À la mode.*"

Mrs. Searsby's face cleared. "Oh, *au courant.*"

"Yes, that's exactly what I said."

"Of course. Silly of me to misunderstand." Mrs. Searsby noticed Jasper and me. "Oh, hello, Mr. Rimington, Miss Belgrave. May I present my great-aunt, Mrs. Prudence Brinkle."

We exchanged greetings, then Mrs. Searsby offered to give us a lift back to the Lodge, but we said we had more shopping to do.

A Rolls-Royce Silver Ghost in the same shade of

yellow as the woman's hat feathers swept across the road, flinging slushy snow, then braked by the saloon. A middle-aged man in a wool coat with a fur collar leaned out the window of the yellow motor and lifted his bowler hat, revealing a head of thick straw-colored hair. "Mrs. Searsby! Can I give any of your guests a lift to Holly Hill Lodge?"

Miss Brinkle looked intrigued, but Mrs. Searsby said, "Thank you, Mr. Sprigg, that's kind of you, but there's no need. We have plenty of room in the saloon. May I present my great-aunt, Mrs. Prudence Brinkle?"

"Great-aunt?" Mr. Sprigg said. "Surely not. A sister, perhaps."

The older woman laughed. "A flatterer, I see. You and I will get along swimmingly, Mr. Sprigg."

A motor behind Mr. Sprigg hooted its horn. "Keep your shirt on, old chap," he shouted over his shoulder, then he called out, "Must get on. Cheerio!"

As the Rolls accelerated away, Mrs. Searsby said, "You shouldn't encourage him, Aunt Pru. He can be rather—um—"

The chauffeur opened the door for the ladies, and Mrs. Searsby held her great-aunt's arm as she got into the motor. "You needn't worry," the older woman said. "I know how to handle men of his sort. A well-placed hatpin does wonders for keeping them in line."

Mrs. Searsby flushed. "Aunt Pru, you wouldn't!"

"I most certainly would—and have."

Mrs. Searsby glanced at the heavens, then seemed to recall Jasper and I were still at her side. "We'll see you back at the Lodge for luncheon?"

"Yes, of course."

"I'll send the motor back for you in an hour."

As we turned away and went into the station, Jasper said, "Rather trying to be a hostess."

"Indeed."

"I believe that's the last of the guests," Jasper said.

"Except for the lady traveler, Miss Windway."

"Oh yes. I'd forgotten her. I believe I see the stationmaster."

The stationmaster did know Bankston and remembered seeing him. "He took the nine-forty. We had a bit of a chat while he waited. He was going up to arrange for the delivery of flowers, but I don't know why the missus at The Lodge didn't use the shop here in Chipping Bascomb. The blooms here are just as fine as those in London, I'm sure."

"I'm sure you're right," Jasper agreed. "Perhaps it was a question of quantity?"

The stationmaster scratched his cheek. "Perhaps," he allowed. "Still, it seems a foolish thing to go to London for, but there you are."

Jasper extended his hand with a note folded discreetly into his palm. "Thank you, you've been very helpful."

"You're welcome, sir."

We were walking away when the stationmaster called out, "Do you want to know what time he came back?"

Jasper and I walked back to the stationmaster. "Bankston returned?"

"Yes. Arrived in on the nine-fifty-three, but it was running over an hour late. Problem on the tracks at Dillingham caused a delay, so the train didn't pull in here until a quarter after eleven."

"You spoke to him?" Jasper asked.

"Yes, sir. I asked him if the Lodge had sent the motor

for him, but he said he preferred to walk. I wished him a good evening and a happy Christmas."

Jasper reached into his pocket again.

"But the snow," I said. "Wouldn't it have been a rather long trek in bad weather?"

"The snow hadn't started—well, a few flakes here and there, but nothing like later. By the time I'd closed the station and made my way home, it was half-past twelve. That was when it started coming down something fierce. Big flakes that covered everything in no time."

"Which way would he have walked?" Jasper asked.

The stationmaster pointed with a gnarled finger. "The path beyond Mr. Sprigg's house."

"So, not the path that comes out by the church," I said, nodding in the opposite direction to the path that Jasper and I had walked to the village.

The stationmaster shook his head. "No, miss. The path Mr. Bankston took is at the opposite end of the village."

"And if we wanted to walk it, how would we get there?" Jasper asked.

"Oh, you wouldn't want to walk it on a day like today, sir. Takes you right through a hollow in the woods. The low point will be wet and muddy now."

"Nevertheless, which way?"

"Well, if you're determined . . . go down the high street. Turn right at the big house of red brick and follow that lane along until it becomes a path. Past the hedgerow, you'll see a trail that strikes out to the east. Follow that, and it will take you to the Lodge. After the hollow, the ground rises, and you'll see the belvedere about halfway along. That's how you know you're on the right path."

"The belvedere?"

"A stone building with open windows. Folks use it as a

65

viewpoint. You can see most of the county from the top. I understand it was built in medieval times for the hunting parties back when the house was a hunting lodge."

"Brilliant. Thank you." Jasper shook hands with the man again. "And you think Bankston would have taken the track that goes by the belvedere to get back to Holly Hill Lodge?"

"'Course. I saw him heading that way myself."

CHAPTER EIGHT

*J*asper and I followed the stationmaster's directions and came to a large red brick house set far back from the road. It was barely visible beyond the high hawthorn hedge that enclosed it.

"I suppose this is our turn," Jasper said. "Ah, here we are. The path is along here. Although, *house* is a rather modest description for Mr. Sprigg's residence."

"Yes, I'd say *manor* is a more apt description."

We followed the track that cut through the woods until we reached the trail that branched off from it. The ground ran steadily down, but it wasn't as muddy as the stationmaster had predicted. The snow was shallower under the tree branches, but at least an inch covered the path. Our footprints were the first to mar the pristine layer of white, except for a few lines of animal tracks that crossed the path occasionally.

We strode along with the sycamore, chestnut, and oak trees sheltering us from the wind. We walked in silence except for the rush of the wind through the apex of the

67

tree branches and an occasional rustle in the underbrush. We moved out of the hollow, and the ground sloped up, making the walk a bit more arduous. I loosened my scarf, and the cold air washed over my throat and neck. Jasper was scanning the white landscape as we walked, his eyes squinting against the glare. "Do you think Bankston had an accident?" I asked.

"That seems the logical explanation. Otherwise, he should have arrived at Holly Hill Lodge." He nodded at a gap in the trees. "See the smoke from the chimneys at the Lodge? We're not that far from it. I imagine we'll arrive there in less than a quarter-hour."

"Yes, with time to spare before the chauffeur departs to pick us up at the village. But why would Bankston go this way—and at night too? Why didn't he wire and have the chauffeur pick him up? With the delay in Dillingham, he would have had ample time to send a message."

Jasper lifted his shoulder. "Perhaps Mr. and Mrs. Searsby don't like to send the motor for the butler. And it was late. Maybe he didn't want to upset the household routine. The night was clear."

"Seems odd, though."

"I agree."

We walked on, our feet crunching through the frosty upper layer of snow for a while, then I said, "Bankston must be quite important for you to be sent down here."

"Olive, you know I can't tell you anything."

"I'm not asking questions. I'm theorizing."

"Oh, that's what it's called, is it? What's your theory?"

"It would seem that whatever concerns Bankston is larger than his disappearance."

Jasper focused on stepping over a fallen tree limb. "Why do you say that?"

"Because of the timing. You were summoned here yesterday morning, the same time Bankston left for London to procure new flowers. You were already on your way when Bankston sent the message that he was delayed. So you can't be here because he was delayed or missing. Those things hadn't occurred. No, Bankston going missing wasn't what set you in motion. Yet you *are* interested in finding Bankston. Is it because he's vital to what you were sent here to do?"

Jasper didn't reply, just grinned at me, then said, "That must be the belvedere."

An octagonal stone pavilion, a narrow tower-like structure covered in ivy, was set a few feet off the path on a steeper rise.

"Let's take a look at the view. I bet it's spectacular. And we can look for any tracks Bankston left." I struck off the path and up the incline, my boots sinking into the deeper snow in the clear area around the tower.

Jasper followed me, his long legs making it easy to catch up. "But if he left the station before it began snowing, Bankston wouldn't have left any tracks."

"Unless he got lost and was wandering around during the storm." I blew out a breath that became a frosty puff of air when I reached the clearing. "Whew! That's a good climb. Look, the architecture is similar to Holly Hill Lodge. It has the same peaked stone facings on the windows and doors—not as well kept, though." Cracks in the masonry laced between the stones, and snow-dusted ivy curled around the broken windowsills. We walked through the pointed archway to the ground floor of the open-air building, where bits of masonry and pebbles had fallen to the flagstone floor. "It's like one of those crumbled ruins you see in Romantic paintings—except the aging is real, not artificial." Each of the walls had a window, and a circular stone bench sat at the center of the room. "It must be lovely in here in the spring and summer."

"No sign of Bankston, though."

"Did you think we'd find him here?"

"He might have taken refuge here from the storm." Jasper nudged the butt of a cigarette on one of the windowsills and pointed to a crumpled Wild Woodbine box on the flagstones. It looked as if it had only been discarded recently. "Perhaps he decided to wait it out."

I moved to an arched door that stood open. "There's a spiral staircase." I climbed the treads, my hand braced against the chilly stone wall because there was no banister. The next floor was exactly the same as the first. Jasper's footsteps rang out behind me as I continued to climb. I emerged at the top and put my hand up to shield my eyes against the glare. I clamped my hat down with my other hand as the breeze whipped around us. "Oh my. It's breathtaking. It *is* a winter wonderland."

Glistening white covered every tree, field, wall, and hedge. It was a world transformed. Jasper nodded at the distant band of gray clouds that contrasted with the bright blue sky. "Looks like there's another storm on the way."

"I wonder if Mr. Eggers knows about this place. It would make a wonderful photo if he can get up here before the next storm."

"He doesn't take landscape photos."

"He doesn't?"

"No. He only photographs snowflakes. I had a rather lengthy discussion with him last evening. He showed us some of his snowflake photographs, but he doesn't consider himself a photographer. Rather, he's a scientist. The photographs are what he uses to record his observations."

"Really? Just snowflakes? I didn't know it was possible to photograph snowflakes."

"He has an apparatus of his own invention. Somehow, he's managed to connect a camera to a microscope."

"That's fascinating. And he seemed such a fussy little man."

"When he's on his subject, he's quite fascinating."

We'd been moving from window to window and stopped at the one that gave the best view of Holly Hill Lodge. "Look, there's someone coming out of the wood and going to the house. I can't make out who it is, can you?"

Jasper shaded his eyes. "No. All I can see is that it's someone wearing trousers—so a man, not a woman. But you know my distance vision isn't good. You'd have a better chance of seeing who it is."

"Well, I can't tell." I was sorry I'd brought up the topic. Jasper hadn't been able to serve in the War because of his poor eyesight. He'd worked in the War Office, but some people looked down on him because he hadn't been in the trenches.

But my words must not have bothered him because his voice sounded normal as he said, "I don't see any traces of footsteps in the snow."

"Oh right. I got so swept up in the view that I forgot to look for Bankston."

We circled the pavilion again, and this time instead of looking out at the snowy landscape, I narrowed my eyes against the sparkling white view and concentrated on looking for any mar or mark in the snow. I didn't see anything in the woods, but something directly under the window caught my attention. The windowsill had completely deteriorated, and the rocks and mortar that formed the wall showed through between the encroaching ivy. At one point, someone had nailed a wooden board across the crumbled section, but even that had decayed. On one side of the window, a nail poked through the ivy and a bit of twine flapped in the breeze, while on the other side, the board hung straight down with only a single nail holding it in place. I braced my hand on the upper portion of the window frame that was still intact and peeked over the fragmented edge.

Jasper reached for my elbow. "Don't lean like that, old bean. Can't have you toppling out."

"But look. What *is* that shape in the snow? Our footprints go right by it, but I didn't even notice it. I suppose on the ground it looks like another bush covered with snow, but from up here, it looks almost like the outline of—"

"—a body covered in snow."

CHAPTER NINE

$\mathcal{W}$e clambered down the spiral staircase, round and round in a dizzying manner, then hurried across the flagstone floor, but once we were in the open air and approaching the snowy mound, we both slowed.

Jasper went to one end of it and used his scarf to dust away the snow. I hoped that he'd uncover a bush or a pile of stones that had fallen from the fractured windowsill, but after a few strokes, he stepped back. "I never met the man, but I'm fairly sure this is Bankston. Poor chap."

Jasper had only removed a small section of the snow, but it was enough to reveal a patch of black hair with silver strands, a pale cheekbone, a sloping nose, and a thick dark eyebrow.

"I believe you're right."

"Blast!" Jasper said under his breath as he stood over Bankston's body.

I looked up sharply at his tone. It was quiet, but there was an intensity to it that I'd rarely heard from Jasper.

He felt my gaze and looked up. "Sorry for the outburst, but his death throws a spanner into the works."

I knew he couldn't say more than that, so I shifted my attention to the belvedere. The window with the decayed sill was directly above us. "Do you think he fell?"

Jasper squatted down and brushed away more snow. Now that I knew it was a person under the layer of white, I could see that Bankston lay on his stomach with one side of his face pressed to the ground.

"No, I don't think so. There's a wound on the side of his head that's not next to the ground. No, don't come around. It's rather ghastly. You'll sleep better if you don't see it." Jasper stood and surveyed the area around us, his hands on his hips. "I would imagine that if he fell, the wound would be on the underside of his head and not visible."

"That makes sense. It's quite flat here at the base of the belvedere. If he had fallen, he wouldn't have—um—rolled after he hit the ground."

Jasper stepped back and brushed a layer of snow away from a large stone that lay nearby. "This is what hit him." Jasper swiveled and looked upward. "It must have fallen from the window."

"The area around the window was crumbling away." I didn't want to look at the pale section of Bankston's face that I could see, so I focused on the belvedere. "Why was he here in the first place? And in the middle of the night too? It was so late when he arrived in Chipping Bascomb. I'd have thought he would have stayed on the path and gone directly to the house."

"He might have popped up to have a smoke. The cigarette butt and pack looked fairly new. Or perhaps he was meeting someone." Jasper moved back to Bankston, leaned down, and gripped one of his shoulders.

"What are you doing?"

"Rolling him over."

"You can't do that. We must wait for the police."

"Ten to one the local chaps will wash their hands of this. A death on a country estate a few days before Christmas? It will be passed up the chain."

"You mean to Scotland Yard."

"Something like that. And I guarantee nothing will be done until at least after Boxing Day. I can't wait that long. I have to find out everything I can about Bankston now."

This was a side of Jasper I'd never seen—intense and focused and unwilling to swerve from his course. Before I could argue further, he pulled at the shoulder. The body rolled over, and Jasper began going through the butler's pockets.

"Jasper!"

"Yes?" He didn't look up.

"I'm . . . shocked. I really am."

He glanced up at me from under his hat brim. "You wanted to see what goes on behind the façade of the foppish gentleman." He tilted his head toward the dead body. "Well, I can say that this is not usual, but . . . in this case, needs must." He pulled out a piece of paper from one of Bankston's pockets.

My curiosity overcame my reservations. "Anything?"

"Nothing of significance. Some loose change. A pencil stub and the receipt for the flowers." Jasper tilted the page so I could read it.

"Well, we do know that he was in London, then. It has yesterday's date."

Jasper nodded and replaced everything. He was about

to return the body to the position it had been in, but I said, "Wait, what's that on the ground? There, under his arm."

I plucked it out and held it by the edges with my gloved fingers. It was a sheet of paper folded in half. One of the corners had a jagged tear. The word "Bankston" was written in thick black letters across the front.

Jasper carefully rolled Bankston's body back onto its side, then came around to look over my shoulder. "What does it say?"

I opened it. "Nothing. It's blank inside. How peculiar."

"Quite." Jasper stepped back and scanned the area. "Bankston left the station and walked this way through the woods toward the Lodge, but he left the path and came up here . . ."

"Where there was a note with his name on it, but no message inside? Why would you leave a note like that?"

Jasper's gaze traveled from Bankston's body to the window of the belvedere above it. "Perhaps there was someone up there waiting for him."

"To drop a rock on his head, you mean. What a horrible thought, but yes, that could be what happened." I traced my gloved hand along the jagged edge of the note. "The note was only to get Bankston into position below the window. There was no need for a message inside." I shivered. "How very cold-blooded."

"Yes, and if it's true, the paper must have been attached to the belvedere somehow."

We both surveyed the ivy-covered stone tower. Jasper strode quickly through the snow and parted the ivy, his motions jarring the leaves and releasing little bursts of snow. "I think . . . yes, there is a bit of paper lodged here among the leaves. It is a slightly different hue. It has a blue tinge to it, rather than the pure white of the snow."

"I can see it. Yes, it does." The slight hint of blue made it stand out from the snow layered on the ivy.

"A hole's been punched in the corner, and a piece of twine's been threaded through it—that's how it was attached."

I held up the note. The diagonal tear at the edge of it fit exactly into the jagged edge of paper that remained in the ivy. "So someone did want Bankston right under the window."

"Wait—the twine isn't tied off to a vine." Jasper reached higher and pushed the ivy out of the way, exposing the rough line of string. It ran straight up through the ivy.

"I saw some twine when we were on the top floor—at the window above us." I shoved the note at Jasper and dashed away, calling over my shoulder. "Wait here. Let me check and see if it's still there." I raced up the circular steps and went to the window.

When I reached the top, Jasper's voice floated up, "Be careful, old bean."

I poked my head out of the window and had a perfect view of the top of Jasper's fedora—and poor Bankston's body at Jasper's feet. "I'm the epitome of caution." He tilted his head back and opened his mouth to speak, but I added, "Most of the time, but most certainly right now."

The ivy curled over the crumpled windowsill and laced up the sides of the frame. The twine was still there, caught on the nail. I gently tugged away a strand of ivy that partially covered the nail. Once I'd pulled the ivy back, I could see that I was wrong. The string hadn't been caught on the nail, which I could now see was shiny, not rusty.

The new nail had been driven through the center of a small piece of wood and deep into the masonry of the window frame. I touched the little strip of wood with my gloved finger. It swiveled loosely on the nail, the far end pivoting up, revealing a hole bored into the end of the wood. The twine had been run through it and knotted. Jasper said, "What did you do? The string moved."

I glanced from the small piece of wood to the other side of the window frame, where the long board I'd noticed earlier still hung by a single nail, pointing downward. "You'd better come up and see for yourself."

By the time he'd sprinted up the stairs, I'd pulled the long board into a horizontal position. It fit across the window opening.

"What's this?" he asked.

"Just watch a moment. See how this small strip of wood, when I swivel it up, holds the longer board in place? If something were placed here, in the middle, and balanced against the long board . . ." I reached over and tugged on the string. "When Bankston pulled the paper away—"

The strip of wood pivoted as I tugged on the string, and the long board fell way. Jasper's gaze went from the board to the figure of Bankston on the ground below. Like the pendulum on a clock that was winding down, the swing of the long board became smaller and smaller as we watched it for a moment in silence. Then Jasper tapped the portion of the sill that was still intact. "Whatever was positioned here on the sill—"

"Like the good-sized rock you found beside Bankston's head," I said.

"—would fall straight down and hit Bankston when he tugged on the note. Clever, in a fiendish way."

"Someone intended to harm Bankston—hurt him severely, if not murder him outright."

"Yes." Jasper sounded preoccupied. His attention was bouncing back and forth between the window and the body below us.

"But why would someone leave the twine and the boards?" I asked. "It's clear what happened."

"Only if you see the string—and it's well hidden in the ivy. Whoever did this probably intended to return and remove the note, twine, and boards. Something must have happened to prevent them from doing it before we found Bankston."

"Oh! Of course! The snow." I swept my arm across the view. "Once it snowed, they couldn't risk returning and leaving tracks that could be identified."

"I bet you're right. The storm blew up more quickly than expected. The forecast had called for snow today, not during the night."

We heard the lilt of voices and scanned the woods.

"There." Jasper pointed. "Coming from the village, down the trail we walked."

Through the trees, I glimpsed two people on horseback. We hurried down the stairs. "That's Francie and—um—Mr. Culwell. Theo," I said, struggling to recall his given name at the moment.

By the time they appeared at the bottom of the slope below the belvedere, we were high stepping through the snow down to the path. Francie waved and called, "You should have come with us, Olive. We found a tremendously handsome bough that will work wonderfully for a Yule log . . ." Her voice died away as she saw our expressions. Francie reined in her horse. Theo slowed his horse and stopped beside her, studying our tracks to and from the belvedere. "What's happened?" Francie asked. "What's wrong?"

"Francie, I'm sorry to tell you this, but something horrible has happened. It's Bankston. He's dead."

Francie's eyes widened, and for a moment I could have sworn a look of relief flashed across Theo's face, but it was quickly hidden as he trotted his horse forward. "We can go for help. Which is closer, the Lodge or Chipping Bascomb?"

Francie's horse shied to the side, and it took her a moment to tighten the reins. "The house." Francie looked around. "Where . . . ?"

"It happened at the belvedere," I said.

"Are you sure? Perhaps I should . . ."

"No, there's no question about it," Jasper said. "And it's a rather gruesome sight. It would be best if you could fetch the police as quickly as possible."

"All right." Francie wheeled the horse around.

Theo called out, "We'll be back as quick as we can," and they galloped away.

80

*J*asper's prediction about the attitude of the local police force proved to be true. First the police constable, then the police inspector echoed Jasper's words, indicating that the death of Bankston was beyond the scope of their abilities to investigate. Lastly, Mr. Daughtry, the chief constable, a stocky, squat man with a despondent attitude, stood over Bankston, his hands linked together behind his back as he studied the body. "Not really our bailiwick—murder."

After a quick look at Jasper, I said, "You suspect murder?" Throughout the preceding questioning, the men had focused on Jasper—they'd said they didn't want to upset me—and had only asked my name and residence. I'd seen Jasper tuck the paper with Bankston's name on it into his coat pocket before the police arrived. He didn't mention it or the string rigged to the wood at the window.

Mr. Daughtry's gaze wandered up to the window. "*Could* be murder. Might not be. Could be an accident. Shame about these old buildings falling into decay." He refocused his attention on Jasper. "Difficult to know which it is, a murder or an accident. Tricky to investigate these things, especially considering Bankston worked at the Lodge. Problematic when there's a party of guests in residence." He sighed and looked even more sorrowful. "And Bankston had been up to London. No, this is a situation for the lads from Scotland Yard." Coming to that conclusion seemed to cheer Mr. Daughtry, and his expression lightened. "We'll put the word about that it was most likely an accident while we wait for the Yard. Pleasure to meet you, Miss Belgrave and Mr. Rimington. I hope this doesn't spoil your holiday. Happy Christmas to you both." He tipped his hat and waddled off through the snow as fast as he could.

A few minutes later, we'd been dismissed and were walking through the woods toward Holly Hill Lodge. I waited until we were a good distance away from the officials who had remained at the belvedere to supervise the removal of Bankston's body before I said, "You never mentioned the note."

"Not to them, no."

"That's rather high-handed of you, Jasper."

"I'll give it to the correct person. Do you think Daughtry and his team would investigate it properly?"

"No, he can't wait to dump it in Scotland Yard's lap, which is the only reason I kept quiet as well."

The path came out of the woods at the snow-covered gravel forecourt in front of Holly Hill Lodge. As we crossed to the manor, a taxi came down the drive, circled around, and stopped by the front door. A slender woman with golden hair peeking out from under her stylish cloche emerged, paid off the driver, and picked up her small case. She wore a tweed jacket and skirt, and knee-high boots. As she strode over to us, I could see her skirt was divided. An aquamarine-colored scarf that matched her eyes fluttered around her shoulders. She extended her hand. "Hello, I'm Blix Windway."

"Oh, you're the lady traveler," I said and introduced myself.

Her handshake became more enthusiastic. "Miss Belgrave! I've read about you. I'm so pleased to meet you. Such adventures you've had! I want to hear all about them."

"They're nothing compared to what you've seen, I'm sure."

"But I've never been involved in a murder investigation. I want to hear about your cases. I quite like a murder for Christmas." I must have looked startled because she added, "Of the literary type, I mean."

"Of course."

My voice was too hearty, and she glanced between Jasper and me. "Interestingly, I did hear there was a commotion in the wood—involving the butler from Holly Hill Lodge . . ."

"An accident, it seems," Jasper said.

"Oh." Her delicately arched brows scrunched together. "Then what I heard in Chipping Bascomb must have been rumors. People do exaggerate, don't they?" Before she could ask any more questions, Jasper offered to take her case.

"Oh no, thank you. Most kind of you, but I can manage it. I'm quite used to toting it around myself."

Because of my chat with Francie and Theo about luggage, I took note of her suitcase, which was a small leather case with worn corners. It was covered with labels. "Goodness, is that all you have?"

"Yes, it's all I need. I've learned to travel light." She demonstrated how easily she could lift it.

"I'm sure Theo—one of the guests—will be intrigued."

"Luggage is his line," Jasper added as we walked to the house. "And where have you traveled from, Miss Windway?"

"Please, call me Blix. Everyone does. Nowhere exotic, unfortunately. Birmingham. I gave a lecture there about my travels."

Before we reached the door, Mrs. Searsby came around the corner of the house. If I hadn't known Mrs. Searsby was the lady of the manor, I would have mistaken her for a poor relation because she had on a worn wool duster and scuffed boots. Two dogs, a black Labrador and the Jack Russell terrier I'd seen yesterday, trotted beside her. She smiled and hurried over to us. "Welcome to Holly Hill Lodge, Miss Windway."

"Thank you for inviting me. I'm delighted to be here," Blix said as the dogs threaded in and out of our little group.

Ford opened the door, and Mrs. Searsby shooed the dogs inside. By the time we entered the Oak Hall, a footman had wrapped the Jack Russell in a towel. He patted his leg as he walked to a small door at the side of the room, and the Labrador galloped to him. The servant and the animals disappeared through the door.

While Ford was taking Miss Windway's hat and gloves, Mrs. Searsby drew me to the side and said in an undertone, "I'm so sorry about this business with Bankston. Mr. Daughtry just stopped by to give us the news. Tragic! Would you like to retire to your room?"

I said, "No, but thank you for your concern."

"I don't understand it. Bankston has always been so

reliable. It's not like him to go and be involved in an accident in the middle of the night. But the chief constable—such a mournful man—came around and informed Mr. Searsby that Scotland Yard will handle it quietly. I hope they get it sorted discreetly. I absolutely cannot have the police nosing around, disrupting our Christmas party. It would ruin the atmosphere completely."

One of the suits of armor caught Blix's attention. She asked Jasper a question about it, and they set off, moving along under the flags as Blix took in the weapon displays and animal-head trophies.

I said to Mrs. Searsby, "If you need anything—anything at all—in connection with your butler's death, I'd be happy to help. I've been of assistance in several situations that were of a delicate nature."

Mrs. Searsby's look sharpened. "I *do* remember hearing something about that recently. You were staying with Lady Gigi Alton when the dowager . . ."

"Yes, that's right."

"And weren't you involved when Lady Agnes had those—um—issues surrounding the death of her uncle, the Egyptologist?"

"Yes."

She nodded decisively. "Let me speak to Mr. Searsby. I'd be delighted if you could clear matters up before Scotland Yard arrives. Frank dislikes anything that causes a hiccup in the running of the household. I'm sure he'll agree with me that you should look into it." Jasper and Blix had made a circuit of the room and were heading back to us. "I'll find you later this afternoon. Ah, Miss Windway, let me show you to your room . . ."

I went up to change, and by the time I'd removed my

sodden footwear, put on a burgundy woolen suit, and combed my hair, a maid arrived with a note.

Dear Miss Belgrave,

I understand you missed luncheon. Perhaps you could join me for an early tea in my room. I'm still feeling rather under the weather, but there is much you and Mr. Rimington and I must discuss.

Your friend,
Miss Ravenna

I WENT along to her room, and as I turned down the passageway, Jasper was coming from the opposite end. We met at her door, and he said, "So you received a summons as well?"

"I did."

Jasper knocked on the door. "Excellent." He paused as a maid passed, then said, "Your company will scotch any rumors about my presence in Miss Ravenna's room."

Miss Ravenna called out for us to enter, her voice scratchy.

I said, "We certainly do want to keep those rumors about you and Miss Ravenna under control. I'm happy to chaperone you at any time," I added as I went through the door ahead of him.

Miss Ravenna sat in an armchair near the fire, swathed in a shawl and with a blanket over her lap. "Do come in—but not too close. I want to keep this cold all to myself. I wouldn't wish my red nose or watery eyes on anyone else."

She wore no makeup, and she must have just risen from bed because when she shifted to put her teacup down, I saw her hair was flattened to the back of her head. Jasper and I went to a settee that was a good distance away from her chair. A lavish tea with scones, sandwiches, and cakes had been laid out on the low table in front of us. "Miss Belgrave, perhaps you could pour out?"

"Of course. Would you like some?"

She picked up her teacup. "Thank you, no. I'm having warm water with honey and lemon. Does wonders for the throat—an old theater trick. It's helping, but I don't think I'll be fully recovered for a few days, and by then it will be too late."

"Too late for what?" I asked.

"We'll get to that in good time. Mr. Rimington, could you give me an update on what happened in the wood? All I've heard are bits and pieces of information that my maid picked up belowstairs."

"Certainly," Jasper said, but then he hesitated, glancing from Miss Ravenna to me.

Miss Ravenna said, "Miss Belgrave is well and truly involved. I've received permission to speak to Miss Belgrave about—um—certain issues, let's call them, here at Holly Hill Lodge. I think there's far more benefit to including her in our discussion rather than excluding her."

"I agree." Jasper crossed one leg over the other and launched into a summary of our discovery of Bankston's body. I ate a fish paste sandwich and a scone during Jasper's quick and businesslike rundown. How could I have thought he and Miss Ravenna were a romantic couple? It was clear they were working together in a professional way—and it appeared Miss Ravenna was the boss.

When he finished, he reached for his tea, and Miss Ravenna sat for a moment, looking at me, her gaze assessing.

"I wanted to speak with you today, Miss Belgrave, for an extremely important reason. At the very least, I want to ask you to keep everything you've learned today to yourself. It's vitally important that the details around the death of Bankston be kept quiet."

I opened my mouth to ask a question, but she spoke before I could. "I can't tell you why—unless you're interested in helping us. Jasper has told me quite a bit about you. I know enough about you to know that you're curious. You like to know the whole story, not the quick veneer that often covers deeper actions. Since you want to know the truth, I think you may be interested in helping us uncover what Bankston has been doing. You do, after all, have a knack for solving difficult problems. You'd be an invaluable asset to our little band and could help us complete our task. Jasper trusts you, so I know I can trust you as well. What do you say, Miss Belgrave? Would you like to help us?"

"What exactly would I be helping you with? Solving a murder?"

"That may come into it, but Bankston's death isn't our primary focus. I can't be more specific unless I have your promise."

"My promise to keep quiet?"

"Yes. Your word that anything that's said in this room goes no further."

I glanced at Jasper. "Very cloak-and-dagger. You said you weren't involved in anything of that sort."

"Oh, I'm not. That's more Miss Ravenna's line. I'm just here as . . . auxiliary, you could say."

Miss Ravenna said, "Jasper has special—um—talents that are needed."

"At least we hope they'll be needed," Jasper amended.

"Indeed. Well, Miss Belgrave, what do you say? Our task is of great importance."

"To the country?" I asked.

She smiled. "I knew from what Jasper had told me that you were sharp. If you do agree to work with us, there will be certain formalities later—papers to sign, that sort of thing. What do you say? Are you willing to help?"

"Yes." How could I say anything else? I was already involved, and my curiosity—about Bankston and about Jasper—was too high to walk away. I still wasn't sure what sort of organization Jasper worked with or how he fit into it. He indicated his role was more of a bit player's, but I wasn't sure if he was on the periphery. Miss Ravenna was right—I did want to know more. I wanted the whole story.

"Excellent. I suggest you pour yourself another cup of tea. My throat is sore, so you begin, Mr. Rimington, and bring Miss Belgrave up-to-date on what we know—and suspect—about Bankston."

CHAPTER ELEVEN

*J*asper brushed the crumbs of his sandwich bread from his fingers and put down his plate. "Unfortunately, our information is limited where the butler is concerned, but we do know a few things. Most important is the fact that Bankston was part of an organization that has, as its top priority, a desire to undermine king and country."

"Goodness." I'd suspected Jasper was some sort of government agent, but seeing his lighthearted manner fall away and hearing his solemn tone conveyed the seriousness of the situation. This wasn't a rag or a lark.

"Sober stuff, indeed. Our knowledge is murky on several points, but we are clear on a few key things. Using various sources, we've been able to piece together fragments of information about this group. The large group is made of many smaller groups that are loosely connected. There's not much contact between these groups or the individuals in them. Each unit operates in a self-contained manner, which is a great strength in keeping their activities secret. With that type of setup, no one person knows everything. Any single individual's knowledge and information are limited. Bankston was a crucial link in the communication chain of the organization. He served as a sort of post office. A courier would arrive here at Holly Hill Lodge with a written communication, a letter. Before the courier arrived, he would have received instructions, which would give him a certain location to leave the letter. Bankston would retrieve it. Then, to keep things absolutely secure, Bankston would move the letter to a new location. Later, Bankston would give the next courier instructions on how to retrieve the letter from its new location. The next courier might be someone who was visiting Holly Hill Lodge at the same time as the original courier, or the letter might be held for a guest who was slated to arrive in the future."

Miss Ravenna took over the explanation. "At some point during the new courier's stay, Bankston would make sure he—or she—received coded directions on where to go to retrieve the letter. He would never speak to the next courier directly about the matter. Instead, he'd leave the directions in the person's room or have them delivered to the person. He'd use something innocuous, like a book or a newspaper, to convey the directions."

"So if someone else saw it, they wouldn't suspect anything," I said.

"Right," she said. "The courier would have a key to decrypt the poem or newspaper article, or whatever it was. Once they'd decrypted the text, the courier would know where to go to retrieve the letter."

An idea stirred, and I looked at Jasper, but I couldn't catch his eye. He was smoothing out a crease in his trousers.

Miss Ravenna continued, "The system was set up so

that there was as little contact between the players as possible."

"What a lot of work, though," I said.

"Yes, but very ingenious." Miss Ravenna put her teacup and saucer down on the table. "And one with many advantages. Oftentimes these sorts of exchanges are done in semi-public areas where people come and go, such as a boardinghouse or a hotel. But the seclusion of Holly Hill Lodge and its exclusive guest lists mean any chance we might have to observe the transfer from afar isn't possible. Since Mr. and Mrs. Searsby like to entertain, large groups of people arrive and depart frequently. A courier would bring their letter and drop it off, then Bankston would retrieve it and arrange for another guest to pick it up. It's made it extremely difficult for us to track the transfers—or even discover who the couriers are. If there are ten guests visiting the Lodge, then there are ten possibilities, and we have no way of identifying the couriers."

"Mr. and Mrs. Searsby, are they . . . ?" I trailed off because it wasn't the done thing to accuse one's host of being involved in treason. I didn't even want to say it aloud.

"Our intercepts indicate Mr. and Mrs. Searsby are unaware their home is being used to transfer the group's letters."

"Intercepts?" I asked.

Jasper said, "Intercepts are what our clever chaps are able to—er—lift from cables." He shifted in his chair. "You might think it's not quite cricket, but the technique was essential to the War effort, and the government now uses it to monitor groups like this. Of course, the people we're interested in are smart enough to know we're listening. The cables don't contain anything truly sensitive. That's why the group uses written communications, the letters that are dispatched by courier. It's a more secure method of exchanging information. Our only chance to discover the identity of the couriers and the information that is being sent back and forth was to arrive as guests and keep Bankston under observation as closely as possible."

Miss Ravenna said, "Mr. Rimington was chosen to accompany me to Holly Hill Lodge because of his . . . additional skills, which should come in handy if we can find the letter."

I looked at Jasper out of the corner my eye. "The letters that the couriers carry back and forth are coded as well, then." He didn't reply, only gave me a small smile as I continued, "You've always been fond of a good mystery—as well as a jigsaw puzzle."

Miss Ravenna raised an eyebrow at me, then said to Jasper, "I see what you mean about her, Mr. Rimington. She's perceptive. I do believe it's a good thing we brought you on, Miss Belgrave, if you can suss out Mr. Rimington's secrets in that manner."

"One of the advantages of knowing someone since childhood."

He tilted his head in acknowledgment of my guess. "Codes and ciphers are quite like jigsaw puzzles, only with words and letters and symbols."

Miss Ravenna cleared her throat, and Jasper and I turned back to her as she said, "Our attempts to gain information through placing someone here at the Lodge have been frustrated because of Bankston's position. As a butler, he had a great deal of authority and autonomy. If he had been, say, a footman, it would have been much easier to keep track of him. But Bankston was able to move freely without supervision, which made it almost impossible to observe him. And with the sheer size of the Lodge and grounds, it's extremely difficult to conduct any sort of clandestine search of the entire place to find any letters from the group that Bankston hid on the property. And it's vital we locate the most recent letter." Miss Ravenna leaned back and gathered the shawl more securely around her shoulders. "Well, Miss Belgrave, I'm curious what you make of this."

"I'll admit, it does sound rather far-fetched—secret organizations, smuggled letters, codes, and ciphers. But I know Jasper, and if he says it's real—then, well, it can't be a joke or a fantasy."

"No, indeed, Miss Belgrave. I assure you this is entirely serious. Do you have any questions?"

"Well, yes. How can you be sure that it's the guests who are bringing the letters in and taking them away? Couldn't it be a servant?"

"Excellent question. We've explored that possibility. Our intercepts and our sources within the organization confirm that Bankston was the sole person from the staff who was involved. In fact, we know Bankston received a letter—a crucial letter—two weeks ago. He had been holding it here until this party of guests arrived. He'd sent word to his organization that everything was in place for the next courier retrieval, which is scheduled to happen after the Christmas festivities. The next courier will receive the coded communication with instructions for where to find the letter on Christmas Day."

"Jolly good news, then," Jasper said. "That gives us a few days."

"Yes, but it will be much more difficult now that we're not able to watch Bankston," Miss Ravenna added.

"So Bankston received one of these coded letters," I

said. "It's hidden somewhere here at Holly Hill Lodge, and the next courier will pick it up soon?"

"Yes, that's it exactly." Miss Ravenna sounded approving. "It's critical we find Bankston's instructions for the next courier. That will give us the location of the letter. Once we know where it is, we can examine it before their courier receives it. Then we can watch and see who retrieves it, which will give us the identity of the courier."

She gave the last phrase a certain note of emphasis that puzzled me. "You make it sound as if knowing the courier is more important than the letter."

"We want to know what's in the letter—that's vital. Finding it is our first priority, but answering the question of who leaves Holly Hill Lodge with the letter is nearly as important. Our sources tell us this letter is going to one of the top leaders of their organization. If we know who has the letter, we can tag along in their wake to the apex of the group and identify the top people." She rearranged her shawl as she said, "But we're getting ahead of ourselves. Let's get back to our first task, locating the letter. Now, we may have a possible shortcut to the letter, which would eliminate the need to find Bankston's retrieval instructions."

"Right," Jasper said. "We know of a few places Bankston has hidden the letters in the past, and we can search those. If the letter is in one of those places, then there's no need to find Bankston's coded communication with the location of the current letter. Our best opportunity to search these known locations will be before the police arrive to investigate Bankston's death. With Miss Ravenna coming down with a cold and my recent arrival, we haven't had the ability to take a discreet look at the locations. We have a small window of time now before the investigators descend. I suggest I check the locations immediately after we finish here. The local officials have decided to hand the case over to Scotland Yard. I imagine it will be at least a few hours before they arrive, or even possibly tomorrow morning."

Miss Ravenna nodded. "Good."

I said, "I suggested to Mrs. Searsby that I might be helpful in sorting out what happened to Bankston."

"Even better," Miss Ravenna said. "Of course, who killed Bankston or why is of little importance."

I was well on my way to completely changing my mind about Miss Ravenna—I was becoming quite a fan of hers, in fact—until she uttered those words, which reined in my enthusiasm for her as quickly as a rider who pulls in a horse short of a too-high hedge. "I disagree. Someone has committed murder."

Miss Ravenna looked chastised. "A horrible thing, indeed. I don't disagree with you, Miss Belgrave. It's just that our primary focus must be on the letter and identifying the courier. The officials will sort out who killed Bankston and why. That's of no interest to us."

"You don't think it was related to his activities with the couriers?" Jasper asked.

Miss Ravenna shook her head. "I doubt it. Very few people knew what he was doing—an extremely small number."

"If the circle of possible suspects is small," I said, "then it should be easy to figure out if someone on—um—our side decided to do away with him."

"Miss Belgrave, I assure you that no one whom Jasper and I are associated with would do such a thing. For one thing, it's completely and utterly in the wrong. Aside from that, Bankston was more valuable to us alive than dead.

His death complicates things enormously. We would have much rather waited and watched. Now we have to act."

"Well, what about this shadowy world Bankston was involved with? Perhaps he became problematic and *they* decided to do away with him."

Miss Ravenna frowned at me, clearly not happy that I continued to pursue the topic. "All our intercepts indicate the other side was quite satisfied with Bankston. If they did want to do away with him, I doubt they'd use such a sloppy manner. The police will investigate, and that brings attention to Holly Hill Lodge—something they'd want to avoid at all costs. No, I'm sure it wasn't related to his clandestine activities."

Miss Ravenna's tone was confident. Her last statement had a final ring. The subject was closed for her. But it was far from closed for me. A slow-burning sensation began in the center of my chest, that disagreeable feeling that comes over one when it's clear one's priorities are different from other people's concerns. She clearly viewed Bankston's death as exasperating but nothing more than that. Discovering who had killed him might not be important to Miss Ravenna at the moment, but I disagreed. Finding out the truth was always important.

However, I squashed my stir of misgiving. I wanted to be involved in what Jasper and Miss Ravenna were doing. There was no reason I couldn't pursue my investigation into who had killed Bankston on a parallel track with Jasper and Miss Ravenna's investigation into the letter and courier.

Jasper hitched forward and prepared to stand. "Then I'm off to check the few hiding spots we know of."

He sent me a questioning look, and I stood as well. "I'll come with you."

CHAPTER TWELVE

*J*asper closed the door to Miss Ravenna's room behind us. "We'd better move quickly. It will be dark soon, and it's begun to snow again."

"So the hiding spots are outdoors?"

He glanced out the window. "Unfortunately, yes." Small flakes were rapidly filling the tracks the taxi had left on the drive.

"I'll get my coat. Where should I meet you?"

"In the morning room. It should be deserted at this time of day. We can slip out of the glass doors and walk around the house to the gardens at the back."

A few minutes later, Jasper and I were crossing the terrace, our breath coming in little white clouds of vapor while snowflakes slanted down around us. We carefully descended the slick stone stairs to the path that ran along the side of the house.

As soon as we rounded the corner, we met a man stepping from the deeper snow that had piled up around the house. His flat cap was pulled low over his eyes, and a brown scarf hid most of his face. It took a moment to recognize him. "Hello, Tommy," I said.

He looked up, his expression startled. He'd been focused on the ground, looking down as he stomped his feet, apparently knocking some snow off his boots. "Oh—hello, Olive. Jasper. Not a good day for a walk, is it?" He gave his feet a final stomp as he lifted his chin, indicating the terraced garden. "I was looking out over the gardens at the snow piling up and wandered off the path into a drift. Serves me right, rambling around, not looking where I'm going." He grinned in a way that invited us to laugh along with him, then touched his cap and said goodbye.

He passed us and followed our footsteps around the side of the house, then we had the gardens to ourselves. We were out of the shelter of the house, and a steady chill wind came at us, driving the small, pellet-like flakes into our faces. The snow was piling higher on the low box hedges that enclosed the geometrical planting beds, adding another layer of white to the bushes that were already mounded with snow.

The gardens at the back of Holly Hill Lodge were a series of shallow terraces that descended from the house. We turned and followed the path that was still distinguishable despite being covered with snow. We set out across the first terrace, moving away from the house. After a few paces, I said, "Leaving aside Miss Ravenna's reluctance to investigate Bankston's death properly, I find I quite like her."

"You sound surprised."

"I am. I thought she was a . . . rival, I suppose."

"In the romantic sense?" Jasper stopped walking and turned to look at me. "You're serious, I see." We resumed pacing along. "Goodness. The mind boggles at the thought."

"Yes, it does. Now that I've met her, I see she's a businesslike sort."

"She is indeed."

"But you did appear in public with her quite a bit."

"That's true, but I was simply a handy escort." He looked back over his shoulder to the Lodge. "Miss Ravenna is very well connected, but those types of events —parties and dinners—go more smoothly if one is part of a pairing."

"I see." So it had been Miss Ravenna's cachet that allowed her to obtain entry to exclusive affairs. A few flakes caught in my eyelashes, and I blinked them away. "If anyone sees us, they'll think we're mad."

Jasper turned up the collar of his coat against the driving snow and leaned closer. "Or in need of a few moments alone." He glanced over his shoulder at the house. "In case someone is watching, we should perhaps demonstrate . . ."

"Definitely." I tilted my face up to his, and he kissed me. "That should certainly let anyone watching us from the house know without a doubt why we're outside on a day like this."

"I believe so. After all, there might be some lingering questions about my arrival with Miss Ravenna. I want everyone to know Miss Ravenna and I are friends, and no more. On this occasion, I'm not officially her escort. The story we put out is that it was simple courtesy on my part to offer her a lift to Holly Hill Lodge."

"After that kiss, I believe it. Now, as lovely as this is, it's beastly cold. Let's get on with our search. Where to?"

"Our first location is through the arched opening in

that tall hedge that surrounds the lowest terrace of the garden."

We tramped through the snow and crossed through the opening in the shrubbery into the sheltered garden dotted with marble statues. Some of them were placed back against niches that had been cut into the hedge, while others were spaced throughout the area along the gravel walking paths, which I could still make out because the protected garden hadn't received as much snow as the more open spaces.

Jasper scanned the garden. "Do you see Diana?"

"Yes, there. At the end." We crossed to the other side where the statue of the goddess stood poised on her plinth, her bow raised. Jasper circled around it. "Apparently, there's a niche in the drapery folds the perfect size to hide something."

"Oh, what about here?" Diana's gown flowed with her movement, and the sculptor had carved undulating waves of fabric that created several crevices. One of them was just large enough that I could put my hand into it. I felt inside. "Nothing here."

"All right." Jasper gave the statue another look. "I don't see anywhere else you could hide something that would be protected from the elements. On to the second location, the sundial. This way, I believe . . ."

We went through a second shrubbery arch located on the opposite side of the garden from where we'd entered and came out at the head of a yew walk. The house blocked the wind here. Once we entered the wide path that was lined on either side with yews cut in perfect conical shapes, it was even more sheltered. A sundial stood at the end of the walk, and beyond it was another hedge with an arch that opened to the woods. "How many possible locations are there to check?"

"Only these two. They're long shots, both of them. I imagine at this time of year, Bankston would be more likely to use a hiding spot inside the house and save these for the summer, but since these are the only places that we know of . . ."

"They must be checked," I said as we approached the sundial, which was set on a small square terrace. The sharp angle of the gnomon poked up out of the snow, its weathered bronze surface covered with a turquoise patina.

Jasper dusted the snow off the sundial's surface. "There's supposed to be a plaque, but I don't see it. . ."

"Here it is, on the base." I shifted the snow away using the toe of my boot. "It was erected in 1602."

Jasper pulled out a penknife, crouched down, and set to work loosening the screws that held the plaque in place. He looked up, squinting against the falling flakes. "We're in the right place. Only one of the screws is well attached. The others are loose." He removed the last one, then lifted the plaque away. "Empty. Well, at least we've made sure."

I ran my gaze over the three stories of Holly Hill Lodge. "What will we do now? The house is immense. There's no way we can search every nook and cranny in it."

He set about reattaching the plaque. "No. Our best bet is to focus on Bankston, get into his rooms. Perhaps we can find the directions he intended to give to the courier —if we're lucky."

I cocked my head. "Do you hear voices?"

Jasper paused.

A clear, strident female voice floated over the tall hedge. "Good riddance—that's what I say."

"Aunt Pru! You don't mean that."

"It's Miss Brinkle and Mrs. Searsby," I said. "Hurry! I think they're coming this way. Can I help?"

"No. Almost done."

"I'm afraid I do mean it." Miss Brinkle's voice was closer. "Odious man—thoroughly unlikable. I can't say that I will mourn him—not even for one moment. And I know you say there's no proof he did it, but I'm quite sure. To think, all that fuss and bother on account of a few G&Ts. Very high-handed—"

The wind whipped the sound of Miss Brinkle's next words away, but then it died down.

Mrs. Searsby said, "But Frank would never cut off your funds—"

Miss Brinkle cut in, her tones carrying over the wind gust. "Julia, you're too soft-hearted. He's a businessman. If he thought I wasn't able to manage the money properly, he'd . . ."

A large black Labrador and the small Jack Russell terrier trotted through the arch in the shrubbery, then the two ladies followed.

The dogs sighted Jasper hunched down near the ground and made a beeline for him, their paws kicking up snow as they shot down the path between the yews. Before he could get to his feet, the Lab bowled him over, planted his paws on Jasper's chest, and licked his face while the terrier zipped around us in a tight circle.

Mrs. Searsby's command rang out, "Zeus, Apollo! Heel!"

The dogs swung around and raced back to her. Jasper

stood and brushed down his coat while I picked up his fedora and dusted it off.

Mrs. Searsby, still wearing the worn wool duster, scolded the dogs, then crossed to the sundial. She'd added a tired-looking beret to her outfit. "I apologize, Mr. Rimington. Their manners are inexcusable." The dogs had stayed by her side as she approached.

Miss Brinkle, who had walked more slowly, her weight on her gold-handled cane, joined us. She wore her sable coat along with a fur-trimmed velvet toque. An abundance of gray vulture feathers set in a fan-like arrangement decorated the center of the hat. "You're too softhearted to train them properly, Julia." Despite her rather harsh words, the dogs trotted over to Miss Brinkle. She ran her hand along the Lab's back. She didn't try to pet the terrier as it darted back and forth around the hem of her coat.

Mrs. Searsby scooped up the terrier and tucked it into her side. "You are a rascal, Zeus," she said to the dog, then turned her attention to Jasper and me. "He thinks he's ruler of all." She addressed the dog again. "Don't you, Zeus?" He licked her nose. "See? Incorrigible!"

Miss Brinkle frowned as she studied the sundial. Jasper had swept the surface clear of snow, and now a thin layer of flakes was covering it again. Her gaze traveled down to the base where our footprints had flattened the patch of snow by the plaque. Jasper hadn't had time to set the last screw completely in place, and the plaque was slightly off-kilter. He reached down to straighten it in the guise of brushing the snow away.

I stepped forward and cut off Miss Brinkle's view. "We were looking at the sundial."

"Odd thing to do during a snowstorm."

"Well, it's odd to be out walking, isn't it, Aunt Pru?" Mrs. Searsby said. "And we're doing that, aren't we?"

"I have quite an interest in sundials," I extemporized. "The history of them, that is."

"How curious," Miss Brinkle said.

"Fascinating subject." Jasper moved to Miss Brinkle's side and extended his arm. "That sundial is a fine specimen. Typical Elizabethan. I had to show it to Miss Belgrave. She's a founding member of SOPS, the Society for the Preservation of Sundials. You've heard of it, of course? No? Fine organization. Does great work to see that history is preserved. So important, don't you think . . ."

Jasper set off, steering Miss Brinkle away from the sundial. Apollo ambled along behind them, then spotted a stick protruding from the snow. He snatched it up and galloped back to Mrs. Searsby. She set Zeus on his tiny paws, then took the stick from Apollo and tossed it. Both dogs shot away, stirring up snow.

Mrs. Searsby fell into step beside me. "My aunt insists on a quarter-hour of fresh air every day, no matter the weather. I don't want her wandering around by herself. She could turn an ankle in this snow. So many steps and elevation changes out here." Jasper and Miss Brinkle moved farther away, his voice fading as he droned on about the merits of different types of sundials.

Mrs. Searsby said, "I spoke to Mr. Searsby about you . . . looking into things around Bankston's death. He'd like to speak to you. He's in his study."

"I'll go directly there, and I'll bring Jasper with me as well. He can be trusted, and he's very good at this sort of thing."

"Two heads are better than one. I agree. Bring him along. I'll get Aunt Pru settled with a warm drink and come find you." She turned and called for the dogs, and we headed into the house.

CHAPTER THIRTEEN

*J*asper held the door of Mr. Searsby's study open for me, and I entered the small, plain space with a weighty keyhole desk of dark wood in the middle of the room. The surface was completely clear except for one sheet of paper and a neatly folded newspaper. A few chairs sat in front of the desk. The only other furniture in the room was a small built-in bookshelf with a set of encyclopedias on the bottom shelf. The rest of the space was taken up with ledgers. There was no sign of our host.

"We must have missed him," I said, but then a man's voice called, "I'm here. Come around."

We followed the sound of his voice and found that the room was actually L-shaped. The desk was at the short end of the L, and the longer section of the room extended out beyond a wall, which had hidden it from our view when we first stepped into the room.

A man in his fifties with pointed eyebrows over hazel eyes and a sweep of dark hair going gray pulled the last

dart out of a board mounted on the far wall. He transferred the darts to one hand and extended his other.

"Miss Belgrave, how do you do? I hope you're recovered from the incident by the bridge."

"I'm feeling much better. Thank you for opening your
home to me."

"Happy to have you. It delights my wife to no end to
have more guests. And Mr. Rimington, are you enjoying
your stay—except for the unpleasantness at the belvedere,
of course?"

"Excepting that incident, very much so."

"Glad to hear it. As you can see, I was having a game of
darts. I'm working out a tricky problem. I find that it frees
my mind up if I do another activity, something mindless.
Care for a turn?"

"Don't mind if I do," Jasper said. "Olive? Are you in as
well?"

"Of course."

If Mr. Searsby was surprised that Jasper assumed I'd
want to play, he didn't show it. Jasper handed the darts to
me. "Ladies first."

My first throw went wide, hitting at the rim of the
target, but my next two were much closer to the bullseye.
Jasper did even better, his darts all striking near the
center. We played a few rounds. Jasper and I acquitted
ourselves fairly well, but it was Mr. Searsby who consis-
tently hit the bullseye. Despite his expensive finely
tailored suit, he looked quite comfortable throwing darts
and seemed to enjoy the friendly competition. Jasper
nearly beat him, but his last shot went wide.

"Jolly good showing, Mr. Rimington!"

Jasper walked down to the target to retrieve the darts.
Mr. Searsby put his hands in his pockets. "Time to get

down to work," he said as he and I strolled to the desk. He gestured for me to have a seat in one of the chairs facing the desk before he went around to the other side. "I understand you're quite good at finding answers to perplexing questions, Miss Belgrave."

"I find I don't like perplexing questions. I like answers."

"So do I, Miss Belgrave. So do I." Jasper sat down beside me in the matching chair. Mr. Searsby looked from one of us to the other. "I take it you two are a team."

"Yes, we work well together."

Jasper added, "I'd say our skills complement each other. Of course, mysterious death is Olive's specialty. She's the one who's been helpful to the police in the past."

"Yes, that's what I understand. I've checked up on you, Miss Belgrave." He gave me a brief smile. "I'm sure you understand. I'm not about to turn someone loose in my household unless I've investigated their bonafides. And yours, Miss Belgrave, seem to be in order."

"I'm glad to hear it," I said. "Did you have any questions for me?"

"If you were to look into Bankston's death, what would that involve?"

"We'd be as discreet as possible. The first thing to do would be to look around Bankston's quarters, then try to work out why he went to the belvedere."

"Foolish thing to do, that," Mr. Searsby said.

"He wasn't in the habit of going there?"

Mr. Searsby shrugged. "I have no idea."

Jasper said, "Then some discreet questioning of the servants would be in order. They will probably have more insight into Bankston's habits. My man Grigsby can take care of that." Jasper glanced at me, and I nodded.

"Grigsby is here now and has a good rapport with staff, I believe."

"Good." Mr. Searsby ran his hand over his chin. "The man from Scotland Yard will arrive tomorrow. We've attempted to keep that news quiet, but it's difficult to do. Have a snoop around—as inconspicuously as possible—and see what you can find out. I'd like nothing better than to wrap this whole thing up and present it to the London man as a *fait accompli*. I'd rather avoid having a man from the Yard invade our holiday. Most likely Bankston's death was an accident—although dashed if I can figure out why Bankston would be at the belvedere."

Mrs. Searsby came into the room, and the men stood as she went around the desk to her husband. She'd removed the worn beret and ulster and wore an elegant silk dress. "I see you've met Miss Belgrave."

Mr. Searsby said, "Yes. Everything is arranged. Miss Belgrave and Mr. Rimington will do some quiet investigation this afternoon."

"Good. I do hope you'll be able to sort this out quickly. Tomorrow we put up the tree and bring in the Yule log. I don't want a police investigation to mar our Christmas celebrations." She sighed. "The housekeeper asked me about Scotland Yard, so the word is already out among the servants. I did my best to downplay it, but I'm sure the news will spread throughout the house."

"Don't worry, my dear. Everything will be fine." Mr. Searsby pushed in his chair, and I stood as well. "Miss Belgrave and Mr. Rimington would like to begin by examining Bankston's rooms."

"Then you'll want to see his bedroom along with his sitting room. I've already checked the silver safe. I used Mr. Searsby's duplicate key. Mrs. Pickering—the housekeeper—and I examined the contents. Nothing is missing."

Mr. Searsby said, "I asked my wife to check it. I'm sure the Scotland Yard people will want to know."

"I didn't have any doubt it was all just as it should be," Mrs. Searsby said.

"But he'd been with you for some time?" I asked.

"Over three years," Mr. Searsby said. "Excellent at his job. No complaints there."

Mrs. Searsby patted her husband's arm as we walked to the door. "Of course Mr. Searsby wouldn't have kept Bankston on if he wasn't good at his job."

"I have little patience with incompetence."

The genial host who had played darts was now frowning, and I could see the businessman in him. I imagined he was the sort of person who had high expectations for his staff, and if those expectations weren't met, then the person would be let go quickly.

"When would you like to begin?" Mrs. Searsby asked.

Jasper waved a hand, deferring to me, and I said, "Immediately."

"Then let me ring for Mrs. Pickering. She can take you to Bankston's quarters."

$\sim$

BANKSTON HAD A SPARSELY furnished bedroom with the other servants' rooms at the top of the house. Mrs. Pickering, a spindly woman with a brisk manner, stood with her hand on the doorknob. She had kept her face blank when Mrs. Searsby informed her that Jasper and I would be making inquiries into Bankston's death and that information was to be kept from the rest of the staff, but now it was clear she wasn't pleased with the idea of leaving us alone in Bankston's room.

The room contained a single bed covered with a thick counterpane in dark blue, a bureau with shaving implements laid out in a neat row in front of the mirror, and a fine walnut wardrobe. The only personal touches were a photograph of a Highland landscape and a stack of books on the bedside table. Jasper tilted his head so he could read the spines of the books, which were perfectly aligned, as I asked Mrs. Pickering, "I suppose Bankston didn't spend much time here?"

"No, miss. He was always busy about his work."

"He had a sitting room as well?"

"Yes, miss. Belowstairs, next to my sitting room."

"We'll need to see it as well. We'll come downstairs and ring for you when we're ready to see his sitting room."

Her brow lowered. "I don't hold with ladies and gentlemen coming belowstairs. It upsets things."

"We'll do our best to not cause a commotion. In fact, we'd prefer to keep our visit as quiet as possible." The attic rooms were deserted at this time of day, so there was no one to see us here, but the basement of Holly Hill Lodge would be bustling. "Our only interest is to discover what happened to Bankston," I added in my most placating tone.

Her gaze, which had been challenging, wavered. "Yes. Terrible, that."

"Do you know why he walked back from the station?"

"No, and it was a foolish thing to do with the storm on the way."

Jasper looked up from the books. "He wasn't in the habit of walking back?"

"Mr. Bankston?" She gave a little scoffing laugh. "No.

He much preferred to have Thompson, the chauffeur, drive him."

Jasper motioned to the bedside table. "A dictionary and thesaurus. Not quite the usual bedtime reading."

A smile crossed Mrs. Pickering's face. "Mr. Bankston was fond of his word puzzles."

"Word puzzles?" I asked.

"The sort with clues and squares that you fill with each letter of your answer."

"Oh, yes. I've seen them in a few ladies' magazines. Crosswords, I believe they're called."

"That's right. Crosswords. That's what he used the dictionaries for. 'To look up possibilities,' he said." Her attitude seemed to have softened toward us a bit. "He would sometimes read out the clues in the servants' hall. I didn't understand most of them, but he could always explain them so that they made sense—a twisted sense, if you know what I mean."

I smiled. "I do. I tried a crossword recently and failed miserably."

Mrs. Pickering chuckled. "It's very difficult to find the crossword puzzles, though. If any of the staff came across one—in a magazine that was in the rubbish or something like that—we saved it for Mr. Bankston. He even made his own crossword puzzles a few times. Stumped most of us, he did."

"What sort of man was he?" Jasper, his hands in his pockets, walked across the room to us. "His attitudes and manner?"

Mrs. Pickering considered a moment, her forehead crinkling. "It's hard to say. Now that I think about it, his fondness for crosswords was the single . . . personal . . . thing I knew about him. Most times, he was standoffish.

Of course one has to be when one is in charge of the staff, but he never made any overtures of friendship toward me —or anyone else that I know of. He was a very self-contained man. Occasionally he would have tea with me in the evening, but not often. During those times, we discussed household matters."

"Do you know if he had any family?" I asked.

"I don't believe so. At any rate, he never mentioned anyone." She shook her head. "I don't understand why he was out at the belvedere. It wasn't like him at all."

"He wasn't a rambler?" Jasper asked.

"No. He much preferred to be indoors." The chime of a clock echoed up from downstairs. "I must return to my duties."

She left, and I closed the door after she was a few steps down the hall. Jasper pulled a pair of driving gloves from his pocket and gave me the right-handed one. "Here. Best wear this." He put on the other one, then used his left hand to open the wardrobe.

"You think the police will look for fingerprints?"

"Perhaps. Better not to leave ours, don't you think?"

"Definitely. We wouldn't want to confuse the issue. I'll look in the bureau." The supple leather glove was too big for my hand. The ends of the fingertips flopped around and got in my way, but I put my other hand in my pocket so I didn't accidentally touch anything with it. I worked my way down through the drawers. "Only clothing. Everything is exceptionally neat." Each article of clothing was carefully folded and precisely placed. I pushed in the bottom drawer and moved on to search under the bed, then ran my gloved hand under the mattress.

"It's the same here," Jasper said. "His own clothes—his day suit—are of the finest quality. The shoes as well.

Everything is of the very best materials and workmanship."

I cocked my head. "Better quality than you would expect?"

He turned from the wardrobe, a pair of shoes in his hand. "From Milford & Dean," he said, his tone reverent.

"Are they?" Even I recognized the name of the exclusive shop. "A butler who shops on Bond Street. Intriguing." I kneeled and pulled out the drawers of the small bedside table. "But it sounds as if he had no family. Perhaps he spent most of his earnings on bespoke shoes and suits."

"Or he liked to indulge in luxurious things, which could be why he's helping with the couriers."

I sat back on my heels. "You mean he was doing it for money, not because he believes in their cause?"

"Money is an incredible motivator—even more so than political opinions."

"Yes, people will do quite a lot for financial gain." I returned to my search. "More books here. An old *Baedeker's*—Egypt—and several books of sermons."

"Odd assortment."

"Yes. They all have paper bookmarks with numbers. Let me see . . ." I flipped open the cover of a book of sermons. The bookplate was stamped with the name *Oscar Quick*. "Yes, they're from the library here." I angled the book so Jasper could see the bookplate. "Tommy told me Mr. Searsby purchased the contents along with the house itself from the former owner, Mr. Quick. Unusual name. That's why I remembered it." I replaced the book in the drawer. "Perhaps the books are for his crosswords. No one has said he was a devout man."

"The library here is quite extensive. It would be a good

resource for him." Jasper closed the wardrobe. "Nothing else that I see here. Ready to do downstairs?"

I took off the glove. "I'll just hang onto this, shall I?" At Jasper's nod, I tucked it into my pocket. "Hopefully his sitting room will be more revealing."

CHAPTER FOURTEEN

*M*rs. Pickering escorted us down a set of plain stairs from the family's domain on the first floor to the servants' hall and kitchens, which were on the ground floor. We met no one on the way, and I suspected that she had made sure the servants were busy so no questions would be raised about our presence. She turned the key in the lock to Bankston's sitting room and stepped back. "I locked the door once we had the news about Mr. Bankston. It seemed the proper thing to do."

"Good judgment on your part, Mrs. Pickering," Jasper said.

The door opened to a large chilly room with polished wood furniture and a richly patterned Oriental carpet in a deep red and white pattern. An armchair sat in one corner by the fireplace, a large desk of polished wood filled another wall, and a grandfather clock stood by the window that looked out on the gardens at the back of the house.

Mrs. Pickering, her manner not nearly as frosty as it had been earlier, said, "The door on the right is the silver

SARA ROSETT

safe." She hesitated. "I can't open that for you. Mr. Bankston had that key with him. Mrs. Searsby brought the duplicate key, and we checked it together. All is in order, but she took the key away with her again."

"We don't need to have a look at it," I said. "At the moment, we're only concerned with his personal effects."

"Then I'll leave you to have a quick look around. I'll return and lock up after you leave," she said and departed.

I moved to the center of the room. "She put a bit of emphasis on the word *quick*. She doesn't want us to linger here."

"Yes, we're making her skittish, being belowstairs. However, I don't think it will take too long." Jasper went to the desk, pulling his glove from his pocket. "I'll start on this. It's so neat and orderly, it won't take long."

Everything on the desk from the ledgers to the inkstand to the carefully placed pencil was aligned with precision. "It does rather look as if he used a ruler to space things exactly one inch apart. Look, even the Christmas cards on the mantel are arranged just so." A card with a row of snow-covered cottages, their mullioned windows glowing with warm yellow light, sat at the exact center of the mantel. A few less-ornate cards were spaced at intervals of two inches apart on either side of the one with the cottages. Christmas packages wrapped in red paper with gold bows were stacked on either end of the mantel, arranged from largest on the bottom to the smallest on the top. I could read the tags on a few of them and saw they were for the servants.

Even with the meticulous placement of all the items, the room still felt more lived-in and homier than the bedroom. The easy chair by the fire looked comfortable, and there were more photos of the Highlands. The

120

Christmas cards and presents gave the room a cheerful holiday touch.

A high stack of books sat on the square side table by the armchair, and I went over to have a look. "More dictionaries. There's a hand-drawn plan for a crossword as well." I'd put the glove back on, and I picked up the sheet of paper that rested on top of the books. A crossword grid had been sketched on it, and some squares had been blacked out with dark pencil strokes.

Jasper looked up from the drawer he had opened. "Any clues listed for the crossword?"

"Only one, 'aristocratic beverage.' Eight letters."

We both fell silent, then Jasper said, "Earl Grey."

"Oh, very good! That fits. Of course, I'd expect a code breaker to be quite good at crosswords. Probably child's play to you."

"Any puzzle, even a simple one, can be baffling if you don't have the key."

I replaced the paper. "Well, there's nothing else here. It looks like it was a preliminary sketch with that one clue listed."

"Then it's not useful to us." Jasper closed the desk drawer and moved to another one. "Except for a couple of unopened packs of Woodbine cigarettes, I'm not finding anything here either."

"So he did smoke the same kind of cigarette you noticed at the belvedere."

"Appears so." Jasper shifted the contents of the next drawer. "Ledgers with the household accounts. He kept the wine cellar well stocked. Correspondence of the sort one would expect. Stamps, ink, and blank writing paper." Jasper pulled out the rolling desk chair to open the lap drawer.

I shifted the dictionary out of the way to have a look at the books on the bottom of the stack, which were another travel guide and a book of poems. A soft leather-bound book didn't have anything printed on the spine. I tugged it out, sat down on the edge of the easy chair, and opened it on my lap.

The lined pages were filled with tidy handwriting, notes about tradesmen to be paid and workmen who were scheduled to arrive to complete repairs. A folded down corner further on marked another section related to Mrs. Searsby's guests. Bankston had detailed which bedroom guests were to have along with any of their preferences, such as whether a lady wanted tea or cocoa served on a tray in her room in the morning, or which newspaper a gentleman read. Mrs. Searsby was a thoughtful hostess, instructing Bankston to see that a guest's favorite flowers were placed in the room along with special soaps for the ladies and cigarettes for the men.

I flipped through the pages. Bankston's personality came through in his short notes. For the first time I got a sense of the man. About Madge, he'd written, "Early riser. Likes tea hot and strong. Will send it back if it's only warm. Mrs. Searsby wants an arrangement of holly and white roses for the sitting room table—although Miss Lambert will never notice." Under Ambrose Eggers, he'd noted, "Fussy about linen and clothing. Must valet him myself. No one else will be up to his standards. Linen closet to be his darkroom. Remind staff to avoid it at all times."

"Find anything?" Jasper asked. "Like a handy notation —perhaps a star—by a name with the words 'next courier' beside it?"

"I'm afraid not."

"No, that would be far too simple." He sighed. "Of course it would be folly to commit something of that nature to paper. He wouldn't write it down."

I slowed as I reached the last pages with Bankston's handwriting, the section devoted to the current guests. I turned a page, and the notebook fell open where a page had been ripped out. "This is curious."

"What?"

"Does Bankston strike you as the sort of man who would tear a page from a notebook in a sloppy manner?"

Jasper glanced at the desk where everything was neatly squared away. "No. I'd imagine he'd take a ruler and use a penknife to cut away a page."

I went across to the desk and pointed out the ragged edge of the page that was still attached to the spine. "It's a book of Bankston's notes on household matters. The missing page is in the section about the current guests."

"Looks as if he was in a hurry to remove it," Jasper said.

I tilted the notebook closer to the light of the desk lamp that Jasper had switched on. "Look, there's some writing on the bit of paper that's still attached to the spine —the first letter of a word, a capital letter *T*. It must be someone's name. See on these other pages how he wrote the names on a single line, then indented his notes about each guest underneath?"

"So it must be either . . . Tommy Phillips or Theo Culwell."

"Let me see who's missing from the entries." I went back to the chair and fumbled with the pages. The glove made my fingers clumsy, but I finally turned the pages and read through the names of the most recent houseguests. "They're listed by given name, then surname . . . there's no listing for Tommy Phillips."

Jasper was glancing through a stack of what appeared to be letters. The pages were folded in thirds and didn't lie flat. His attention was on what he was reading, and he murmured a noise that indicated he was half-listening to me. I went through the entries again to double check that I hadn't missed Tommy's name—I hadn't—but this time I read slower and noticed one of Bankston's jottings underneath Prudence Brinkle's name. Bankston had written, "Too fond of gin. Can probably get twenty pounds out of the old girl."

I sat up straighter and read the note aloud to Jasper.

He looked up from the papers. I had his complete attention now. "That's . . . curious. Sounds rather nefarious, in fact."

"Yes, it does sound like Bankston intended to indulge in a spot of extortion, doesn't it? And—remember in the garden—Miss Brinkle was talking to Mrs. Searsby about an 'odious man.'"

"I don't recall what they were saying. I was focused on getting the little plaque in place."

"Well, I do. Miss Brinkle must have been talking about Bankston. She said she wouldn't mourn him. She mentioned a fuss over G&Ts and Mrs. Searsby said 'Frank'—Mr. Searsby—wouldn't have cut off Miss Brinkle's allowance."

"Then it does sound as if Bankston intended to ask for hush money," Jasper said. "I guess that answers our question about what motivated him."

"It certainly appears to," I said. "He was in a position to know the habits of the guests. Perhaps he threatened to send off an anonymous note if Miss Brinkle didn't pay him. Twenty pounds isn't an outrageous amount. Bankston probably hoped she would pay up without much of a fuss to make it go away."

"We're not building a flattering picture of Bankston." Jasper tilted his head, indicating the stack of books at my elbow. "His interest in crossword puzzles seems to be the only redeeming feature we've uncovered."

"He was good at his job. Mr. and Mrs. Searsby said he was an excellent butler."

"But if Miss Brinkle is right," Jasper countered, "Bankston used his trusted position to his advantage."

"That's true. Let me see if there's anything else here . . ." I looked over the entries carefully. "Yes, there's more. I missed these notations earlier because I was focused on the names, not the details about each person. Under Theo Culwell's name, Bankston wrote, 'Research Culwell Luggage Company, headquarters in Kansas City,' and then there's—"

Jasper held up a finger. "Wait. Kansas City . . . didn't I see . . . ?" He flipped back through the letters, then plucked one from the pile. "Yes, here it is. A letter from the Kansas City Rotary Club." As he skimmed the contents, his eyebrows moved up his forehead. "I didn't read it earlier. I was only checking the return addresses, but listen to this. 'Dear Mr. Bankston, regarding your inquiry into Culwell Luggage Company, we are unable to provide any further information as the company is not located in Kansas City. However, Anderson Fine Luggage and Trunks is located here. Their owner, Mr. Stephen Row, is astute and stays on the forefront of all things in his industry. He assures me that there is no such company as Culwell Luggage in Kansas City. He would be familiar with it if it did exist. I enclose Mr. Row's address, if you would like to correspond with him. I can vouch for the quality of Mr. Row's luggage. It is excellent. Please let us know if we can be of any further assistance.'"

I jumped up. "But then that would mean—Culwell Luggage Company doesn't exist. Theo told me himself the headquarters are in Kansas City." I went across and read the letter, then handed it back. "How incredibly bizarre. He's clearly passionate about luggage, and Francie said she'd seen samples of his aeroplane case."

"Anyone could have a prototype made and travel about in another country, raising investment funds and then . . ."

"Disappear with the money. Oh, dear. We'll have to tell Francie. That will be upsetting."

Jasper refolded the letter. "Perhaps a word with Mr. Searsby might be the better course. At least let him know the situation before he invests, then he can tell his daughter."

"Yes, that would be better. But more to the point for us, Bankston apparently intended to put what he'd learned from the helpful Kansas City Rotary Club to work." I found my place in Bankston's notes. "There's more to his entry under Theo's name. Bankston used a very fine pencil, so it's difficult to read, but the amount of two hundred pounds is written beside the note about Kansas City." I tapped the notebook with my gloved finger. "There's no question about it. Bankston was blackmailing the guests."

"It certainly looks that way. This whole stack of letters is of a similar nature as the rotary letter. At first, I thought perhaps Mr. Searsby was having Bankston make inquiries about certain companies and persons, but that would be more the purview of a secretary, not a butler. Bankston was checking up on everyone. He inquired about Mr.

Eggers' scientific research, then had a private detective check on Miss Ravenna's habits regarding paramours as well as drugs—she'll find that amusing, I'm sure."

"And you? Did he have you investigated?"

He shook his head. "Nothing. I was a late addition to the guest list. He probably didn't have time to research me."

"Thank goodness for small favors," I said. "Such secrets you have—you could have been a veritable treasure trove!"

"Quite." He met my teasing tone with a smile, then went on. "I also found a letter about Madge Lambert—checking what school she attended and what her connections are. And finally, the last related to our little group is a letter to a reporter asking if there's any dirt on Blix Windway. It's couched in more civilized language, but that's what it boils down to. The single response that was —unflattering, shall we say—was the one about the Culwell Luggage Company."

"Nothing about Tommy Phillips?"

Jasper looked again. "No. Nothing."

I ran my gloved finger down the jagged edge of the missing page. "Odd that Tommy's page is missing from Bankston's notes and that there's no letter about him."

Jasper said, "Maybe there *was* a letter and it was removed when the page was torn out."

I leaned back in the chair. "Remember when we set out on our walk earlier and came around the corner of the house and met Tommy. He was stomping snow from his boots. If my sense of direction is right, he would have been coming from somewhere around this area of the house."

Jasper and I both looked at the room's single window,

which gave a view of the back gardens where the wind was dragging at the tree branches and driving snow against the hedges. Jasper crossed to the window and examined it without touching it. "This catch is unlocked." He popped up on his tiptoes to look at the ground directly below the window. "Large prickly holly bushes on either side, but not a hedge of them. It wouldn't be a comfortable experience, but it would be possible for Tommy to get to this window. The latch is a simple one. It could be opened with the blade of a penknife. Very lax, considering this room has the entrance to the silver safe."

I felt the rug under the window. "Damp. You know what this means, don't you? I didn't share Miss Ravenna's assurance that Bankston's death had nothing to do with his involvement with couriers, but she may have been absolutely correct. His killer might have been a blackmailed houseguest."

CHAPTER FIFTEEN

*T*hat night after dinner, when the card games in the drawing room broke up and everyone began to retire for the evening, Jasper and I left the room together. Once we'd climbed the stairs to the next floor and were alone in the long corridor, Jasper asked, "Any luck?"

"No, it was a complete washout for me."

Jasper and I had decided to keep our discoveries about Bankston to ourselves for the moment. The police would arrive tomorrow, and we'd share what we'd found with them. Our plan for the evening had been to watch the interactions of the guests and try to glean any details we could about Bankston. We'd planned to divide and conquer, with Jasper concentrating on Tommy while I focused on Theo. However, I'd only had a chance to exchange a few words with him.

At dinner, I'd been seated between Jasper and Mr. Sprigg. I'd heard quite a bit about Mr. Sprigg's London-based import-export business, but Theo and Francie were too far down the table for me to overhear their conversa-

129

tion. "I learned Mr. Sprigg didn't know Theo before meeting him here. When I asked him about Culwell Luggage, Mr. Sprigg said, 'Never heard of it—although I've become quite well acquainted with the man's merchandise now.'"

In the drawing room after dinner, several couples had played bridge. I'd volunteered to join in, angling to be paired with Theo and Francie, but Mrs. Searsby had steered me to another table where I was Jasper's partner in a game with Mr. Sprigg and Blix. Mr. Sprigg, who had been quite chatty with me at dinner, transferred his attention to Blix, complimenting her clever tactics. Blix was unfailingly polite, but her cool rejoinders conveyed that warmer attentions from Mr. Sprigg wouldn't be welcomed. I'd suggested a change of partners, but Francie said she wanted to get Theo's opinion on an antique trunk in the Oak Hall and whisked him away. "I had no luck at all with Theo. What about you?"

"I had a few moments to speak with Tommy when the gentlemen stayed behind in the dining room. He has a long scratch on his jaw. He says it's from shaving, but it could have been made when he pushed through those holly bushes outside Bankston's sitting room."

"Interesting. Oh, I did sit with Miss Brinkle for a bit. She'd had several cocktails. In fact, it almost seemed as if she was celebrating. She was quite jolly by the end of the evening. I tried to ask her about Bankston, but she dodged the subject both times I brought it up. First, she wanted to know more about my deep interest in sundials"—I threw a look at Jasper, and he grinned—"but I managed to dodge the subject by asking her about her cocktails. Her all-time favorite is the Pink Lady, and she says people are 'too precipice' and dismiss it too quickly."

"Falling off a cliff over it, are they? Conversation with Miss Brinkle is entertaining," Jasper said, then turned more serious. "It's not surprising she avoided the topic of Bankston. People wouldn't want anyone else to know they'd been blackmailed. Of course they would keep quiet about it."

As we came to a stop outside my door, Jasper looked at the ceiling. "I must see about having a sprig of mistletoe put up here."

"That could be a very good idea." There was no one else in the hallway, and I went up on my toes to plant a kiss on Jasper's cheek. He slipped his arm around my back and held me close as he turned his face to me.

"That was nice. I think"—he looked away as if contemplating something grave like economic policy—"we should do that again."

I matched his sober tone. "I agree."

The sound of a throat clearing signaled that we weren't alone, and we stepped apart.

Apparently, we'd shocked Mr. Eggers so much that we'd rendered him motionless. He'd played bridge at the other table and won every game. He'd looked quite pleased when we left the drawing room, but now his frown radiated disapproval, and he reminded me of my headmistress.

Jasper bowed. "Good evening, Mr. Eggers. I was telling Miss Belgrave goodnight. She's an old family friend."

Mr. Eggers sniffed, wished us goodnight, then moved with small mincing steps to the far side of the hallway as if we might contaminate him. I waited until the faint jingle of his watch chain had died away before I said, "What a prissy little man. He might as well be an old maid."

"In case there are any more disapproving old biddies around, I bid you good night." Jasper kept his gaze linked with mine as he kissed the back of my hand. Even though I was wearing gloves, it was extremely pleasant.

~

24 DECEMBER 1923

The next morning before I came fully awake, I realized something was different. It took me a moment to work out what it was. A stillness permeated the house. The wind that had lashed the windows yesterday, rattling the panes, had disappeared. One set of drapes wasn't completely closed, and a shining bar of light blazed across the bed. The bright luminescent quality of the single strip was enough to tell me that the snow hadn't melted during the night.

A tap sounded on my door, and Laura came in with my cup of chocolate. "Good morning, Miss Belgrave." She set down the tray and drew back the curtains. "It snowed all night, miss. It's at least a foot deep now."

"Goodness."

"Makes it nice and Christmasy, doesn't it? Cook said if it was to snow, she'd prefer it on Christmas Day, but I still think it's nice."

"That's right. Today is Christmas Eve." I propped myself up on my elbow so I could see out the windows, but they were fogged over, which distorted the view into an abstract picture of lines and curves. "And the roads?"

She shook her head. "Blocked with drifts. Mr. Ford went and checked at the gates. Up to his knees, it was. The girls who were to come in from the village to help today won't be able to get here. Everything is at a standstill. Even the trains aren't running today."

Which meant that investigators from Scotland Yard wouldn't make it either. "Is the telephone still working?"

"Yes, miss. As far as I know."

I reached for my dressing gown. "Then I had better dress and make a telephone call right away in case it goes out." I'd been so wrapped up in the events around Bankston's death that all thoughts of traveling to Parkview had gone right out of my head. Gwen expected me to arrive today, which certainly wouldn't happen.

Someone was splashing about in the adjoining bath, but they finished quickly and went out through the door that opened to the corridor. I washed, then Laura helped me into a velvet dress in a deep shade of green.

On my way down to breakfast, I met Mrs. Searsby in the hall. She carried a small basket, and the Jack Russell terrier and Labrador were at her heels. "Oh, you are awake. Good." She walked down the stairs with me. "I wanted to make sure you're still feeling well."

Zeus zipped down the steps, his little terrier legs a blur. Apollo followed him at a chipper lope.

"I am." I touched my forehead. I'd again combed my fringe down over the cut. It was tender and turning an unlovely shade of puce. Other than the unflattering color of the bruise, it wasn't bothering me.

"I'm glad to hear it. You really mustn't even consider leaving." She motioned to the tall windows on the landing, which weren't as foggy as those in my room. The view of the grounds showed a contrast of pure white layers of snow cut through with the sharp dark shadows from the bare tree limbs. "It would be foolish to attempt to drive, and the trains are canceled. You will stay on with us through Christmas, won't you? There's no chance of it melting by tomorrow."

"I'd be delighted."

"Good. That's settled, then."

"I'm so thankful that I landed here."

"I consider it a happy coincidence, especially if you're able to help sort out the trouble around Bankston. Any luck?"

"Nothing yet," I hedged. I didn't want to bring up Bankston's possible blackmail activities unless we were sure it was connected to his death. "Do you mind if I use the telephone to contact Parkview Hall?"

"Of course not. It's in the alcove outside the Oak Hall. Help yourself. You must let them know you've been delayed. Otherwise they'll worry you've crashed into a snowdrift." She half turned away, then said, "I almost forgot. Let me give you this." She held out the basket. "A few things to make your stay more comfortable. All the guests receive them, so you must have one too."

"Thank you. You're too kind." A card with my name written on it rested on top of several bars of lavender soap.

"Nonsense. I enjoy giving gifts. It's one of the things that delights me."

A footman walked by, toting an enormous ladder, and Zeus shot out after him. Mrs. Searsby called the little dog back. He wheeled around and zoomed back to her side. Apollo gamboled over and leaned against my leg while I rubbed his ears.

"We're bringing in the tree today. I hope you'll join us in the Oak Hall and help decorate it after luncheon."

"Count me in," I said.

"Wonderful. I'll leave you to your telephone call, then."

After listening to a series of clicks, pauses, and dead air followed by crackling static, I was connected with Parkview Hall. I explained what had happed, and Gwen's voice, tinny and choppy, came over the line. "Not coming?"

"I'm sorry," I said. "I'm afraid there's nothing I can do. I'm snowed in. Drifts blocking the road, and the trains have been canceled. It's amazingly beautiful, though."

"Sounds like a Christmas card, but I do hate for you to be stranded among strangers. Where did you say you were?"

"Holly Hill Lodge." I gave her a brief, highly abridged recap of the last couple of days, and ended by saying, "And Jasper is here as well."

"Jasper—!"

"And he's still speaking to me—in quite a nice way, actually."

She laughed. "Oh, I see how it is. Everything makes sense now. So your snooping worked out. Lucky you, snowed in with him. I won't worry about you now. I'll miss you, of course, and I expect you to come along to Parkview as soon as you can. In the meantime, I hope there's plenty of mistletoe scattered throughout the house. Let us know when you're arriving. Lucas' parents are staying on until the new year, and Violet's invited James to come up as well. They're quite devoted to each other and can't be apart for more than a few days. I hope you can make it."

"I do too. I'll do my best to be there."

I returned to my room and unpacked the gifts from Mrs. Searsby's basket. The envelope contained a Christmas card with a row of cottages, a match to the one propped on Bankston's mantel. Mrs. Searsby had written a lovely welcoming note inside, and both she and her husband had signed it. I put it up on the mantel, just as Bankston had done, then I picked up the lavender soap and headed for the bath that adjoined my room, but I stopped short with my hand poised to knock before I entered. A sharp male voice sounded on the other side of the closed door. "Scotland Yard, Maggs! *Scotland Yard.*"

I pulled my hand back as I recognized Tommy's voice.

"Keep your voice down," a higher-pitched woman's voice answered.

I felt my eyebrows shoot up. That was Madge. They were arguing in the bath! An image of Mr. Eggers' disapproving face from last evening popped into my mind. If he were standing outside the door of the bath that opened to the hall, how scandalized he'd be—two single young people in there together! He'd probably faint dead away and require smelling salts.

Tommy's voice was impatient. "That room is empty. No one is staying there. Forget about that. I don't know why you can't understand that I had to do something."

"And a foolish thing it was. I told you I'd taken care of Bankston."

The fine heating system of Holly Hill Lodge clicked on. I must not have closed the door between the bath and my room firmly enough. As soon as the air gusted out of the vents, the bath door swung open, releasing a waft of damp air scented with powder. Wearing only a slip, Madge stood in front of the basin holding a hairbrush. Tommy leaned against the tub in a brightly patterned dressing gown, smoking a cigarette.

CHAPTER SIXTEEN

"*I*'m sorry—um—" I couldn't come up with any sort of coherent response that would smooth over the highly inappropriate fact that Madge and Tommy were in the bathroom together, both in a state of undress.

Madge shot a furious look at Tommy, then said, "No, we're sorry to disturb you. You'd better come and let us tell you about it." Madge turned away and went through the opposite door in the bathroom into a spacious room where she slipped on a pale green dressing gown.

Tommy made a motion indicating I should precede him into the bedroom. The velvet lapel of the dressing gown lay against his collarbone, leaving his neck and jaw exposed. The long red scratch stood out starkly against his pale skin.

I was still holding the lavender soap. I put it down on a table in my room, then walked through the steamy bath. I felt my face flushing at the awkward situation, and my velvet dress suddenly seemed too warm, but I certainly couldn't shut my door and walk away—especially not after discovering the missing pages from Bankston's notebook contained information about Tommy.

Madge gestured with the hairbrush she still held, indicating I should take the upholstered armchair, then she plopped down on the dressing table stool and spun around so that her back faced the mirror triptych. Tommy went to the far side of the room near the window and lit another cigarette.

Madge said, "It's not nearly so scandalous as it seems. The long and short of it is that Tommy and I are married."

"Married? But your wedding is in February." The newspaper-reading public was fascinated with the two lawn tennis stars. Since they'd announced their engagement, I'd seen several articles about them and their upcoming wedding.

Madge aligned the edges of her dressing gown over her knees. "The wedding in February is all for show. We'll be married twice over."

Tommy, with his gaze on the blurry view out the fogged window, said, "We'll have tied the knot good and tight."

I looked from one of them to the other. "I'm sorry, but I'm frightfully lost. You're married, but you're having a wedding?"

Madge rotated the hairbrush handle as if it were a tennis racket. "Let me tell you the whole thing. Tommy and I did a mad, impulsive thing. We married last June. We were determined to do it despite the fact that my family didn't welcome Tommy as a son-in-law. We had the banns read in a little church in London. I used my middle name, and Tommy used his real name."

"Tommy Phillips is quite a common name." His words had a bitter undertone to them.

"Don't be like that, Tommy. It was a lovely day even though we did it in a hidden way." Madge turned back to me. "Two charwomen were our witnesses. It was really quite romantic—a secret wedding." She lowered her chin and looked up at him in a flirtatious way. The corners of his mouth went up, seemingly reluctantly.

Her face broke into a wide smile. She kept her gaze focused on Tommy as she spoke to me. "That's why I love Tommy. He never stays upset for long." They exchanged a look that made me feel quite like a gooseberry, but then Madge collected herself and turned back to me. The happiness went out of her expression. "We didn't tell my family. Daddy would have cut up rough, and well—he threatened to cut me off when we announced we were engaged, so I'm sure he would've done it if he found out we were married. We decided to keep it quiet. With all the travel we do, it's not been difficult to keep it from our families. But then in the fall, the situation changed."

Tommy crushed his cigarette in the ashtray. "My sister became engaged to Kippy—Lord Higgenbotham. Now I am not a grasping fortune hunter, but a man with connections and expectations."

Madge put the hairbrush on the table and crossed her arms. "My family did a frightful about-face. It was tacky of them, but it seemed to solve all our problems. The barriers were down. We could marry with my father's blessing. He'd be quite put out if he discovered we'd deceived him. We decided to go along with my mother's plans for a London wedding." She sighed. "We didn't realize there would be such an interest in the wedding. It's all gotten rather out of control, what with the articles and the photographs. However, no one realized the truth about us."

"Until Bankston found out about it," I said.

Madge's arms were still crossed, and her fingers tightened on her upper arms. "You know?"

"Yes."

"How?"

That was a question I didn't want to answer, so I countered with one of my own. "Does it matter? You have bigger issues to worry about, I think."

Madge's shoulders rounded, and she closed her eyes briefly. "Yes, that's true. He had a copy of the marriage certificate. Of course, something had to be done. We couldn't let him go to the newspapers."

"So what did you do?"

She twitched her shoulder back and straightened her posture. "I paid him off." She said it as if it were the most logical thing in the world. Her heavy brows came down. "It was Tommy who took an unnecessary risk."

He shoved the ashtray away, and it skidded across the table and hit a lamp with a jarring clink. "If you think Scotland Yard won't be thorough, then you're the thickheaded one, Madge. I'm the one who's saved us from being exposed."

"So you broke into Bankston's sitting room and tore the page about you out of his notebook," I said. And probably took the copy of the marriage certificate as well since Jasper hadn't found it in the desk.

Tommy caught his breath, but he recovered quickly. "That's right—you saw me on the path near the window of his sitting room."

"Yes, coming out of the bushes, although you tried to make it seem as if you'd wandered off the path because of the snow."

Madge leaned forward and braced her hands on her legs. "Olive, please—you will keep our secret, won't you?"

"That depends. I certainly don't want to upset you or your family, but Bankston is dead."

"But we had nothing to do with that. It was an accident, wasn't it? The Scotland Yard investigation is a formality. That's what everyone is saying—a horrible accident."

Tommy had come away from the window and picked up a tennis racket that had been propped against the wardrobe. He swung it back and forth, his arm moving in an easy arc. "I wanted to rough him up a bit—let Bankston know he couldn't threaten us and get away with it, but Madge talked me out of it."

Madge nodded. "I did." Her voice was firm, but I thought a flicker of concern crossed her face as she watched Tommy go through the motions of a backhand. This time, he whipped the racket through the air in a strong, decisive stroke.

Despite being on the other side of the room, I instinctively flinched. I'd thought Madge was the competitive one of the pair, but the power of his tennis stroke and the intense look on his face reminded me that Tommy was a fierce player in his own right. He spun the racket handle as Madge had spun the hairbrush. "In any case, old Bankston couldn't have come to a better end, in my opinion."

CHAPTER SEVENTEEN

*J*asper and I strolled to the far end of the Oak Hall and paused in front of a large display of swords, which were attached to the wall with the points at the center and the handles arranged in a fan shape. With his attention on the military hardware, Jasper said, "So Tommy did break into the sitting room and tear the pages out of Bankston's notebook."

"Yes. He freely admitted it."

As soon as we'd met in the Oak Hall after luncheon, Jasper and I had moved away from the group. It was our first opportunity to talk alone. As we'd circumvented the Oak Hall, I had brought him up to date on my discussion with Tommy and Madge. At the other end of the Hall, Francie and Mrs. Searsby were supervising the placement of the Christmas tree, installing it near—but not too near —the monstrous fireplace that would soon contain the Yule log. Francie looked jaunty in a navy corduroy sport suit with knee-length knickers, socks, and Oxford shoes. Mrs. Searsby was dressed more traditionally in a long-sleeved berry-red wool dress. The main door of Holly Hill Lodge stood open, letting in chilly air, which added to the already glacial atmosphere of the Hall.

Jasper and I ambled on to the next display, a full suit of armor complete with a jousting pole. "Bit extreme of Tommy, don't you think? Breaking into a locked room at a country house where one is a guest just to keep news of a wedding from getting out."

"But Madge's father is incredibly wealthy. If he were to cut her off, they would only have their tennis winnings to live on, which I'm sure are significant, but . . ."

"Yes, one can't keep playing lawn tennis and winning tournaments forever." Jasper jingled some change in his pocket as we strolled. "Her father's estate is substantial?"

"Very. It would certainly be something worth keeping Bankston quiet about. It was obvious Madge and Tommy disagreed on how to handle the situation. In fact, I heard them talking about it in the motor right after the accident. They didn't think I was listening—I had a ghastly ache in my head and was lying back with my eyes closed—but I heard Madge say they had to stop 'him.' I didn't know who they were referring to, but now that I've thought about it, I remember she said something about the man poking his ski-slope nose into their business. I should have made the connection when we discovered Bankston's body."

"His nose was the shape of a ski jump," Jasper allowed, "but there was quite a lot going on at that time. It's not surprising you didn't connect those details until now. Did Tommy or Madge tell you anything else?"

"Oh, yes. Tommy insists he simply wanted to rough Bankston up, but Madge maintains that she'd paid him off and that Tommy didn't go near Bankston."

"Did Madge say how much Bankston wanted?"

It was one of the questions I'd asked before I left Madge and Tommy. "Fifty pounds."

Jasper's lips quirked down in a thoughtful expression. "A surprisingly moderate amount to demand for keeping a secret that could lead to financial calamity."

"I expected her to name a much higher figure too. I suppose Madge could be lying about the amount, but I don't think she was."

"And you're quite good at reading people." We moved around the suit of armor, looking at it from all sides as Jasper said, "Of course, that may have been Bankston's play, request small amounts over time. Nothing to rouse someone to do anything—drastic, shall we say."

"It does agree with the amounts written in his notebook," I said, "but then we have the fact that someone killed him."

"Perhaps Bankston threatened someone with a small thing, but they had something bigger to hide."

I looked across the flagstones to the group at the other end of the Hall. The tree was now in place, a towering evergreen that looked exactly the correct size by the substantial fireplace. A footman closed the wood and iron front door, then another pair of footmen set up a tall ladder beside the tree. "Perhaps like being involved in something treasonous?"

"Possibly."

We moved on in our slow circle around the room, pausing to tilt our heads back and study a stag's head that was mounted high on the oak paneling. I wrapped the lapels of my cardigan over my chest and crossed my arms in an effort to warm up after the cold breeze that had flowed in through the open door. "On my way down here,

I tried to picture Tommy setting up the note and the string, then arranging the carefully balanced rock for Bankston and"—I shrugged—"I couldn't imagine it. It doesn't seem at all like the sort of thing Tommy would do. He strikes me as impulsive and spontaneous."

"I agree. He's a bit of a wildcard. Madge, on the other hand . . ."

"Completely the opposite. Much more strategic."

"Have you ever seen her play?" Jasper asked.

"No. Have you?"

Jasper nodded. "Last year, at a tournament in France. She's very"—his gaze, which had been on the stag's antlers, drifted to the group by the tree—"mechanical in her play. Technically, her strokes are brilliant. Clean and precise."

"You make her sound rather dispassionate."

"On the contrary. Her execution in her strokes is flawless, but there's an underlying drive, or passion, that she keeps in check. It surfaced a few times. I remember a long series of volleys in particular. The whole crowd seemed to hold their breath as the ball went back and forth, back and forth. When she finally smashed the ball home and won the point, she clenched her fist and looked triumphant. I remember thinking at the time that she only seems to be passionless."

Francie's husky tones carried across the room as she laughed at some quip from Theo. Mr. Eggers stood off to the side, smoking and staring out the window, while Mr. Sprigg chatted with Blix as she untangled the tinsel.

Miss Brinkle sat in a chair, her russet-colored gown with tufts and ruffles spread around her. She braced her hands on her cane as she leaned forward to tell Mrs.

Searsby something. Miss Brinkle's hair ornament, a decorative spray of peacock feathers that stuck straight up from her coiffure, quivered as she emphasized her point. With her plump figure and the feathers bobbing over her head, she reminded me more than ever of a pineapple.

Tommy shifted the ladder around closer to the tree as Madge distributed ornaments. "I can see Madge executing all the little details perfectly to get rid of their problem," Jasper said.

"I can too. But I suppose the question is, would she have had the opportunity to do it? No one knew Bankston would go to London until the morning he left."

"Yes, but Mrs. Searsby mentioned it at breakfast."

"How do you know that? You didn't arrive until later that day."

"I dropped by and gave Miss Ravenna an update before luncheon. I asked her about it, and she said everyone was in the breakfast room when Mrs. Searsby mentioned it."

"Everyone?"

"Yes—Madge, Tommy, Mr. Eggers, Mr. Culwell, and Francie. That's everyone except Mr. Searsby."

"How is Miss Ravenna?"

"She's running a fever and would only speak to me from across the room."

"Poor thing." What a difference a few days had made in my feelings about Bebe Ravenna. "I hope she feels better soon."

"If I know Miss Ravenna, she won't be confined to her room long. She'll be up and about soon, I'm sure."

We walked on to a glass display case of daggers, and Jasper said, "But getting back to our original topic—we won't have much longer alone—everyone knew Bankston was leaving."

"Did everyone know his destination?"

"Yes. Mrs. Searsby mentioned the name of the flower shop and that it was in London."

"Then it would be simple for someone to go into the village and send a telegram to be held at the flower shop until Bankston arrived. The telegram could set up a meeting with Bankston and instruct him to return to Holly Hill Lodge by way of the belvedere."

Jasper leaned over the case to take a closer look at the jeweled handle of a dagger. "That would give someone plenty of time to set up the—trap, let's call it—at the belvedere."

"We need to find out if anyone went into town. I doubt a murderer would entrust that type of task to anyone else's hands."

"It'll be difficult to track down everyone's movements."

"Not if we check with the servants," I said. "They'll know who stayed in and who left the house."

"Good idea, but Mr. and Mrs. Searsby want us to be discreet. Questioning the staff would certainly draw attention."

"Not if we use Grigsby, as you suggested. He's the embodiment of discretion. As long as I don't ask Grigsby, I'm sure it will work out fine." Jasper and I occasionally used the telephone to communicate, and that had put me in Grigsby's bad books. Proper young ladies did not telephone single gentlemen's residences.

"All right, I'll have him begin inquiries. He will do it quietly, of course."

Mr. Sprigg called out to us, "Are the two lovebirds joining us for tree decorating?"

"In a moment," Jasper replied good-naturedly. "The armaments are rather intriguing."

"Armaments? Hmm. I imagine it's your companion, rather than those dusty old things, that is keeping you occupied. If I were a younger man, I'd give you a run for your money with the lovely lady," he said with a flare of his eyebrow in my direction before returning to the group by the tree.

I fixed a smile on my face as I said in a low voice, "You know, it isn't necessarily only someone at Holly Hill Lodge who could have set up the trap for Bankston. It could have been Mr. Sprigg. If Bankston took the path that runs by the belvedere when he went to the village, Mr. Sprigg might have seen Bankston when he departed for London."

Jasper tipped his head to the side as he thought. "But how would he know Bankston was going to London?"

"You've got me there, I'll admit. Perhaps Mrs. Searsby or one of the other guests told Mr. Sprigg."

"And what would Mr. Sprigg's motive be?"

"The same as everyone else's, to stop Bankston from blackmailing him."

"Mr. Sprigg wasn't in Bankston's notebook," Jasper countered.

"No, but I've learned that if I draw the circle of suspicion too small, I may miss an important suspect. Mr. Sprigg is a randy old thing. Perhaps Bankston discovered a liaison that Mr. Sprigg would rather keep quiet."

"Possible, but if we're including him, we must also add Miss Brinkle to our theoretical list."

"I know you're joking, but you're right." I watched the feathers quiver on Miss Brinkle's hair ornaments as she made a point while chatting with Blix. "She seems unlikely. I don't think her cane is for show."

"Yes, I agree. I do think she appears to need the help of it to get around. Managing the stairs would be difficult for her."

"And then there's also Blix," I added, playing devil's advocate. "She's like Miss Brinkle. Both of them are late arrivals and weren't here—as far as we know—when the trap was set. Either one of them could have arrived earlier, positioned the rock to fall at the belvedere, then made a show of arriving later to put themselves out of the running."

A footman arrived with a yellow-hued cocktail on a salver and held it out to Miss Brinkle. She scooped it up, sipped, and sighed with satisfaction. I studied her for a moment. "No, it's too far-fetched. I can't imagine Miss Brinkle climbing the stairs of the belvedere or balancing the stone so that it would fall. Blix, on the other hand—"

Jasper nodded. "She seems quite capable."

"One would have to be to travel the world alone as she does."

As we began to move slowly across the flagstones toward the tree, Jasper said, "I've had a very busy morning myself."

"Really?"

"You sound as if you don't believe me."

"You must admit, you're not generally an early riser."

"Normally, no. But at the moment I'm searching for a certain valuable item—rather motivates one since the clock is ticking away."

"Yes, we only have one more day to locate Bankston's directions to the letter. What have you been doing?"

"I had a look in Mr. Theo Culwell's room."

"Really?"

"Don't look so shocked. You may be the daughter of a vicar, but I don't suffer from your moral impediments. I had a very unconventional upbringing."

"That's no excuse."

"However, the security of the nation is."

I dipped my head. "I can see your point. Find anything?"

"Yes. Mr. Culwell is carrying several letters of introduction. Most from businessmen in America. Including one from a familiar name in Kansas City—a Mr. Row."

"Forgeries?" I asked as we moved across the flagstones to the tree.

"I'd imagine so. However, Mr. Culwell certainly hasn't been lying about his travels. He has orders for his aeroplane cases from citizens in Birmingham, Manchester, and Yorkshire, and a stack of checks to go with them."

Jasper stopped walking while we were still out of earshot of the group. "One other thing—I had a peek in the linen closet that Mr. Eggers is using for a darkroom. Grigsby told me that the staff has been instructed not to use the closet while Mr. Eggers is in residence. Something that is strictly off-limits fairly cries out to be examined."

"I agree wholeheartedly. And what did you find?"

"All the accouterments that one would use to develop film—chemicals, drying racks, tongs, shallow baths. Everything as it should be, except for one thing."

"What was that?" I asked as Francie handed Theo a small box of ornaments and motioned to the ladder. From where I stood, I could see Theo's Adam's apple bob as he eyed the ladder before he climbed a few rungs.

"A red light. As talented as Mr. Eggers may be, I doubt he can develop photos in complete darkness."

"Perhaps the light broke, and he threw it away?"

"Then he'd have requested something to use instead. A lamp covered with red fabric, perhaps. But Grigsby tells me he's made no such request."

"So Mr. Eggers is here under false pretenses too? What a lot of scoundrels at this Christmas celebration."

Francie's voice carried to us as she called out, "Not there, Theo. Higher. Those ornaments must go at the top of the tree."

He gave a jerky nod and ascended several rungs of the ladder.

Jasper picked up a pile of tinsel and began to unwind it, his voice low enough that only I could hear. "I took a gander around Mr. Eggers' bedroom as well."

"How industrious of you."

Jasper grinned. "I do try." Then his face turned serious. "Mr. Eggers does have many photographs of snowflakes in his room—more than he showed us at dinner. Fascinating and rather beautiful. They certainly weren't taken by a dilettante, so I'm not sure about him."

"Then he bears further investigation as well."

Jasper let out a sigh. "Yes. It's all very interesting, and I understand you're keen on finding out who the murderer is—I'm interested in discovering the truth around that as well. But unfortunately, I found nothing that resembled a cipher or code that Bankston could have passed along to Culwell or Eggers which they could use to find the location of a letter to carry away from here."

"Theo!" Francie's sharp voice cut through the chatter. "Don't tilt the box! You'll—"

He jerked his hand up, and the ladder rocked with his sudden movement. Theo, his face going the color of snow, leaned into the ladder, and his sudden shift caused it to teeter even more.

The box of decorations listed lower in his hand, forgotten. The ornaments fell in a cascade, shattering as they hit the stone floor, sending out tiny explosions of glass shards. The ladder swayed and tilted, and Jasper sprinted toward it.

CHAPTER EIGHTEEN

*J*asper, Mr. Sprigg, and Tommy converged on the ladder at the same time and steadied it. At the apex of the ladder, Theo had wrapped his arms around one of the rungs and clung like the limpet to the underside of the ship. He stayed that way, head tucked and shoulders drawn in for a few seconds, until Francie called up, "Are you all right, Theo?"

He lifted his head and unwound his arms, then began to inch down. "Everything's Jake," he said, but there was a definite tremble in his voice. He stepped off the last rung and brushed down his suit coat. "I'm sorry about the ornaments, Mrs. Searsby. I do apologize. Foolish of me to be inattentive like that."

"Don't fret about it. As long as you're fine, then there's nothing to worry about. Although you did give us quite a fright."

He chuckled, but it sounded forced. "I gave myself a fright too." Drops of perspiration beaded his hairline. His face was still pale, and I thought he probably needed to sit down, but a maid arrived and began sweeping up the glass shards. We all stepped back, and Theo took out his handkerchief and wiped his forehead. Once the floor was swept, Mrs. Searsby said, "It's looking lovely. I've rung for tea, so if someone will hang these last ornaments, we can relax and admire our handiwork."

Jasper and I did our part, placing glass decorations and arranging sparkling garlands. With the fire crackling and the scent of evergreen filling the Hall, it was a festive scene.

A maid brought in tea, and Mrs. Searsby declared, "Looks delightful! Thank you, everyone. Time for a well-earned break."

Francie was eyeing the tree, her head tilted to the side. "Oh, bother. We forgot to put the star at the top."

Theo's gaze darted to the tree, the ladder, and then to Francie in a way that made me think of a mouse triangulating an escape route from a cat. Francie, her head down as she dug through a box, didn't notice. "Ah," she said. "Here it is."

Mr. Sprigg stepped forward. "Allow me. Young Culwell has had enough of ladders today, I think."

"Oh, thank you, but it won't take a minute, and I haven't done nearly enough today." Francie was already climbing as she spoke, moving up the ladder with an agile lope. Once she reached the upper rungs, she held onto one side of the ladder, leaned out, and positioned the star on the top bough. Still leaning out over the tree, she looked down. "Theo, is it straight?"

He opened his mouth to say something, but only a choked sound came out. He cleared his throat. "Looks swell."

"Good." She came back down the ladder as rapidly as

she went up. Beside me, Theo let out a shaky breath when Francie's feet were on the flagstones.

Mrs. Searsby motioned for the ladder to be removed, then said to the footmen, "You may bring in the presents now." She poured out the tea, then came over to me. "I forgot to mention to you earlier that you don't need to fret about gifts. We'll open presents after our Christmas feast tomorrow, but because so many of the people in our little gathering are not familiar with each other, Mr. Searsby and I are providing presents for a Lucky Dip."

"Oh, wonderful." With everything that had happened, I hadn't even thought about gifts for guests. "Thank you. That's a perfect solution." With Mr. and Mrs. Searsby providing a pool of presents to choose from, we'd get the fun of opening gifts without the anxiety of trying to find an appropriate gift for people we didn't know well.

Several footmen arrived with baskets of wrapped packages, and Mrs. Searsby said, "Here they are. The presents will be just the thing for the finishing touch."

As the gifts were arranged under the tree, a realization hit me. "A Christmas present," I murmured.

"Did you say something, Miss Belgrave?"

I'd been lost in thought, but Mrs. Searsby's question brought me back to the present. "Nothing of importance."

I caught Jasper's eye. He disengaged himself from Miss Brinkle. I drew him away from the crowd. "A wrapped Christmas gift would be a perfect place to hide something that isn't supposed to be seen until Christmas day."

Jasper had been about to take a sip of his tea, but he paused with the cup halfway to his lips, then turned to me as the realization dawned on him as well. "And there were presents in Bankston's sitting room."

"Yes! They were the only thing we didn't check."

He handed his drink to a passing footman. "We'd better remedy that right away."

～

WE SLIPPED AWAY from the group around the Christmas tree. I went to find Mrs. Pickering, while Jasper rang for Grigsby and set him onto the task of discovering who had left the house on the day Bankston went to London. By the time Jasper rejoined me, I'd convinced Mrs. Pickering that we needed to see Bankston's sitting room once more.

It was even colder in the butler's sitting room than the Oak Hall. I crossed my arms. "Chilly in here, But I didn't like to ask Mrs. Pickering to have a fire lit."

"No, indeed." Jasper removed a pair of gloves from his pocket. "She was reluctant to let us in as it was. Ah, good. The presents are still here."

Above the empty fireplace, the gifts were stacked on the mantel on either side of the Searsby Christmas card. The presents were all labeled with names, some of which I recognized, like Ford. Only one box, a small red package tied up with gold ribbon, didn't have a name. The tag on it read, "Place under tree in Oak Hall."

I fingered the tag. "I bet Bankston would have handed this off to a footman and told him to place it under the tree."

"Yes, it wouldn't have been associated with him at all. Probably Mrs. Pickering will see that the other gifts are distributed," Jasper said, "and she would likely do the same with this one, just place it under the tree as the tag instructs." Jasper balanced it on the palm of his gloved hand as if he was weighing it. "A book, possibly. Do you want to do the honors, or should I?"

"Well, it depends. Are you going to try to wrap it up like it's never been opened after you see what's inside?"

"That's the idea."

"Then you'd better do it. I'd be sure to tear the wrapping in a way that couldn't be hidden. You know patience isn't one of my strong suits."

"I think it best for me to refrain from commenting on that," he teased, then went to the desk. "You've convinced me. I'll do the honors."

He put the gift in the center of the blotter and switched on the desk lamp. He smoothed the gloves over his hands, then sat down and examined each side before taking a letter opener from a drawer. He carefully loosened the knot that held the bow together. I watched over his shoulder for a few moments, then he said, "Your breathing on the back of my ear, while delightful, is a bit distracting."

"Sorry." I crossed the room and sat down in the easy chair. I let my gaze range around the room while Jasper hunched over the desk, making tiny movements with the letter opener. Everything was positioned just as we'd left it—the rug placed at the center of the room, the easy chair angled beside the little side table that held the stack of books. I ran my hands up and down the arms of the chair. Jasper moved the letter opener and repositioned the package. I shifted and sighed and looked around again for something to occupy myself with. I noticed a bit of paper protruding from behind the small table. Something must have been knocked off the back of the table and lodged between it and the wall.

I leaned forward and used the tip of my fingernail to pull it out. It wasn't a single sheet of paper. It was a magazine folded open to a crossword puzzle, each square filled with neatly written letters. I could picture Bankston sitting in his chair working through the crossword with a fire burning in the grate. I pulled the sleeve of my cardigan down over my hand and picked it up. I dropped it onto my lap and, with my sleeve still shielding my fingers, turned clumsily to the cover.

I wasn't familiar with the *New England Home Companion*. "I found a magazine that was dropped behind this little table. It must be one of the magazines that the servants saved for Bankston. It was published in America. Probably one of the guests who stayed here left it."

Jasper didn't look up. "Most likely."

I flicked the pages, then stopped and sat up straight as a headline caught my attention. "Jasper, you must see this."

"I'm rather engaged at the moment. Finally! Got it." The red wrapping paper fell open to reveal a small wooden box. "Curio box," Jasper said as he used the letter opener's blade to lift the lid. "Empty . . . but there's something folded to fit exactly into the lid." A twist of the letter opener dislodged it. "A paper." He unfolded it, then turned toward me, his face alight with satisfaction. "It's a crossword. Of Bankston's own making, it looks like." He rattled the paper. "It's got to be the cipher, which will give us the location of the letter. Now, what was it you said?"

"Listen to this headline. 'World's Only Snowflake Scientist.'"

Jasper's forehead wrinkled. "I can see you're quite worked up about it, but I fail to see . . ."

"It's a long article about a man who photographs snowflakes with a camera and a microscope—the sole person in the world who does that—and his name *isn't* Ambrose Eggers."

CHAPTER NINETEEN

I held the magazine so Jasper could see the headline about the snowflake scientist, then turned it around and scanned down until I found the line I was looking for. "It says that the New England scientist is Wilson A. Bentley. He's a farmer in Vermont and has a hobby of photographing snowflakes with a microscope attached to a camera. And he doesn't look like Mr. Eggers. His hair is receding, but it's dark, not light brown, and he has narrow eyes with flat brows as well as an extravagantly thick mustache." I stood up. "I think we need to have a chat with Mr. Eggers."

"I agree." Jasper was already gathering up the red wrapping paper, the wooden box, and the crossword. The items were small enough that he could fit everything into his suit coat pocket.

I'd heard a hint of reluctance in Jasper's voice and said, "I can speak to Mr. Eggers alone while you sort out the message Bankston left in the crossword."

He glanced at his watch. "No, there's not enough time

to work on it properly before dinner. I'll tackle it later this evening."

We ran Mr. Eggers to earth in the billiard room. The billiard room was oak paneled in a square board and batten pattern. Narrow diamond-paned windows bracketed either side of the fireplace, where the flicker of orange flames reflected on the tiled hearth. Mr. Eggers stood, his cue angled over the billiard table at the center of the room. After he made his shot, Jasper reached for a cue. "Care for a game?"

"By all means."

"Are you playing as well, Olive?"

"No, you two go ahead. I'll sit over here and read this magazine."

I'd slipped the *New England Home Companion* inside another magazine. I settled down in one of the chintz-covered chairs beside the fire. The men began their game, and I flipped through the pages. When I'd read the article earlier, I'd focused on the details about the snowflake scientist and the photo of him, but now I studied the images of the snowflakes that accompanied the article.

Some were star-shaped and spiky with many facets, while others were plainer with more of a column shape. Even though some of the shapes were similar, each one was unique. Placed on a black background, the close-ups of the individual flakes showed each facet of the intricate shapes. The flakes didn't look delicate. Instead, the complex and varied flakes looked as if they were made of crystal instead of frozen water.

For a while, the only sounds were the pops from the fire, clicks as the billiard balls knocked against each other, and an occasional murmur of "jolly good," and "well done."

Mr. Eggers took a long time between each of his shots, mincing around the table with his small, exact steps, studying the layout of the billiard balls from every angle before taking up his position with deliberation.

During one of these excessively long preparatory periods as Mr. Eggers paced back and forth, checking his shot from several angles, Jasper crossed his eyes, and I covered a laugh that bubbled up with a cough, which caused Mr. Eggers to go back to the beginning of his routine again. Jasper shot me an agonized look, and I mouthed the words, *it's your own fault*, at him.

I waited until Mr. Eggers was poised over the table with his elbow in the air, his cue lined up on the ball, and said, with what I hoped was a note of genuine surprise, "How extraordinary! There's an article in this magazine about a man who photographs snowflakes—just like you do, Mr. Eggers."

His cue juddered across the surface of the billiard table before hitting the ball off-center, which sent it skittering off at a right angle. He pushed up his spectacles as he straightened, then focused on tugging his sleeve and cuff back into place. "You don't say. What an unusual coincidence."

I folded the page back and showed him the article. "It says this man is the only man in the world who studies snowflakes."

Jasper laced his hands together and leaned on his billiard cue. "Rather odd that you're also studying such an obscure topic. Makes one wonder." Jasper smiled as he said the words, but a smidge of doubt tinged his words.

Mr. Eggers paused, his cue braced on the ground as his gaze darted back and forth between Jasper and me. "Surely two men can study snowflakes!" He changed his grip on the cue and lifted it up, readying himself to play again. "Not to be rude, but I don't see what business it is of yours. Now where were we . . . ?"

I leaned forward in the chair. "We do have an interest in hearing about it, Mr. Rimington and I. Wouldn't you rather explain it to us instead of the Scotland Yard inspector when he arrives after the snow melts?"

Mr. Eggers had been walking around the table to assess the game from a different angle, but he stopped dead. "The Yard sending down a man is nothing but a formality. Mr. Searsby told me that himself."

"That may be what Mr. Searsby says to the guests, but he's engaged us to look into certain—irregularities, let's call them—around Bankston's death."

"What do you mean, irregularities? It was an accident."

"Perhaps not," Jasper said. "That's why Scotland Yard is sending a man down. To clarify exactly what happened. But in the meantime, it's come to light that Bankston had a nasty habit of blackmailing guests."

I tapped the magazine. "This magazine belonged to Bankston. He worked the crossword puzzle in it, so he most likely knew of the only snowflake scientist in the world—who wasn't you."

Jasper leaned his hip against the billiard table, his arms crossed. "And that's dangerous knowledge in the hands of a man who has a tendency to extort money from guests. It might lead someone to do something rather rash . . ."

Mr. Eggers remained motionless for a moment, but he was breathing heavily, his nostrils flaring with each breath. Then he laid his cue down on the table and went to the door. I thought he was going to leave the room completely without another word, but he glanced up and down the passage, then closed the door quietly. As he sat down in the chintz chair across from me, he took off his glasses and polished them with his handkerchief. "Let me clear things up. I hope this can be kept between ourselves."

"I suppose that depends on what you tell us," I said.

"I think you'll be quite satisfied and see that there's no need for anything I say to go farther than this room. I don't study snowflakes—that was a little ruse—but I *am* a scientist."

"What do you study?" I asked.

"Snails."

"Snails?"

Mr. Eggers hooked his glasses over his ears and leaned forward. "Fascinating creatures. The library here at Holly Hill Lodge has several important monographs written by Archibald Virgil Potheroe." Mr. Eggers paused. He seemed to be waiting for Jasper or me to say, "Oh, I see."

When we stayed silent, he added, "The famous naturalist. You haven't heard of him?"

"No, I'm afraid not," I said and glanced at Jasper.

"Neither have I."

"That is unfortunate. Old Potheroe was one of the foremost scholars in the field. His monographs—the ones here in the library—are very rare. Extremely difficult to find. I must see them to complete my research."

Jasper asked, "Then why not simply ask to see these monographs?"

Mr. Eggers pinched his lips together for a moment. "I'm a common man. My pedigree is not quite as exalted as some. I don't move in the highest academic circles, but I am devoted to my studies. I didn't have the connections to reach out to Mr. and Mrs. Searsby and ask for an invitation to Holly Hill Lodge." He adjusted his cuffs. "I did try. Twice! I sent letters and received the same reply each time from one of Mr. Searsby's secretaries. My requests were declined. The only way I could see those monographs was to come up with something completely different, a more enticing request."

He motioned to the leaded-glass window where snow was mounded up in the corners of the windowsill. "Snowflakes are much more . . . *romantic* than snails. A person studying snowflakes creates a genuine interest and curiosity." He threw up his hands, palms angled to the ceiling as he shrugged. "That's what I had to do to make myself attractive as a guest. I'd read an article in a newspaper about the man in New England who studies snowflakes, so I borrowed the idea."

"And his snowflake photographs?" Jasper asked.

Mr. Eggers smoothed down his lapels and fussed with his cuffs. "Well, yes. I found that magazine article you have there and cut the photos out and mounted them on cardboard. It's not cricket, I admit that, but I had to have some pictures to show in case anyone asked to see the photos of snowflakes, but I assure you that I only did it because there was no other way to get at those monographs."

"So you're here under false pretenses, but your motive is pure—scientific knowledge," Jasper said.

"Yes, that's it exactly. I'm so pleased you understand. I'm taking down the information in the monographs by hand, transcribing them word for word. My little fib had nothing to do with Bankston. It's a small matter. A trifle. Nothing to trouble anyone else with."

"Perhaps," Jasper said, and Mr. Eggers seemed to stiffen.

I put the magazine down on the table. "There's the

small matter of Bankston's death. Did he approach you and demand remuneration in exchange for keeping your secret quiet?"

"No, of course he didn't! The single interaction I had with Bankston was telling him which newspaper I preferred."

"And that was all?" Jasper asked, doubt heavy in his voice.

"I assure you that was the extent of our conversation, if one could call it that. It's a shame Bankston was struck down like that." Mr. Eggers removed his glasses, squinted at the lenses as he angled them to the light, then whipped out his handkerchief again as he continued, "In the prime of life, as they say. He was a fairly young man, you know. Always a pity to hear of someone so young dying." Mr. Eggers put his glasses on again, tucked the handkerchief into a pocket, and pressed his hands to the arms of the chair, preparing to stand. "Really, most inconsiderate of you to continue to insinuate that there's something underhanded in my actions."

"Then perhaps you can answer one more question," I said, my tone conciliatory to counteract his huffy manner. "Just a curiosity of mine. One small thing."

He sighed and relaxed his grip on the chair. "Yes?"

"Your camera and microscope, and the need for a darkroom . . ."

He tipped his head forward in mock contrition. "That, I'll confess, is all for show."

"But also you went outdoors to take photographs," Jasper said. "I saw you leave the house myself on the day I arrived. You were carrying your camera and equipment."

"I had to make my little fiction appear to be true. I put it about that I was looking for the perfect place to set up if heavy snow came. I'm sure you understand. In reality, I walked with the camera until I was out of view of the house, then I waited in the garden in that sheltered bit with the high hedge around it. Putting on a good show, you know."

"Did you go toward the village?" I asked.

"No," he said quickly. "The opposite direction. I returned through the glass doors in the morning room. It was easy to put my equipment away in my room without being seen, then go to the library to continue copying the monographs with no one the wiser. There are several nice little alcoves in the library. I can work for hours without anyone noticing me."

"Did you see anyone while you were outdoors?"

"Not a soul. Completely deserted," he said, his words still coming quickly. "Now, I trust I've cleared up any doubts you have?" He didn't wait for an answer.

Jasper and I sat in silence until he left the room. Jasper followed Mr. Eggers to the door, made sure he'd actually gone, then closed it again. "Well, what do you think?"

"I'm not sure. His story could be true, but I do have the feeling that he wasn't completely honest about everything."

"I suppose the first thing to do would be to check and see if there are monographs in the library by this snail expert—what was that outlandish name?"

"Archibald Virgil Potheroe." I brushed down my skirt as I stood. "Let's go now. We'll just have time to do it before dinner."

~

Jasper and I went directly from the billiard room to the library. I drew a breath as I took in the stone walls and high vaulted ceilings with Gothic arches. "It feels more like a church than a library."

"Indeed. A temple to learning. It appears some Elizabethans took their book collecting rather seriously."

Instead of pews, a series of bookshelves stood on either side of the room, creating an aisle. Delicate vases lined the top of the shelves, and marble busts on plinths ringed the room. At the far end of the oblong room, three tall leaded-glass windows set high on the wall were bright with sunlight reflecting off the snow. Under the windows, three sets of glass doors looked out on the snow-covered terrace. Several tables and a few comfortable chairs were arranged at the end of the room near the glass doors and windows. A circular staircase in one of the room's corners curved up to a book-filled gallery that lined the three walls without windows. "What a delightful room. It may take a while to find a series of monographs about snails, but I shall enjoy looking for them."

"If you don't mind, I'll take a moment and copy out the crossword that was in the present. I'll feel better once I have a duplicate. I'm sure I can find some writing paper here."

"Of course. I'll start looking for the monographs." I headed for the first row of shelves.

"Let me know if you find any crime books," Jasper said over his shoulder as he moved down the aisle to the tables under the windows.

"I will, but these all look rather antiquated. I doubt if they'll have any shilling shockers or detective stories among this lot." The books were grouped by theme. I worked that out as I browsed the section devoted to fiction. From there, I moved on and found bookshelves of poetry. On the other side of the aisle, the bookcases held titles related to geography, history, and travel. "Nothing scientific yet," I said. Bookshelves were arranged between the glass doors, and as I went to examine them, I passed by Jasper's table. "How's the copying going?"

"Nearly done." He held up his sketch of the empty crossword grid. Under it, he'd also copied down the clues in his neat handwriting.

"Do you think the cipher is in the clues, or in the crossword puzzle itself?"

"Since Bankston was so fond of crosswords, I suspect it may involve both." He folded the original and tucked it into his pocket, then centered his copy in front of him on the desk. He picked up his pencil again. "Let's have a go at it, shall we?"

"All right, what's the first clue?" The books by the glass doors were encyclopedias and other reference tomes, but nothing related to nature studies.

Jasper said, "A vicar's daughter should be able to help me with this one. First clue, 'angel salutation.' Four letters."

I paused, my hand on the circular staircase's banister. "Easy—'hark.'"

"I agree," Jasper said, "but I shall write it in pencil."

The first books I examined in the gallery were biographies. Jasper's voice floated up. "Second clue, another religious one, 'action of faithful.'"

"Could be 'prayer.'"

"No, only five letters."

"Then it can't be 'give' either. What about 'share?'"

"No. That doesn't fit."

I moved on to the next section of books. "Seems rather

peculiar for Bankston to have several religious clues. It doesn't seem the sort of topic he'd be interested in."

"Indeed," Jasper said. "We'll come back to that one. Third clue. 'Triad of potentates followed it.'" His pencil beat out a quick tattoo on the table. "Hmm . . . not the right number of spaces for 'law.'"

"But kings would make law, not follow law," I said, then went to the banister as a thought struck me. "It's 'star.' The three kings followed the star."

"Of course. Jolly good."

"The crossword has a theme. It's about Christmas carols—'We Three Kings' and 'Hark the Herald Angels Sing.'"

"By George, you're right. Then 'action of the faithful' would be . . . yes, 'adore,' as in 'Oh Come Let Us Adore Him.'" Jasper wrote in the answer. "Next clue, 'abounding happiness.' That would be 'joy.' And 'quiet evening' would be 'Silent Night.' Yes, that fits."

I went back to the shelves. "Here we are, a whole wall of books relating to the natural world."

"What about this clue," Jasper said. "'Transparent twelve?'"

"I don't know—wait, what about 'It Came Upon The Midnight Clear?' Do any of those words fit?"

"Yes, midnight does."

I moved along the wall, searching the shelves for the name Potheroe, but I didn't see it. "You're making much better progress than I am. I'm beginning to have severe doubts about Mr. Eggers' truthfulness. I see nothing here by Potheroe."

"Perhaps Mr. Eggers took the monographs to his room."

"He didn't say that, though. He said he was copying

them in the library." I pulled out several thinly bound volumes that were so small no title had been printed on the spines. I opened the first one to the title page. "Oh, I take back what I said about Mr. Eggers. I found one, *A Study of Hygromiidae*. And . . . yes, there are several more by Potheroe—all of them on the subject of snails. Well, that will teach me to be a doubting Thomas."

"I'm almost finished here as well. Only a few more . . ."

"It looks as if the monographs have been taken down and read recently. They're not nearly as dusty as the books around them."

I replaced the monographs and went down the stairs. "It appears Mr. Eggers was telling the truth—at least about the monographs. And since obscure monographs about a specific type of snail aren't generally well known, I doubt he could come up with the name Potheroe and the specific monograph unless he really was copying it out."

"Yes, rather surprising, isn't it?" The dinner gong rang out, indicating it was time to dress for dinner. Jasper put down his pencil. "There. First step completed, and just in time too."

CHAPTER TWENTY

*T*hat evening, I was the last one to arrive in the drawing room. I'd wondered if Jasper would make an excuse and stay in his room so he could work on decoding Bankston's message in the crossword puzzle, but Jasper was in the drawing room as well. He stood beside the fire, talking to Theo.

Theo had his back turned to me. "Good evening, Jasper," I said as I approached. "Theo—" I broke off when I saw his expression. Head lowered and chin tucked, his intense gaze was concentrated on Jasper. Theo reminded me of a drawing I'd seen of an angry bull readying itself to charge a matador. It was such a change from the affable, cheery young man's usual demeanor that I was shocked into silence.

Jasper said, "I've just asked Theo how his nonexistent company will be able to manufacture aeroplane cases."

Theo angled his head from side to side, reminding me more than ever of a dangerous animal about to charge forward. "You have it all wrong. Let me put you wise.

Culwell Luggage is a good, strong company. I don't know who you've been talking to, but—"

"The information came from Bankston," I said.

The butler's name checked his anger. "Bankston? The butler fellow who tumbled out of the stone tower?"

"Yes, that's right," I said. "The butler, Bankston, knew that Culwell Luggage wasn't a real business."

Theo's neck and face flushed as he took a card from his waistcoat pocket and shoved it at me. "See there?" He pointed to the card. "Culwell Luggage. Headquarters, Kansas City."

"But the Rotary Club in that city has never heard of Culwell Luggage," I said.

"The Rotary—? What do you mean?"

"The Kansas City Rotary Club," Jasper said. "Bankston contacted them to check up on you. He knew about your deception."

"Did you pay up?" I asked. "The amount was two hundred pounds, I believe."

Theo's head reared back. "Pay a butler? You're all wet."

"What?" I said. "I'm afraid you're not making sense."

"I mean, you're all wrong—that's what 'you're all wet' means. You're wrong, Olive. Completely wrong. Bankston didn't want money from me. He didn't want anything from me, in fact."

"Oh, but he did," I said.

Jasper added, "And we have written proof of it."

"You're talking about blackmail, but you can't have proof that the butler blackmailed me because it didn't happen."

"Then we seem to have reached an impasse," I said.

"And we'll have no choice but to tell the detective from

Scotland Yard about Bankston's knowledge of Culwell Luggage's lack of bonafides," Jasper added.

The red flush drained from Theo's face. "But they're not serious about it. I mean, I heard—"

"That it's a formality?" I tapped the card against my palm as I shook my head. "I'm afraid not."

"They're on the way to investigate Bankston's death," Jasper said. "Olive and I are making a few inquiries on behalf of Mr. and Mrs. Searsby. We intend to clear things up before the investigators arrive."

Theo stepped back and scrubbed a hand over his mouth, then drew in close to us. In a voice barely above a whisper, he said, "Look, I'll grant you that my business is —er—in the beginning stages, but that has nothing to do with Bankston."

I glanced at Jasper. He made a small movement with his cocktail and raised his eyebrows a minuscule amount, which I took to mean he wasn't sure if he believed Theo. I wasn't convinced either. I said, "Tell us about it, Theo—unless you'd rather tell Scotland Yard."

Theo took a gulp of his sidecar as he shot a quick look around the room. "If I talk to you, you'll keep it quiet? There won't be any need to talk to the police—or for the Searsby family to know?"

"It depends on what you have to say," I said.

Theo tossed back the rest of his drink, then put the empty glass on the mantel. "Let's move over there." He strode across the room to a far corner. Jasper and I followed, moving to stand on either side of him so that it appeared we were all admiring a life-size oil painting of a general.

"It's like this. I have a factory lined up to make the cases." Theo put his hand on his chest. "I swear I do. It's in

London, Stanislow Manufacturing. Once I've got two hundred orders, they'll manufacture the cases and ship them. It's all square."

"Then why the deception about a location in Kansas City?" I asked.

"No one wants to invest in something that's got no record." Theo's gaze wavered from mine. "I admit Culwell Luggage doesn't exist—not officially, on paper. But it *does* exist." He tapped his lapel. "*I'm* Culwell Luggage. My word is good. I know my onions—at least when it comes to luggage. I worked at the Anderson Fine Luggage and Trunks company for two years. I know quality luggage. I took my idea for aeroplane cases to them, but they didn't want it, so I've struck out on my own. I had some savings, so I had the sample cases made. I've been taking orders since I arrived in England. A few more months and I should have enough to begin manufacturing. I've promised my customers the best aeroplane cases, and that's what they'll get. I just need a little more capital to get the business off the ground."

"And it's easier to deceive people in a foreign country," Jasper said. "It's difficult to check up on a business based across the pond."

Francie's throaty laughter floated across the room, and Theo closed his eyes for a moment. "I came over here to build up a clientele. I'm legit. I'm not a black hat."

"And Bankston?" I asked.

Theo shook his head, his eyes wide. "I don't know anything about him. He said maybe five words to me the whole time I was here. Honest!"

Francie joined our group. "Why are you all hiding over here in the corner? What's so intriguing about old

General Yardley's portrait?" She looped her arm through Theo's and drew him back to the main room.

He threw us a pleading expression over his shoulder, then turned back and bent his head to hear something Francie was saying.

Jasper said, "It's difficult to catch Theo alone. He and Francie have been inseparable, so when I saw him standing by himself tonight, I decided I'd better approach him. What do you think? Is young Mr. Culwell an honest businessman? He certainly seemed surprised when we mentioned blackmail."

"But was it because he didn't know anything about it, or was he surprised that we knew about it?"

Ford entered the room and, after a nod from Mrs. Searsby, announced that dinner was served.

"I have news from Grigsby, but that will have to wait until after dinner," Jasper said as we went to the dining room.

I was again seated between Jasper and Mr. Sprigg. Jasper and I didn't speak about blackmail or coded messages during dinner. Instead, Jasper told me about a play he'd seen recently—not one of Miss Ravenna's—and then we discussed a new crime book we'd both read.

I turned to Mr. Sprigg during the fish course. "I believe I passed your house when I was returning from the village. It's charming."

"Thank you. I'm quite fond of the old place myself."

"Have you always lived there?"

"No. I bought it last year. Picked it up for a song. The exterior is in good shape, thank goodness. But the interior"—he shook his head—"terrible, terrible mess. I've had the carpenters in to repair the floor. The situation was much worse than we expected. In fact, I had to miss choir practice on Saturday because of it."

"Choir practice? I didn't realize you're a singer, Mr. Sprigg."

"Not I. I'm the organist." He chuckled at my expression. "I can see that I've surprised you."

"It's only that you seem—"

"More of the horse and hound type of squire?"

I grinned at him. "Exactly. You strike me as someone who enjoys the outdoors."

"I certainly enjoy a good hunt. I do have some musical ability—only a little, I assure you. The vicar needed someone to pitch in and"—he angled his shoulders toward me and said in a soft voice—"his wife is rather persistent." He made a waving motion with his knife. "I surrendered. I decided it would be much easier in the long run to participate than to avoid her."

"Sounds like a wise decision."

"Terrifying woman. Best to stay out of her bad books." Returning to his normal volume, he said, "Yes, I was hoping for a brisk walk in the winter air before the snow, but that wasn't possible. The workmen took much longer than I expected. Never buy an old house, Miss Belgrave, unless you're flush with cash."

After dinner, instead of going into the drawing room, we went to the Oak Hall and gathered in front of the fireplace, where the Yule log blazed. As long as one stayed in that vicinity, the room was pleasantly toasty. The men joined us, and Jasper and I spent some time mingling with everyone except Theo and Francie, who went off to a corner to play a game of chess. When the coffee trolley was brought in, Jasper handed me a cup, then picked up his and tilted his head toward a pair of chairs on the outer edge of the fire's warmth.

A box with a jigsaw puzzle sat on the table between us. I put down my coffee cup. "Perhaps we should give this a go while you tell me your other news." The puzzle was a Christmas scene, a snowy, wooded landscape with a family bringing in the Yule log.

"Yes, let's."

I dumped the pieces out of the box as Jasper said, "Grigsby was able to pin down the movements of several of the guests during Saturday, the day before the first snowstorm."

"That was quick work."

"Grigsby isn't one to lallygag. He was able to verify that Mr. and Mrs. Searsby were both indoors at all times. Mrs. Searsby was with the housekeeper in the morning, then she and Francie were together in the afternoon, going through the Christmas ornaments. Mr. Searsby was closeted in his study. He was with his secretary throughout the day."

"And there's no exit from that room to go outdoors."

"That's right. Now for the other guests. Mr. Sprigg has a valet. He says Mr. Sprigg was at home all day."

"That confirms what Mr. Sprigg told me at dinner. He said he had some carpenters in to work on his house and that the work took so long he missed choir practice."

Jasper looked up from sorting puzzle pieces, his face surprised.

"He's the organist and is apparently deathly afraid of the vicar's wife."

"That explains it."

I shifted puzzle pieces, looking for the ones that made

up the edge of the puzzle. "Any word on the rest of the party?"

"Oh, yes. I have oodles more to tell you. Mr. Eggers left with his camera after luncheon and was not seen again until teatime. He told one of the maids he was off to look for locations to take pictures in case it snowed."

"Which tallies with what he told us, but it also means he's basically unaccounted for."

Jasper propped the lid of the box up so we could see the image of the puzzle. "Theo and Francie went riding after luncheon."

"I wonder if they saw Mr. Eggers?"

"Francie says no. I asked her about it tonight during dinner. She said she and Theo didn't see anyone, and that they didn't go near the vicinity of the belvedere at all."

Francie and Theo still sat across from each other, but they'd abandoned the chess game. They'd pushed the board aside, and Theo was sketching in a notebook he'd taken from his pocket. After a few moments, Francie took the pencil from him and made her own edits on the drawing.

"Theo seems to be back to his amiable and eager-to-please demeanor," I said. "I suppose it's possible that Bankston hadn't approached Theo with a blackmail demand. Perhaps Bankston was planning to do it later."

"Yes, but there's one small piece of information that *is* quite suspicious. Theo requested a hammer."

I left off looking for the corner pieces. "A hammer? That's a rather unusual request for a guest at a country home. He'd need that for . . . what?"

"According to Grigsby, Theo's excuse was that he needed to fix some tacks that had come loose in one of his sample aeroplane cases. He says he worked in his room, repairing the cases and writing letters on Saturday until he and Francie went riding."

"I suppose that could be true."

"Yes. However, he didn't return the hammer until the next morning. If he took it when he and Francie went riding, he could easily have used it to nail the boards in place at the top of the belvedere."

"But did you notice how frightened he was when he was on the ladder?" I asked.

"He did look shaken."

"When he came down, his hairline was beaded with sweat, and his hands were trembling. And his face when Francie asked if he'd go back up! I thought he might pass out."

"So you think it's impossible that he could have set up the trap for Bankston because of the height of the belvedere?"

"I think if Theo wanted to do away with Bankston, he would have chosen some other method that didn't involve leaning out of a stone tower several feet off the ground."

Jasper took a drink of his coffee and studied the pair. "Of course Francie had no trouble with the ladder. She seems to have an excellent head for heights."

I spotted two pieces that matched and fitted them together. "She does, but would she help someone do away with the butler in her home?"

"People have done stranger things for love."

"Yes, but their romance is quite a sudden thing, isn't it? They've only known each other for a few days. Would she do something that quickly?"

"I don't know her well enough to say." Jasper sipped his coffee again, then returned to working on the puzzle. "I do know that when we played cards on the night you arrived, Francie was quite decisive. No dillydallying with her. Let's see, who else did Grigsby find out about? Oh yes, Madge and Tommy. They had two long practice sessions at the indoor court. One in the morning, and the other after luncheon. No one can confirm they were there throughout the whole day."

"So they could have slipped out." We shifted puzzle pieces around for a few moments, then I said, "So that accounts for everyone."

"Not exactly." Jasper compared the shade of green on a puzzle piece he held to a few pieces I'd fitted together at the edge of the puzzle.

"But we already agreed that Miss Brinkle is too infirm to manage the stairs. And in any case, neither she nor Blix had arrived."

"That's the case for Miss Brinkle. Her maid says Miss Brinkle lives nearly seventy miles away. Miss Brinkle was at home Saturday. They traveled by train the next day and arrived before luncheon." Jasper discarded the puzzle piece and picked up another. "Blix, on the other hand, hadn't arrived at Holly Hill Lodge the day before Bankston died, but she *was* in the village."

I stopped searching for the match to the puzzle piece I held. "Blix was in Chipping Bascomb?"

"Yes. She was visiting her former headmistress, a Mrs. Cox, who lives in a charming Tudor cottage off the village green. Blix arrived on Saturday and stayed one night at Mrs. Cox's cottage before she came to Holly Hill Lodge."

"But she told us she'd come from Manchester."

"It seems an odd sort of thing to lie about," Jasper said. "Especially since she didn't attempt to keep it secret that she was in the village. Mrs. Cox's parlor maid is the sister of one of the maids here at Holly Hill Lodge and told Grigsby all about it."

"Hmm." Blix was chatting with Mr. Sprigg and Mrs. Searsby, her bright hair shining in the light of the fire. "She completely fooled me. I believed her when she said she'd come from Manchester. But wait a moment—Blix wouldn't have known about Bankston going to London if she was staying in a cottage in the village."

"No, she did," Jasper said. "Mrs. Searsby sent down a mince pie specifically for Mrs. Cox. The footman who delivered it passed on the news about Bankston going to London to the cook, who told the parlormaid, who mentioned it to Mrs. Cox and Blix."

I was turning a puzzle piece around and around in my fingers, lost in thought. "But Blix? We saw nothing about her in Bankston's notes."

"Agreed. But you never know. Perhaps he'd found out something but hadn't written it down."

I spun the puzzle piece faster. "So, let's see where we are . . . Miss Brinkle was miles and miles away on Saturday. Mr. Sprigg was at his home all day. Mr. and Mrs. Searsby appear to have been occupied in the house all day, as were Tommy and Madge, as far as anyone knows. Everyone thinks Mr. Eggers was out all afternoon, but he told us he only slipped out into the gardens, then returned to the house. Francie and Theo went riding in the afternoon, but Francie says they didn't go near the belvedere. Blix was in the village, even though she said she'd come from Manchester."

"That's about the sum—" Jasper's gaze shifted to a point behind my shoulder. "Mr. Eggers, care to join us? Are you a jigsaw puzzle fan?"

He pulled over a chair and surveyed the puzzle.

"You've not sorted by color. It will go faster if you do that." He was already sliding the pieces around. Within a few moments, he'd arranged them into color-coordinated piles.

After a few minutes of silence, I asked, "How is your snail research going?"

Mr. Eggers stiffened, but after a quick survey to make sure no one else was near, he took off his glasses and wiped them down with his handkerchief. "Quite well. I should finish the last bit of copying soon."

Jasper said, "I suppose you know an old college tutor of mine. He's quite the expert on *Hygromiidae*. At the time, I was just a lad and didn't really take it in, but he's one of the authorities in the field, I understand. Do you know old Sweetwater? Thomas Sweetwater?"

"Never met him," Mr. Eggers said. "But I hear he's a fine chap."

"Come and have some mulled wine," Mrs. Searsby said, and we left the puzzle to join the others by the fire. Mrs. Searsby informed us that the servants had shoveled a path through the woods to the village. As long as it didn't snow again during the night, we'd be able to walk to the Christmas service in the morning. It wasn't long afterward that everyone began to retire.

On the way up the stairs, I said to Jasper, "Old Sweetwater? A test for Mr. Eggers, I think?"

"Right you are. A name drawn from thin air."

"And Mr. Eggers took the bait." We paused outside my door. "But Mr. Eggers did admit that he's not in the 'first circles' of that field of academia. Perhaps he doesn't personally know the top scholars. He could still be what he says he is—"

"A snail scholar?" Jasper asked, unable to keep a straight face.

"Well, there are some scholars who study snails, aren't there? Mr. Eggers certainly knew about Potheroe's monographs in the library. Perhaps he said he'd heard Sweetwater was a good egg simply because he didn't want to admit that he doesn't know the top chaps in—er—snail studies."

"Enough of snails and scholars. Let me kiss you goodnight."

CHAPTER TWENTY-ONE

25 DECEMBER 1923

*T*he organ music floated through the church, and I drew a breath before we launched into the final verse of 'Hark! The Herald Angels Sing.' If Jasper were there, we would have shared a glance of secret understanding as we began the last carol, but he hadn't appeared that morning. I assumed he'd worked late into the night sorting out the cipher in the crossword puzzle. Miss Ravenna had also not accompanied us to the church. She'd sent word to Mrs. Searsby that her fever had broken, but she intended to remain in her room and rest during the holiday celebrations.

The sturdy little church was a hodgepodge of styles. The building itself was Norman, but it also had medieval stained-glass windows and a Victorian tiled roof. Today it was full of Christmas morning worshippers. I was wedged in at the end of a pew. Blix and I shared a hymnal, and her clear alto voice hit every note perfectly as we sang the chorus of the Christmas carol for a final time.

The skies had remained clear during the evening, and we'd been able to walk from Holly Hill Lodge through the woods along the shoveled path to the village to attend Christmas service. We'd taken the short route that Jasper and I had walked when we went down to the village the morning after my arrival. It was shorter than the path that went by the belvedere. It hadn't taken more than a quarter-hour of walking in the bracing air to reach the point where the path emerged from the woods near the village church.

The interior of the church was rather plain and austere, which showed off the stained-glass lancet windows. Lit by sunlight reflected off the snow outside, the colorful panes glowed in ruby, sapphire, emerald, and topaz tones, casting splashes of color over the holly and ivy decorations. It was quite moving as the voices and the organ chords blended in a swell that filled the church.

As the last notes of the organ faded, the vicar said the blessing, then there was a hubbub of movement as everyone shuffled out of the pews. Once outside, I pulled my hat brim a bit lower to shade my eyes against the glare of the sunlight on the snow. A tattered line of clouds had moved in, which created some relief from the constant brilliance.

Blix had followed me out, and we paused in the churchyard to wait for the group from the Lodge. A petite woman with white hair and vivid hazel eyes approached Blix.

"Happy Christmas, Mrs. Cox," Blix said. "Lovely service."

"Yes. Wasn't it? I do enjoy it when the church is full. So

nice to have it resound with song—and Christmas songs, at that."

Blix shifted so I was included in their conversation. "Let me present Olive Belgrave. She's a guest at Holly Hill Lodge. She's a detective. Olive, this is Mrs. Cox, my former headmistress."

"How do you do?"

I expected to see shock or surprise in Mrs. Cox's face at the description of me as a detective, but she only said, "I've read about you, Miss Belgrave. Very good work you've done."

"Why, thank you."

She examined me, her head nodding with several little bobs as if confirming some assessment. "Yes, clearing up nasty situations is so important, isn't it? False accusations cast a long shadow, you know. Essential to get at the truth."

"What a refreshing perspective," I said. "I find that often the truth is the last thing people want."

"They'd rather have a pretty façade over the facts."

"Yes, that's it exactly."

My surprise at her attitude must have come through in my voice because she added, "Working with pupils—and parents—has given me a rather realistic outlook. You must continue in your chosen profession, Miss Belgrave. Don't give up."

"I don't intend to."

Blix was smiling broadly. "Mrs. Cox is a wonderful encourager. In fact, she was a driving force in my decision to travel."

Mrs. Cox made a noise that was very nearly a snort. "I had very little to do with it, I'm sure. The trouble with Blix was keeping her attention so that she could finish her lessons. You always were intrigued with the next new thing."

"A good quality for a traveler, I imagine," I said. "Was the school here in Chipping Bascomb?"

"No, I moved here after I gave up teaching. I have my own little cottage and garden."

"Which is even more delightful than she described in her letters," Blix said. "If I ever settle down, I want a cottage exactly like yours, Mrs. Cox." To me, Blix said, "I stayed with Mrs. Cox before coming to Holly Hill Lodge."

I'd been looking for a way to turn the subject to Blix's early arrival in Chipping Bascomb, and I seized the opportunity she gave me. "But you said you'd come from Manchester."

A tiny line appeared between Blix's eyebrows. "But I did come from Manchester. I was there before I arrived here in Chipping Bascomb."

Mrs. Cox tilted her head toward me as if letting me in on a secret. "I do believe we are a little too quiet here for Blix—excepting poor Mr. Bankston's tragic accident." She patted Blix's arm. "After all, we're a small village. I know it's not as exciting as the world capitals that you're used to staying in," she added, her tone apologetic.

"Nonsense. Chipping Bascomb is refreshing," Blix said. "A taste of old-world charm. You can't find that elsewhere."

Mrs. Cox leveled her gaze at Blix, and Blix laughed. "All right, yes. I admit it, I have itchy feet. I get a bit restless. I had to go out for a walk."

"Were you able to see some of the countryside before the snow?" I asked.

"Yes, I had a good tramp across the fields and into the woods."

"Did you go to the belvedere? The view is spectacular."

"No, I went in the opposite direction. I stopped in for tea at an inn on my way back, a quaint little place called The Thistle."

Mrs. Cox tightened her scarf around her neck with a shiver, and Blix said, "It's awfully cold, even with the sun shining. Shall I accompany you back to your cottage, Mrs. Cox?"

"There's no need, my dear."

"I insist. I wouldn't want you to slip on the slushy bits."

Blix looped her arm through Mrs. Cox's, then glanced at the group from Holly Hill Lodge that was assembling near the shoveled path. "Don't wait for me, Olive. I'll catch up."

Blix and Mrs. Cox set off at a slow pace around the village green. I joined the group returning to the Lodge, thinking that Blix had certainly seemed to be open and honest about her visit to her old schoolmistress. If she did visit the belvedere on Saturday instead of The Thistle, she was an excellent liar.

The sun was bright, but a layer of snow still blanketed everything. The ice on the bare tree branches was melting, though. The plink of water dripping into the mounds of snow accompanied us as we walked through the woods. The ground rose gradually to the knoll where Holly Hill Lodge stood.

Mrs. Searsby dropped back and fell into step with me at the rear of the group. "I believe the snow will have melted on the roads by tomorrow, and I heard after the service that the trains will begin to run."

"Then you expect Scotland Yard representatives to arrive tomorrow."

"Yes, if not tonight. They may motor instead of

waiting for the train." She slowed her steps and put more distance between us and everyone else. "What have you found out?"

"Nothing definite yet."

She puckered her lips in disappointment. "I had so hoped to have this wrapped up before our Christmas feast today."

"I know. Mr. Rimington and I are making every effort to do just that." I debated whether I should launch into the details of Bankston's blackmail scheme, but a snowy walk in the woods didn't seem to be the best time to share the news with her. "We've discovered a few important things. Would you like us to share them with you later today?"

"Yes, I'd like to hear what progress you've made, and I know Mr. Searsby will as well. Let's see . . . we'll have our Christmas feast and then open presents. Perhaps after those festivities are over? I'm afraid I'll be quite busy seeing to things before then."

"Whenever you like."

"Then let's meet in my husband's study later today."

Holly Hill Lodge came into sight. With its layer of snow, eaves dripping with icicles, and smoke drifting from the chimneys, it looked like a Christmas card.

I slipped off my coat, hat, and gloves and made a quick tour of the public rooms. I didn't find Jasper in any of them. I went upstairs to the corridor where the bedrooms were located. In the dim hallway, a thread of light came from under Jasper's closed bedroom door.

I hesitated a moment, glancing up and down the hall to make sure it was empty. Then I did a scandalous thing.

I tapped on his door.

CHAPTER TWENTY-TWO

*J*asper called out, "Come in."

I poked my head around his door. "It's me—"

I broke off as I took in the state of the room. The words *have you been successful* had been on the tip of my tongue, but I bit them back. "Gracious!" I slipped in and shut the door.

In a rumpled shirt with the sleeves rolled up, Jasper sat at the writing desk, which was littered with paper. Discarded pages covered the floor around him like a layer of snow. Elbows braced on the blotter, he sat with his head tipped down and his forehead resting in his palms. He'd obviously been running his hands through his hair because it stood nearly on end. He spoke without glancing up. "I can't do it, Olive. This cipher has gotten the better of me."

I went across the room, picking up sheets of paper from the carpet. They were covered with his precise handwriting and contained lists of numbers and letters. Some had been scratched through, some circled, others underlined. Other squiggles and lines that were meaning-less to me looped over the pages. "Surely it can't be that bad."

He leaned back and rubbed his eyes, which were shad-owed with deep circles. "Oh, but it is. I've tried everything I know." He jabbed at the paper on the top of the stacks around him. It was his sketch of the crossword we'd found in the gift. "It's a devilish piece of work. Something I've never seen."

"But you must be able to do it, otherwise—"

"Otherwise, we won't know where the letter is hidden, so we won't know what's in it because I haven't been able to accomplish my task." He slapped his hand down on the papers as he said the last word.

His words were so sharp that I halted instead of coming closer. He dipped his head into his palms again. "I'm sorry, Olive. That was unfair of me to snap at you like that. I'm rather cross this morning."

Jasper was not one to fling out words in anger or give in to despair. He was more upset than I'd ever seen him. "Have you slept?"

"No, I've been up all night. I've tried everything." He picked up different piles of paper on the desk. "As far as I can make out, it's not a substitution cipher or a transla-tion cipher. It's not any type of cipher I've ever seen." He dropped the pages onto the desk.

"You need food. Have a wash and ring for tea and toast. I'll change from my tramping-through-the-snow shoes into a festive dress for the Christmas feast, then I'll come back. I may not be much use with the decoding or deciphering, but I've found that it's often beneficial to talk over things with someone else. It often shows one what is missing."

Jasper rubbed the heels of his hands against his eyes. "I suppose we might as well try that."

"You've often listened while I've talked out my problems—and been very helpful too."

He looked up. "Have I?"

"Yes. Quite often, actually."

Jasper pushed back the chair and went to the bellpull. "I'm sure you're right. Sorry I flared up at you, old bean."

In all the years that I'd known Jasper, I'd never seen him stay in a funk for a long time. And if he was calling me 'old bean,' then he'd be back to his typical good-natured self soon. "You're forgiven, old thing."

~

WHEN I RETURNED, Jasper had changed his clothes, and only crumbs remained on the plate in front of him. He poured me a cup of tea and brought it to me. "Thank you, Olive. That was just what I needed."

"Good," I said. "A cup of tea always does wonders. Now," I said briskly, "tell me about these codes."

I settled into an armchair by the fire, which had been built up and was burning nicely. Jasper launched into a detailed explanation of the difference between a code and a cipher as well as his attempts to decipher the page with Bankston's crossword puzzle. He paced back and forth across the carpet, talking more to himself than to me. After a few moments, I was lost, but I nodded and murmured sounds to indicate agreement until his words petered out. He plopped into the desk chair, his long legs sprawled out in front of him. "And that, my dear, is all I know to do. Any thoughts?"

"I wish I could say something frightfully erudite, but

honestly, I'm baffled. In fact, I was in that state after you'd spoken about five sentences." I put down my tea and walked to the leaded-glass window. "I have no knowledge of codes or ciphers beyond the simplest things."

He wiped his hand down over his mouth, then blew out a long sigh. "Well, I must speak to Miss Ravenna." He began to search through the papers on the desk. "I'll have to tell her I can't work it out and that we are well and truly in a hole." But he didn't get up. He picked up the crossword puzzle and sat staring at it.

The servant who had built up the fire had done a good job. The windows were beginning to fog up as the room warmed. I took a handkerchief and cleared a section of the window so I could see out.

The motion caught his attention. "What is it?"

"It's this old leaded glass. I saw something moving— oh, it's Blix returning from the village. I couldn't see out the window." I gave the surface a last wipe. "What you've been doing sounds frightfully complex. Bankston didn't seem to have an extremely complicated personality. Perhaps it's a simple cipher, if there is such a thing?"

Jasper was staring at me in a fixed way. "Simple. What if . . . ?" He jumped up, paced back and forth, then came over. "Yes, it's possible. It might be a mask. It's the only thing I haven't tried."

"What is that?"

"It's one of the simplest ways to send messages. It doesn't involve encryption at all. The message is revealed when you place the mask—a piece of paper with cutouts —over the text." He came over and tapped the window. "The leaded glass creates a pattern across the window. You wiped away the fog on a few of the panes and created a little opening to see outside. That's what a mask is—a small opening, or several small openings that show the important parts."

He turned and began to pace again, his gaze focused on the carpet. "The mask is usually made of paper. It's placed over the text—in our case, Bankston's hand-drawn crossword puzzle. The top sheet of paper masks the inconsequential words, while the cutouts show the words or letters of the message. It's like that foggy window. You can only see certain pieces of information. The cutaways in the top sheet of paper, like the section of the window you wiped clean, let you see the crucial bits."

His pace had become more rapid as he spoke, but he stopped as if he'd run into a wall. "But it's a useless idea if we don't know the shape of the mask."

I sat on the broad windowsill. The room was getting stuffy, and the coolness of the air coming off the windows felt good on my back. "These masks can be any shape?"

"Yes, anything—circle, square, rhombus, even an hour-glass shape. Or they might have many individual openings across a page." Jasper hurried across the room, flung open the wardrobe, and removed the wrapping paper and box that had contained the crossword puzzle from his jacket pocket. "The person who receives the message must have the mask." He dumped it all on the desk. He checked the red wrapping paper, turned the box upside down, then examined the lining of it. "Nothing. The mask isn't here."

"Perhaps it's already in that person's possession."

Jasper's hands went to his temples again. "Then we're finished. There's nothing to be done."

"Unless"—I hopped down from the window and crossed the room—"it's something that every guest received when they arrived." I plucked the Christmas card from Mr. and Mrs. Searsby off the bureau where Jasper had propped up his. It was exactly like mine. "Mrs. Searsby told me she gave Christmas cards to all the guests. Look how they're made. The windows of the cottages are cut away. Gold tissue paper behind the cutouts makes it look as if there are lights glowing inside."

"The windows! Yes, it's possible . . ."

I brought him the card, and he pawed through the papers on the table to find Bankston's original hand-drawn crossword that had been in the box. He folded the paper so the crossword grid was all that was visible. He slipped it inside the card. "It fits exactly." He leaned forward and gave me a quick hard kiss on the lips. "Well done!"

"Thank you. For the compliment—and the kiss. I'll expect more of both later. What does it say?"

We bent over the card. My shoulders dropped. "But it doesn't spell anything."

"Wait . . ." Jasper snatched up a pencil and flipped over one of the papers to a blank side. He jotted the letters down. Intent on the task, he hunched over the desk. I pushed the chair up to his legs, and he took a seat automatically as his pencil scratched across the page.

I leaned over his shoulder, fascinated as he shuffled, then reshuffled the letters. "It's got to be . . . yes, first word is 'Baedeker's.'" Jasper scribbled down the rest of the letters. "And the next is . . ."

He stopped as the next word became obvious to both of us.

"'Egypt,'" I said. "The letter is in *Baedeker's* guide to Egypt."

"It will be in the library." Jasper shrugged into his jacket, raked his fingers through his hair, and straightened his cuffs. He was far from his usually perfectly turned out appearance, but I didn't mention it. I could tell he was too focused on his task to care. He returned Bankston's hand-drawn crossword to the wooden box, then shoved it, along with the wrapping paper, into his pockets.

"You carry it around with you?"

"Of course. Safest place for it, what with servants coming and going from one's room, not to mention the flimsy locks on the doors."

If anyone had seen us as we hurried to the library, they would have thought we were moving with unseemly haste. Thankfully, we didn't meet anyone on the way. As we neared the library, my steps slowed. "Wait a moment. Bankston had a *Baedeker's* guide in his room, remember? It was on his bedside table. What if that is the copy we need?"

"Then we'll have to get back into the bedroom, but as we're here . . ." Jasper opened the library door. "There might be two copies of the *Baedeker's* guide."

"Yes, you're right. I did see a whole line of *Baedeker's* guides when I was looking for the monographs."

We entered the cathedral-like silence of the library. "The books on travel are over here." I led the way to a set of shelves on the main floor.

It was easy to spot the *Baedeker's* guides. Their red spines and gold lettering stood out from the other more soberly bound books. One of the guidebooks rested apart from the others on an empty section of one of the upper shelves. Jasper picked it up as I ran my finger down the row. "This is *Baedeker's* guide to Northern Germany."

I located the *Baedeker's Egypt*, pulled it out, and flipped it open. I expected to find a folded piece of paper or a letter tucked between the cover and the endpapers, but there was nothing except the usual list of *Baedeker's* guides on the front endpaper and the foldout maps after the title page. A colorful map of Egypt filled the endpaper attached to the back cover. Disappointment darted through me. "No."

I fanned the pages to make sure I hadn't missed anything. About a fourth of the way through the book, I stopped and let it fall open. "Look, some pages have been hollowed out."

CHAPTER TWENTY-THREE

*T*he hollowing out of the book had been neatly done with a sharp instrument, probably a penknife. It was only the center of the pages that had been removed. When the book was closed, the edges of it looked normal. It was only when one opened the book that someone would realize the book had a cavity.

Jasper had been returning the other *Baedeker's* to the shelf. He paused with the Germany guidebook halfway inserted into the gap between the other books. "I say! That's not cricket. I knew these people were scoundrels, but defacing books!" He shoved the *Baedeker's* into place with a jerk. "A new low, even for them."

"I agree, but there *is* something inside." I took out the sealed envelope that rested inside the cavity and handed it to Jasper. The paper was of good quality. A round cursive hand had written the address on the front to Mr. Jack Straw in London. "If I saw this letter in the post or on someone's desk, I wouldn't think for a moment that it was anything suspicious."

"Except for the name, perhaps?"

"What—? Oh, I didn't pick up on that. Yes, if someone noticed the name was actually a children's game, then it might draw some attention."

"And isn't 'jackstraw' a synonym for nobody? Having a little joke, aren't they?" Jasper flipped the envelope over and examined the flap, running his fingernail along the edge. "It's not that well sealed. It shouldn't be hard to steam it open. They should have given more attention to sealing the envelope and less to being clever with the addressing of it."

As I replaced the guidebook on the shelf, Jasper glanced at his wristwatch. "I believe I'll just have time to open it and get it copied out before our Christmas feast."

"I thought just knowing who retrieved the letter was the point," I said.

"Yes, that's the most important thing. Be we have it now and should take advantage of that. It won't take a moment to open it, copy it, and return it."

We left the library and retraced our steps to the bedrooms. "What about the gift that was in Bankston's room?" I asked. "Doesn't it need to go under the tree? We're to open presents after we eat."

"That's right." The deep boom of the dressing gong rang out, and Jasper increased his pace. "I should have time," he said under his breath.

I hurried along, almost at a jog as I tried to keep up with his long stride. "I can take care of the present."

"Brilliant!" We reached Jasper's room. "Let me get the ribbon for you—*that* I did hide."

I followed him inside his room a few steps. "Where?"

"The toe of my least-used pair of shoes." His voice came from within the wardrobe. "Yes, still here. Safe and sound. I never wear the brown, although Grigsby said it was essential to bring them." He handed off the gold ribbon. As we re-entered the hall, he murmured, "Water out of the tap should do it, I think . . ." The hall door to the bath that adjoined my room was closed, and the muted sound of running water came from beyond it. Jasper set off down the hall to the bath at the opposite end.

I went to my room and deposited the little wooden box and red wrapping paper on the writing desk. The sound of running water cut off, then alternating voices, one deeper and the other higher, came from beyond the door. It sounded as if Madge and Tommy were still covertly sharing the bath—and probably the bedroom as well. I was surprised that no one except myself had noticed, but I supposed if they were careful, it would be possible to prevent a guest from seeing Tommy coming and going. The servants, though—that was another matter. I was sure they knew exactly what was happening, but they probably assumed it was an affair, not a marriage.

"Come on . . ." The words carried clearly through the door. " . . . late to Christmas dinner . . ."

A few moments later, I had wrapped the ribbon around the box and was tightening the bow so that it held the paper in place. The sound of a door opening came from the direction of Madge's room, then the low voices passed outside my door. I hurriedly combed my hair, tucked a new handkerchief into my pocket, and picked up the gift.

I went to my door to go downstairs and found Jasper standing with his hand raised to knock. "Is something wrong?" I asked.

"No, why should it be?"

"I expected you to still be copying out the letter."

"All done. Wonderfully steamy hot water here. Jolly good place, old Holly Hill Lodge. They kept the old-world whatnots with the timber and armor but brought in modern heating and hot water."

"If only every country house was as well equipped," I said. "So no problems with the envelope?"

"None. It was easy to open. Copying out the letter took no time at all—no crossword this time, just a plain old letter. It was short and to the point. And the flap of the envelope had just enough sticky bits left on it that I was able to reseal it without any trouble."

"Could you tell anything about it? Do you think you'll need a mask for that one as well? Or—" We'd started down the hall, but I gripped Jasper's arm as I came to a halt. "Perhaps it uses the same mask?"

"Unfortunately, no. I checked it against the Christmas card, but the openings didn't match up with the letters. The whole thing was off. I think the letter is a true cipher. I'll work on it after dinner."

"I think I know why Bankston had a copy of *Baedeker's Egypt* in his room," I said as we rounded the corner of the corridor. "If there are two copies of the guidebook, one could be whole and the other hollowed out. When he was ready to place the envelope or letter or package for the courier, he could place it in the hollowed-out book, then switch it for the real book in the library."

"Oh, clever of you to work that out. He'd take the real book back to his room until after the courier had picked up the letter," Jasper said. "By George, I bet that's what happened. Besides the *Baedeker's*, he did have an inordinate number of books of sermons in his room for a blackmailer."

I laughed. "Yes, that was odd. But I bet it was an intentional choice. He picked books that wouldn't be read often. I doubt there's much demand for leisure reading of sermons among the houseguests. It wouldn't be difficult to find duplicate copies of old guidebooks or sermons in bookshops. Normally, the regular book would sit on the library shelf, but Bankston could switch it out for the hollowed-out copy whenever he needed to. He probably picked the Egyptian travel guide because he assumed it wouldn't be consulted very often."

"Perhaps Blix might want to read a guide to Egypt," Jasper said. "But overall the chance of a house guest selecting *Baedeker's Egypt* would be slim."

I paused at the top of the circular staircase. "Here, let me give you the gift. It doesn't fit in my pocket nearly as well as it does in yours."

He twisted the present around, looking at it from all sides. "Well done. I'd never know it had been opened." Being careful of the bow, Jasper slipped it into his suit jacket pocket. "Now, after dinner when we go into the Oak Hall to open presents, I must make sure I'm the first person to admire the Christmas tree. I'll put it with the other gifts. Then we'll only need to keep an eye on it and see who retrieves it." He extended his arm. "Shall we?"

～

THE MEALS that had been served at Holly Hill Lodge had been excellent, but the cook outdid herself with Christmas dinner. From the tender roast turkey to the flaming Christmas pudding, the meal had truly been a feast, but I was too preoccupied with everything that had happened to enjoy it thoroughly.

Mr. Eggers was also in an abstracted state. Our conversation had been stilted, and I'd had to repeat my questions to him a few times. It was only when Miss Brinkle announced, "Oh, I found one of the charms," that he seemed to shake off his pensiveness.

Miss Brinkle let out a trill of laughter. "Well! I look forward to seeing this come true in the new year. Indeed, I do. It's the ring!"

Theo looked confused, and Francie explained, "The charms are baked into the pudding. It's said they're signs of what will happen in the coming year. The ring means that Miss Brinkle will get married."

"And that tells you, Mr. Culwell, how reliable this little game is." Miss Brinkle's headgear—today a sprig of holly and red feathers—quivered as she shook her head. "I like my solidarity too much to give it up."

Theo looked even more confused. Mrs. Searsby said, "Yes, you're quite fond of your *solitary* state, aren't you, Aunt Pru?"

Miss Brinkle said, "Yes, that's exactly what I said."

Theo's face cleared, then he peered more closely at his pudding. "What does a button mean, then? That's what I have."

"It means bachelorhood," Francie said, a trace of disappointment crossing her face.

"Not if I have anything to say about it," Theo said, and Francie's cheeks flushed a bright red.

My spoon connected with something solid. "Oh, I have the wishbone."

Jasper said, "A year of good luck for you, which is more promising than what I've found." He tilted his spoon to show a silver thimble.

A ripple of laughter ran around the table as Francie explained to Theo, "The thimble symbolizes a year of spinsterhood."

Mr. Eggers announced, "I have one as well, the coin." He dipped his head toward Theo as he explained, "The coin indicates a prosperous year. Nothing but an old wives' tale, of course," he added, but he looked quite pleased.

Blix said, "And I have the anchor."

Mrs. Searsby said, "Safe harbor is an excellent thing for a traveler," and Blix agreed. Then Mrs. Searsby glanced from Miss Brinkle to Jasper. "For some of us, it seems it will be a topsy-turvy year."

As the plates were cleared, Mr. Eggers transferred the coin to his napkin and wiped it clean.

I said, "Perhaps that means your research will be well received."

"What?"

"The coin. Perhaps it means your research will catch the attention of the leading—er—snail experts."

"Oh. Indeed. Yes." His manner was abstracted again. He put the coin into his waistcoat pocket, then gave me his full attention. "Might I request a moment of your time later today? I must speak with you and Mr. Rimington." His voice dropped to a whisper. "In private."

"Of course." Had he looked up Dr. Sweetwater and found he didn't exist? "Perhaps after the gifts are opened? Shall we say in the billiard room?"

He considered. "As long as it's empty. If not, we'll have to go somewhere else."

"You're worried about being overheard?"

"Yes." He hesitated a moment, then removed his glasses

and shook out his handkerchief. "You see, I've remembered something—something I think could be quite important." While Mr. Eggers polished his spectacles, he focused his attention across the table on Theo, who was in what looked like a deep discussion with Francie. "On Saturday, when I was out, I saw—"

Theo must have felt the weight of Mr. Eggers' gaze because he looked across the table to Mr. Eggers, who immediately shifted to examining the lenses of his spectacles as he said to me, "I must say no more now."

The men decided to forgo their port, and we all went along to the Oak Hall, which looked especially festive and cozy with the tinsel and bright ornaments, and the Yule log flaming and sparking. The blaze had warmed the room, and the leaded-glass windows were fogged over, creating a blurry white view of the grounds.

I looped my arm through Jasper's and said a little more loudly than necessary, "Let's admire the tree."

He shot me a quelling glance. I lifted my brows. "Too contrived? Amateur theatrics isn't a strong suit of mine."

"Your delivery was perfect, but the volume—you sounded as if you were calling 'all aboard' before a train departed. However, it did get us here first."

Apollo was stretched out near the hearth, his back to the fire. He raised his head and thumped his tail. I paused to rub his ears. Zeus trotted over, a red ball in his mouth. I would have tossed it for him, but he zipped away, weaving in and out of the guests' legs. Jasper slipped the present out of his pocket. While seeming to lean close to examine one of the ornaments on the tree, he deposited the red package at the bottom of the pile of gifts.

"Well done," I said.

"I hope so. Since the presents aren't marked with names there is a chance the wrong person may pick it up."

"A slim chance, I think. You buried it deeply enough that someone will have to make an effort to get it. I bet the courier will ensure he or she is one of the first guests to select a gift." We took a seat on the sofa with a good view of the presents. "Mr. Eggers would like to meet with us in the billiard room after we open presents. He says he's remembered something he saw on Saturday that could be important."

Jasper said, "That's intriguing."

"Yes, especially because he was staring at Theo when he told me, but he stopped speaking as soon as Theo noticed."

A footman came with a tray of mulled wine in small porcelain mugs, each garnished with an orange slice. Jasper and I took a mug, and I inhaled the aroma of cinnamon, nutmeg, and cloves.

Mrs. Searsby said, "We'll do Lucky Dip for gifts." She indicated that Blix and I should start.

I picked up a green package with red ribbon, while Blix selected a white gift with silver ribbon. I returned to the little sofa, and Mrs. Searsby said, "Go on, open them. See what Father Christmas has brought you." She motioned for another set of guests to pick gifts.

I pulled the paper away and found a set of fountain pens. I said to Mrs. Searsby, "They're beautiful. Thank you."

Blix removed the paper from her gift. "A writing desk. How perfect! I'll get lots of use out of this. It should fit in my suitcase easily. Thank you."

Francie and Miss Brinkle were selecting their gifts when an odd noise—a retching sound—cut through the chatter. It was such an incongruous sound that everyone stopped what they were doing.

I looked around and saw Mr. Eggers had shifted forward in his chair. His mug dangled forgotten in one hand as he pressed his other hand to his mouth. His complexion was the color of chalk. He made the horrible sound again and surged to his feet. His mug clattered to the floor, sending a spray of mulled wine across the flagstones as the porcelain shattered. Droplets spattered over my shoes as Mr. Eggers paused, his gaze going to the door at the other end of the room that led to the main part of the house. A panicked look came into his eyes as his shoulders heaved again.

Theo, who had been sitting in the chair beside Mr. Eggers, jumped up and put out his hand. "Mr. Eggers—golly! You're pickled! Here, let me—"

But Mr. Eggers shoved Theo's hand away. Mr. Eggers spun and lurched to the Lodge's front door, which was much closer than the door to the rest of the house. He pawed at the handle, flung the door back, and reeled outside. An icy blast of air surged in as Mr. Eggers was sick outside.

For a few seconds we all remained frozen in place. How embarrassing! Poor Mr. Eggers—so neat and particular. I was sure he was mortified to be taken sick in company.

Mr. Searsby crossed to the door, but before he reached it, Mr. Eggers came back inside, his handkerchief pressed to his mouth. His skin looked even paler, but his complexion had a sallow undertone to it now. His spectacles reflected the light of the blazing Yule log. He leaned against the doorframe. "Poison," he gasped. "You"—he pointed his handkerchief at Theo— "poisoned me."

Theo looked from the splatter of mulled wine on the flagstones to Mr. Eggers. "What? Poison? You're off your head, old man."

"You poisoned me!" Mr. Eggers repeated as he moved forward a few steps, then collapsed.

CHAPTER TWENTY-FOUR

*I*t was Blix who moved first. She hurried over and kneeled beside Mr. Eggers. "Let me have a look. I've had a little nursing experience."

Mr. Eggers had fallen on his side, then rolled forward so that his face was pressed to the flagstones. His glasses had come off when he collapsed. I picked them up so no one would step on them.

Jasper helped Blix turn Mr. Eggers onto his back, while Mr. Searsby sent a footman to telephone for the doctor. "Tell him to come along the path that runs by the church, and he shouldn't have any problem getting here."

Blix felt for Mr. Eggers' pulse, then watched his chest a moment. "His heart rate is a little fast, but his breathing seems normal."

Mrs. Searsby, her hands pressed to her chest, said, "It can't be good for him to lie on the cold stone floor, though." She glanced at the front door, which still stood open. The cold air was pouring in, dousing the warmth coming off the fire.

Theo moved toward it. "I'll see to the door."

Mrs. Searsby said to Blix, "Do you think it's all right to move him?"

"We could move him to the sofa," Mr. Sprigg suggested.

"No, let's take him up to his room," Mrs. Searsby said. "He'll be more comfortable there, and we can warm that room much more quickly than this one." She turned to the footman. "Send Laura up to Mr. Eggers' room. She has assisted the doctor in the past. Mr. Rimington, perhaps you and Mr. Sprigg could . . . ?"

"Of course." Jasper came forward and eased his arms under Mr. Eggers' shoulders while Mr. Sprigg gripped his ankles. They heaved him up and carried him carefully out of the Oak Hall, following Mrs. Searsby up the circular staircase. Holding Mr. Eggers' spectacles, I trailed along behind them but paused in the hallway outside Mr. Eggers' room.

Jasper emerged from the room, pulling his sleeves down and straightening his lapels. Mr. Sprigg held the door for Mrs. Searsby. He wiped his palm over his forehead, then followed her out and pulled the door closed. Mrs. Searsby said, "Blix and the maid will stay with him until Dr. Harris arrives. Thank you, Mr. Rimington. Mr. Sprigg."

Mr. Sprigg inclined his head, and Jasper said, "Happy to help," his breathing only a little labored.

I handed Mr. Eggers' glasses to her.

"Thank you, Miss Belgrave. I'll see that these are put in a safe place. Now, I think a break in the festivities—"

"Is he awake? I want to talk to him," Theo said as he and Francie joined the group around Mr. Eggers' door.

"He awoke briefly when the gentlemen settled him on the bed, but I told him to rest," Mrs. Searsby said firmly.

Francie glanced around and took a step closer to Theo. "There's no call to look at Theo in such a disapproving manner. Mr. Eggers was obviously off his head. He didn't know what he was saying. I'm sure once he's recovered, he'll retract his absurd accusation."

Theo added, "I have no idea what he was talking about. Poison! That's bunk, I tell you. Bunk!"

"Of course it is," Francie said.

Mrs. Searsby cleared her throat. "As I was saying, I think a break in the festivities is called for. Perhaps we could gather in the Oak Hall around teatime?"

A murmur of agreement went around the group. Francie said, "I'm in the mood for a game of billiards, Theo. Care to join me?"

He looked at Mr. Eggers' door, but Mrs. Searsby sent him a disapproving glance, and he turned away with Francie.

As everyone dispersed, Jasper came to my side. "Dashed irregular Christmas, this."

As we walked slowly down the corridor, I added, "Mr. Searsby said nothing about notifying the village constable."

"He's probably waiting to see what the doctor's diagnosis will be."

"Or intending to keep it altogether quiet if he can."

A maid came along the hall. She was carrying the set of fountain pens I'd unwrapped and the little writing desk that had been Blix's gift. She said, "Good afternoon, miss. We're tidying up the Oak Hall. Shall I put these in your room?"

"Yes, do. And I'm sure it will be perfectly fine to do the same with Miss Windway's gift."

The maid departed, and I gripped Jasper's arm. "The present!"

Jasper didn't need any further explanation than that. He knew I was thinking of the red gift with the gold ribbon that he'd discreetly placed under the tree only a short time ago. Without another word, we hurried down the stairs.

The glass mugs and discarded wrapping paper had been cleared away in the Oak Hall. Another maid was rising to her feet after scrubbing the floor where Mr. Eggers had dropped his mulled wine. When she saw us, she curtsied, picked up her mop and pail, and departed.

I said, "We'll never know what was in Mr. Eggers' drink now."

"Yes, very efficient of the servants," Jasper said, but he sounded abstracted as he went to the tree. I stayed behind, looking at the place where Mr. Eggers' mug had fallen, but not a drop of liquid remained.

Jasper turned from the tree. "It's gone."

I whirled around and went to his side. "Are you sure —?" I broke off. None of the packages under the tree were the small red box with gold ribbon.

Jasper dropped down into a chair and rubbed his hand across his forehead. "It must have happened when Mr. Eggers collapsed."

"Yes. Everyone was distracted. I certainly wasn't looking at the gifts."

"I wasn't either." He blew out a sigh, then pressed his hands to his knees and stood. "Well, I haven't completely blotted my copybook. At least we do know where the courier will go to retrieve the letter. I've suddenly developed a deep and abiding interest in books and plan to spend the rest of my time in the library."

"You *do* have a deep and abiding interest in books, so that's not a recent development."

"True, but it's not the behavior of a good houseguest. One shouldn't secret oneself in the library for hours on end." He checked his wristwatch. "In fact, I'd better go now. It won't take long for the recipient of the letter to complete the crossword and use the mask of the Christmas card to figure out where to look. I'll write a quick note to Miss Ravenna and pop it under her door so she knows the situation."

"I'll be along in a moment." After Jasper left, I examined the chair where Mr. Eggers had sat and the floor around it. I also had a look at Theo's chair, but the servants had done a thorough job of cleaning up, and nothing remained.

I stood still and looked around the quiet room. The only sound was the popping of the fire as the Yule log continued to burn, warming the Hall again. A flash of movement outside one of the leaded-glass windows caught my eye. I went over and wiped away the condensation.

A servant carrying a shovel disappeared around the side of the house. He must have been given the unenviable task of cleaning up the place in the snow where Mr. Eggers had been sick. I continued to stare out the window, lost in thought. If Mr. Eggers had seen Theo near the belvedere and Theo had realized Mr. Eggers intended to share that news with Jasper and me, then Theo would have known that he was about to be exposed. It would make sense for him to try to silence Mr. Eggers as quickly as possible.

The raggedy clouds were moving across the sky, and the pattern of sun and shadow checkerboarded the blanket of snow. The wind was whipping the clouds along, and their shadows rippled over the lawn. One of the shadows engulfed Holly Hill Lodge. A few moments later it sailed away, and the view was brilliantly bright again. Something glinted in the snow not far from where the footman had been working.

I went to the front door and stepped outside. The frigid air hit me, and I wrapped my arms around my body as I squinted against the reflected light. Again, the glitter showed up. There was definitely something shiny in the snow. It was several feet away, lying in one of the drifts around the plantings next to the house.

I went inside, through to the main part of the house, and climbed the stairs quickly. I changed into a pair of boots, pulled on my thickest cardigan, and went back down. I closed the heavy front door behind me. I picked my way across the snow, scanning the drifts. The clouds had plunged the scene into shadow, but they slipped away, and sunlight flooded down. I spotted the bright flash a few feet ahead and used my handkerchief to pick it up.

It was a small glass vial no bigger than my pinky. A bit of dark brown liquid stained the rim of the vial. I imagined that at one time, there had been a cork stopper in the top. I wrapped it in my handkerchief, put it in my pocket, and returned to the house.

CHAPTER TWENTY-FIVE

A little while later I was sitting in the library with Jasper. The vial and my handkerchief lay on the table between us with a chessboard hiding it from the view of anyone who might enter the room. I'd just told Jasper how I'd found it in the snow not far from the front door of Holly Hill Lodge.

"Do you have any idea what it is?" Jasper asked.

"No. It has a musty odor, but I don't recognize it."

Jasper used the handkerchief to pick up the vial. He sniffed, then jerked his head back. "I would know that scent anywhere. It's ipecac." He put it down quickly. "Nasty stuff. I had to take some when I was a child once. Horrible. Someone only wanted to make Mr. Eggers sick."

"Possibly, but I suppose it depends on how much was poured into his wine. Even medicinal things can be deadly." I folded the lace edge of the handkerchief over the vial. "Theo would have had the opportunity to toss the vial into the snow when he went to close the door."

Jasper began setting up the chess pieces on the board. "Chancy thing, though. If Mr. Eggers hadn't staggered outside, Theo wouldn't have had the opportunity to throw it away."

"I'm not saying Theo planned to pitch it into the snow. He saw an opportunity and took it. He could have easily discarded it in his room later—or even returned it to a medicine cabinet in one of the bathrooms."

"Yes, that's probably where he got it," Jasper said.

Blix came through the doorway, a stack of books in her hands. I put the handkerchief in my pocket as Jasper stood to greet her.

"Oh, don't get up," she said. "I'm just returning this book. It's a brilliant biography of a Victorian lady traveler."

"Are you off nursing duty?" I asked.

"Yes. The doctor came. I'm not needed anymore."

"How is Mr. Eggers?" Jasper asked as she deposited the books on the table.

"Better, in a way. He came around but was extremely upset. Kept banging on about Mr. Culwell poisoning him. He said Mr. Culwell moved his mug on the table, and that's when he must have put the poison in it. He got so worked up, the doctor gave him a lecture and told him he had to rest."

"Did he say why he thought Theo would poison him?" I asked.

"That was the odd part." Blix frowned. "When the doctor asked him, Mr. Eggers became downright cagey and wouldn't say anything more. He demanded to speak to the police immediately, but the doctor said he wouldn't allow it until at least tomorrow."

Jasper asked, "But the doctor *did* think he was poisoned?"

Blix tilted her head side to side, indicating the statement was iffy. "He said Mr. Eggers ingested something that didn't agree with him. He said he couldn't confirm what it was without testing everything that Mr. Eggers had consumed."

"Well, I sat next to him during the Christmas feast," I said. "He didn't have anything different from the rest of us."

"And Mrs. Searsby had already checked with Cook about the wine," Blix added. "The mugs were poured out from a single large pot."

Jasper said, "Then if someone did put it into his drink, it would have happened in the Oak Hall."

Blix nodded. "It certainly seems that way. Mr. Culwell knocked on the door while the doctor was there—to check on Mr. Eggers, he said—and Mr. Eggers began shouting about the poisoning and Mr. Culwell moving his mug of wine. But Mr. Culwell insisted he only shifted Mr. Eggers' mug a little to the side so he could put his own mug down on the table. It was at that point that the doctor insisted Mr. Culwell leave." Blix leaned against the table and crossed her arms. "The whole situation is distinctly odd. Why would Mr. Eggers accuse Mr. Culwell of poisoning him in the first place? That's quite a leap. Wouldn't it be more likely he'd assume there was something off with his drink?"

"Yes, it is quite strange behavior," I said, and Jasper agreed.

Blix studied us both, then said, "You two know something."

Jasper made a scoffing sound, and I said, "No, unfortunately. We aren't any clearer on what's really going on than you are."

She leveled a look at me, then switched her attention

to Jasper. "So that's how you're going to play it, is it?" Her words could have been sarcastic, but a little smile played at her mouth while her tone conveyed that she was party to our secret. "You fooled me when I first arrived. You said there was nothing mysterious going on here at Holly Hill Lodge. Well, I'm not fooled this time. Something is definitely strange here. Either you've decided not to share what it is, or you're sworn to secrecy."

Jasper and I exchanged a glance. She was too perceptive to fob off. "Something like that," I allowed.

"Well, I'd intended to depart tomorrow, but it looks as if we will all have to stay another day. Scotland Yard will want to speak with us all."

Jasper, his attention on aligning the pawns, asked, "Because of Mr. Eggers' accusations?"

Blix nodded. "I'd heard Scotland Yard was on the way because of Bankston's death, but their activities would be a formality—that it was obvious the butler had met with an accident. I don't think that will be the case now. I overheard Mr. Searsby tell the doctor that there is no need to call in the constable to investigate Mr. Eggers' allegations about Mr. Culwell. Mr. Searsby said Scotland Yard was on the way, and they could look into Mr. Eggers' statements. So, I assume that all the guests will need to stay on until the Yard finishes their investigation."

"Yes, I would think that would be the case," I said.

Blix straightened. "Well, I can see that you intend to keep your counsel. Tomorrow should be a rather interesting Boxing Day."

Ford entered. "Telephone call for you, Miss Windway."

"Oh, someone's been frightfully extravagant and rung up with Christmas greetings." Before she followed Ford out of the room, she said, "When this is over, I'd like to hear the whole story. As I said earlier, I'm quite fond of a jolly little Christmas mystery."

Once she'd left, I said, "I wonder if she came to retrieve *Baedeker's Egypt* but decided not to take it because we were here."

"I don't think our presence would prevent her from doing that. There's nothing suspicious in simply taking a book off the shelf. And in her case, selecting a book about Egypt would be nothing remarkable."

I gestured to the chessboard. "Perhaps we should have a game if we're going to stay here all afternoon."

"Good idea. If we spend a couple of hours in here, it will look less odd if we're playing chess." He adjusted the position of several chess pieces. "Shall we say best two out of three? That should cover several hours."

"At the pace you play, definitely." Jasper did not play chess in the same expeditious manner he played billiards.

I won the first game with a stealthy move of my knight and succeeded in taking Jasper's king. The second game went in his favor. I was merely shifting my chess pieces around the board in a futile attempt to avoid losing. It was only a matter of time before he cornered my king.

A voice from the gallery floated down. "That looks like a difficult position for you, Miss Belgrave."

I looked over my shoulder. Miss Ravenna stood at the gallery's balustrade.

Jasper said, "How did you get up there, Miss Ravenna? I refuse to believe we were so absorbed in the game that we didn't notice you sneak in."

"It's not that at all. I came in the hidden door."

I swiveled fully around. "Hidden door?"

"Yes—all the best manor houses have them. Come up. I'll show you."

We left the chess game and climbed the circular staircase. The pallor of Miss Ravenna's skin was gone. Her complexion was now creamy, and her cheeks were a healthy pale pink. She moved with energy as we followed her to a bookcase against the wall in the back corner of the library. "None of these are real books. They're all fashioned to look as if they are, but they're simply part of the door." She put her finger on the top of a book, *Gulliver's Travels*, and tilted it forward. A little metallic click sounded.

She tugged on the edge of the bookcase, and it swung back.

I poked my head out the door. "But this is the hallway where our bedrooms are."

"Handy, isn't it?" Miss Ravenna said. "My maid learned about it from the household servants and told me. Apparently, one of the family members from years ago was quite the bookworm and didn't like the idea of having to go down a flight of stairs to get to the library. The jib door was made so they could dart into the library if they wanted a new book."

"Well, I have to say I approve of that," Jasper said.

Miss Ravenna gestured to the door. "Go ahead and take a closer look. I'll keep watch over the library." She moved to the balustrade and looked down into the empty room below.

Jasper stepped out into the hallway and studied the seam of the door, which was fitted so that the frame was flush with the wall.

I made a face. "Obviously, I'm not nearly as observant as I think I am. I've walked by here for several days and never noticed it."

Jasper ran his hand along the wall. "Don't be too upset, old bean. The wallpaper disguises it rather well."

I closed the door, and we joined Miss Ravenna in the library. "Of course it's not really a secret," she said. "All the servants know about it, and the family uses it often." She looked down into the main floor of the library.

"Nothing to report?"

"Not so far."

"I'm glad that you've recovered, Miss Ravenna," I said.

"Thank you. I'm frightfully glad to be well. And thank goodness no one else has come down with it. Now, Jasper, you can't skip tea as well as dinner. It will raise questions. I've kept my recovery quiet, but I think I shall feel the need to compose some letters during dinner. I'll use the bookcase door and work there." She gestured to a small writing desk at the end of the gallery. "I'll have a good view of the lower floor. I'll be able to see if anyone comes before or after dinner while you mingle with the guests."

Jasper said, "Capital idea."

"Yes," Miss Ravenna said. "We certainly don't want to raise any eyebrows at this point."

"But you mustn't tire yourself out, Miss Ravenna," I said.

"That's right," Jasper said. "I'll keep watch after dinner —all night if necessary."

"Oh, I don't think it will come to that," Miss Ravenna said. "The courier will want to retrieve the letter and be packed and ready to go tomorrow."

Jasper leaned against the railing. "No one will leave tomorrow."

We told her about the news that the much-delayed Scotland Yard man was on his way, and she said, "So they will finally arrive, only a few days late. Thank goodness the poisoning of Mr. Eggers and the death of Mr. Bankston—and his sordid activities—aren't our responsibility."

Jasper shot a glance out of the corner of his eye at me, and I knew what he was thinking—that I certainly was interested in finding out the truth behind Bankston's death and Mr. Eggers' poisoning, even if Miss Ravenna was not. However, I kept my thoughts to myself. There was nothing to keep me from pursuing both lines of inquiry up until Scotland Yard actually arrived—and perhaps after.

Miss Ravenna pushed away from the balustrade. "I'll return to my room for now and let you get back to your game. No need for all of us to congregate here and draw attention." As she headed for the bookcase door, Miss Ravenna said, "And you might consider your rook, Miss Belgrave. Some intriguing possibilities there."

Jasper let out a mock sigh. "Ladies—they always gang up on a chap."

CHAPTER TWENTY-SIX

*D*inner that evening was a cold buffet and very informal. Mr. Eggers was still recovering and remained in his room. Francie and Theo made themselves roast beef sandwiches and disappeared back to the billiard room, where they'd been holed up most of the afternoon. After dinner, Jasper and I returned to the library, where we found Miss Ravenna sealing her letters. She came down the curving staircase to meet us.

Jasper asked, "Anyone drop by for a book?"

"Not a soul."

I glanced at the row of red spines. "That seems rather odd, doesn't it?"

Jasper said, "It will probably happen this evening. I'll take the night watch."

"I don't think that's a good idea," I said. "You were up last night working to decipher the crossword. You and I should split the evening, Jasper. You need at least a few hours' sleep, and I feel a need to catch up on my corre-spondence. That writing desk that you used, Miss Ravenna, will be the perfect place to do it. Then I'll find a

227

book and become immersed in it until midnight—no, one in the morning—and that will give you a few hours of sleep, Jasper. You can relieve me then."

He opened his mouth, but before he could speak, Miss Ravenna said, "Excellent idea. She's right, Jasper. We can't have you nodding off at a critical moment. I'll relieve you at six in the morning in case nothing happens during the night. Right, that's settled, then. Good night."

Once she'd departed, Jasper let out a huff. "I really must keep you two away from each other." He strolled over to the *Baedeker's Egypt* guide. He pulled out the bright red book, opened it, and snapped it closed.

My heart did a funny dip. "Still there?"

"Yes. Just ensuring someone hadn't swiped it out from under us without us noticing. Well, I'll leave you to your letters, then."

"I think you forgot something."

Jasper glanced back to the shelf and pushed the book in a fraction so that it was lined up perfectly with the other books. "What?"

"A goodnight kiss."

"Ah, yes, indeed. Critical oversight on my part."

～

I PUT my pen down and massaged my fingers, which were a little cramped. I was seated at the writing desk in the gallery. I had a marvelous view of the lower floor of the library, which lay quiet as a church at midday during the week. I'd switched on several lamps on the main floor of the library before climbing the spiral staircase to take my place at the writing desk. They cast pools of golden light, spotlighting the rich colors of the bindings and the glitter of the embossed spines. The uncurtained high lancet windows on the far wall were tall inky rectangles.

I straightened the pages in front of me and read over them. I hadn't written any letters. I'd drafted a summary of everything that had happened since I'd arrived at Holly Hill Lodge. I came to the end and went back, skimming along the lines. As I'd written the notes, something had caused a ripple of disturbance. What was it?

I reached the end and went back and looked again, but I couldn't isolate what had produced a flare of unease. With a sigh, I folded the pages and went downstairs to find a novel. Perhaps, like Mr. Searsby and his darts, completely leaving the puzzle would free my mind to work it out.

It was clear the current owners of Holly Hill Lodge weren't fiction readers. The most recent crime fiction title I could find was A. E. W. Mason's *At the Villa Rose*. I took it off the shelf and considered staying on the main floor, but then decided I liked my bird's-eye view from the gallery and returned there. A few easy chairs were placed between the bookcases, and I dragged one over so the travel books were in sight, but I was still mostly hidden by the edge of a bookshelf.

I settled down to read, but even the entertaining Inspector Hanaud couldn't hold my attention. The patter of movement sounded from the library's main floor. I leaned forward to peer through the railings. The tension drained out of me when I spotted Zeus, his red ball in his mouth. His short terrier legs skimmed along the rug as he trotted down the aisle between the bookcases. Apollo stood at the doorway. The Labrador surveyed the room, then backed away from the door and loped off.

Zeus wove through the chairs and tables at the far end

of the library, then zipped up the spiral staircase and made directly for me. Tail wagging, he dropped the ball at my feet and fixed his dark, expectant gaze on me.

I couldn't shoo him away immediately. "All right, we'll play, but only for a bit. I'm the night watchman. I can't have you here too long. You'll give away my hiding place."

I tossed the ball along the gallery. He darted after it, hemmed it in, snapped it up, and raced back to me. We repeated the sequence until his steps weren't quite so quick and sharp. "One last time," I warned and released the ball. He zipped away after it but misjudged and bumped it, sending the ball off in a different direction. It shot through the railings and fell down into the main floor.

My heart plummeted along with the ball as I shot out of the chair and sprinted to the railing. I sagged with relief as the ball bounced harmlessly between the book-cases. For a moment, I'd had a horrible vision of the ball hitting one of the valuable items displayed in the library, like the stone busts or the delicate vases that lined the top of the bookshelves. Thank goodness nothing had been struck down. I stood frozen there, the thought repeating in my mind.

Beside me, Zeus' head had been angled down through the railings. He wiggled backward and fixed his attention on me, his head tilted.

"Don't look at me. It's your ball. You go get it."

He dashed down the staircase and snatched up the ball. He must have heard a noise from the hallway because he went still, his gaze focused on the open door, then he forgot about me and scurried out. I waited motionless for a few moments, but no one came into the library.

On my way back to my chair, I retrieved my notes

from the writing table and read them again, the detective novel forgotten. I had it now. I knew what had bothered me earlier. I turned the pages until I found the section and went over it slowly.

I dropped my hands to my lap and stared unseeingly across to the other side of the gallery. "That turns everything on its head," I murmured. I leaned back in the chair, my mind busy rearranging what I'd thought I'd known into a new pattern.

A quarter-hour later, I was pacing up and down the gallery, lost in thought as I worked out the last small details. A male servant entered through the main door of the library. I faded into a corner, hoping he wouldn't come upstairs.

It was Ford. He checked the locks on the three sets of double glass doors. He pushed in a chair and began switching off the lamps. While his back was turned, I turned off the small lamp on a nearby table that I'd been using to read by.

When he finished downstairs, the gallery was dark. He didn't even glance at the spiral staircase. He left by the main door, closing it behind him.

The room was plunged into darkness except for the high leaded-glass lancet windows, which were no longer black rectangles. Milky white moonlight flowed through them, casting faint diamond-shaped patterns across the tables and bookcases.

I didn't want to pace about in the darkness, so I sat down in the chair to wait. The clocks chimed half-past ten. Jasper would relieve me soon, and I could share what I'd figured out.

The house became quiet. Except for an occasional creak or groan, it settled into its nighttime stillness.

Before dinner, I'd told the maid who attended me—Laura was still sitting with Mr. Eggers—that I'd see to myself that night. She would have retired by now along with the rest of the servants. The minutes dawdled along, marked by the chimes of the clock every quarter-hour.

Finally, the clocks pealed a single stroke throughout the house, and the bookcase door swung open, letting a bar of light from the hallway fall across the gallery. Jasper's tall figure blocked it for a moment as he stepped into the room, then he closed the door, and blackness descended again.

"Over here," I whispered. He moved slowly along the gallery. Since his vision wasn't good, I supposed it was even more difficult for him to see in the gloom than it was for me. "Down here at the end of the gallery." He followed the sound of my voice, and I met him halfway. I gripped his outstretched hand. "I've worked it out."

"Someone's been in and taken the letter? Who?"

"Oh, no. Nothing's happened with that. Except for a visit from Zeus, it's been as quiet as a crypt down there. What I meant was, I've worked out who set the trap to kill Bankston."

"You have?"

"Yes. It came to me when I was throwing the ball for Zeus. He bumped into it, and it went through the rails and sailed down into the main library. I thought it was a good thing nothing had been struck down. That was what did it."

"Did what?"

"The words 'struck down' helped me realize what had been bothering me. Earlier this evening, I jotted everything down that had happened, but something wasn't quite right. I couldn't put my finger on it until that incident."

"The ball going over the edge of the gallery?"

"No, it was what I'd thought, *thank goodness nothing had been struck down.*"

"I'm afraid I'm not following you."

"It reminded me of something Mr. Eggers had said." I drew him along the gallery. "Here's a chair where you can sit and keep watch over everything. Wait a moment . . ." I dragged the chair from the writing desk over and sat beside him. "Let me tell you the whole thing. Remember when we spoke to Mr. Eggers? Do you remember what he said when we asked him about Bankston's blackmailing him?"

"Not his exact words, no. But he denied having anything to do with it."

"That's right. He also said it was 'a shame that Bankston was struck down like that.'"

Jasper didn't reply. In the darkness, the clock on the main floor of the library ticked on in the silence.

"Don't you see? Mr. Eggers knew Bankston had been struck by a rock falling from the window above. Bankston had been *struck down.* Those were the exact words Mr. Eggers used."

"But that's a common expression."

"I know it is," I allowed, "and Mr. Eggers tried to follow up by saying something about how sad it was that Bankston was young when he died, but he'd taken off his glasses and was polishing them again. He'd already polished them once. He didn't need to do it again. I think he polishes his glasses when he's lying. It gives him some-thing to do with his hands, and he doesn't have to look anyone in the eye."

"A tell."

"Yes, exactly! He did it again tonight at dinner when he told me he'd seen something important when he was outdoors on Saturday."

"And you think he was lying about that?"

"Yes."

"But your theory doesn't fit with everything else that's happened. Someone attempted to poison Mr. Eggers."

"Oh, but there's more. Much more. I've been working out all the details for the last several hours. It all fits."

"I'm afraid I don't see how."

"Let me explain the whole thing from the beginning. Bankston must have tried to blackmail Mr. Eggers, and Mr. Eggers decided to set up the trap for him at the belvedere. Balancing the rock and setting up the cord so that it would fall when Bankston pulled the note—it's exactly the sort of thing Mr. Eggers would do. It's very detailed and depends on careful timing. It fits with his personality perfectly."

"I suppose if one were to match a murder method with a man's personality, that would certainly seem about right for Mr. Eggers."

I heard the hesitancy in Jasper's voice and went on, "Mr. Eggers admits he was out of the house on Saturday afternoon. Mr. Eggers says he stayed out a short time, then returned to the library. But he told us himself that no one saw him in the library. He had ample opportunity to set up his trap and send a telegram to Bankston in London. I'm sure that if we inquire, we'll find that Mr. Eggers went into Chipping Bascomb and sent a telegram that day."

"Rather foolish to do that, though. If anyone inquired, the game would be up."

"But Mr. Eggers was counting on the fact that no one would realize Bankston's death was murder. No one would care what Mr. Eggers' movements were or whether or not he had sent a telegram to London."

Jasper made a murmuring noise, indicating he was intrigued.

"Bankston went to London," I said. "Mrs. Searsby announced the fact to all the guests, and Mr. Eggers decided to seize the opportunity to do away with Bankston. Mr. Eggers sent the telegram to London to draw Bankston to the belvedere on Bankston's return to Chipping Bascomb. That afternoon, Mr. Eggers arranged the stones at the window of the belvedere so they'd fall when Bankston pulled the note with his name on it. The movement would jerk the string, which would release the stone. The variable that Mr. Eggers didn't account for was the snow. He intended to return to the belvedere the next day and remove the note and the string so it would appear as if Bankston had been unlucky. Can't you hear the narrative? *Poor chap, at the wrong place at the wrong time.* Mr. Eggers even left some fresh Woodbine cigarette butts near where the rock fell so it would appear as if Bankston had gone up there to have a smoke."

Jasper was quiet a moment, and I knew he hadn't dismissed my idea out of hand. "But what reason would Bankston have to be at the belvedere in the middle of the night?"

"It wasn't supposed to be the middle of the night. The train was delayed. It would have been late, but not after midnight. The path through the woods was commonly used. It wouldn't have been unusual for someone to walk from the station to the Lodge that way. Granted, he preferred to have the family's motor pick him up at the station, but I'm sure the motor wasn't always available to him. I'm sure he had to walk back to the Lodge at times."

"Yes, I'd agree that was probably the case with the motor," Jasper said.

"But with the snow, Mr. Eggers couldn't retrieve the note and remove the traces of the trap without leaving his footprints. The string was well hidden in the ivy. Mr. Eggers had to hope that the note was either overlooked, or that he was on hand when the body was first discovered. Do you remember before Francie and Theo arrived, I saw a flash of light down the path that went to Holly Hill Lodge? I believe it was the light shining on Mr. Eggers' spectacles. He must have spotted us at the top of the belvedere and retreated. Then Francie and Theo went that direction to call the police, so any tracks he might have left from the house to the woods would have been covered over."

"It all sounds possible, except for the fact that someone poisoned Mr. Eggers."

"No one poisoned Mr. Eggers. He dosed himself with the ipecac."

Jasper drew a breath, and I assumed he was about to argue with me, but then he stopped. "I suppose you're right. He could've had the vial of ipecac in his pocket, added a few drops to his cup, then thrown the vial away when he was outside being sick."

"Yes, that's exactly what I think happened. Theo did go outside, and he could have tossed the vial away, but Mr. Eggers went outside as well. Either one of them could have thrown the vial. Remember when we were working on the jigsaw puzzle and Mr. Eggers edged up without us noticing? He could have overheard us talking about Theo, so he'd know Theo was a good candidate to divert suspicion from himself. Mr. Eggers 'poisoned' himself and created a scenario that would make Theo look even more guilty."

"A rather risky—not to mention distasteful—plan, dosing himself with ipecac. As I said, I know how foul-tasting that concoction is. Not something one would take on a whim."

"But to make sure you were clear of suspicion?"

Jasper shifted in his chair. "Well, yes, I suppose one might swallow something as revolting as ipecac to prevent oneself from being charged with murder."

"And he may have exaggerated his symptoms so that he appeared to be more ill than he really was."

"Quite devious," Jasper said. "But the question remains, why would he kill Bankston in the first place?"

"I suppose it goes back to Mr. Eggers' deception around the snowflake research."

The ambient moonlight made it bright enough to see that Jasper was staring across to the other side of the gallery. After a moment he shook his head. "I don't see it. It's not as though Mr. Eggers was a scholar with an eminent university. If he were exposed, what did he really have to lose, except access to the snail monographs?"

"Yes, that is the weak spot in my argument. I confess I haven't worked out that part yet. I can't see Mr. Eggers killing Bankston over the fact that he had discovered Mr. Eggers was researching snails and not snowflakes."

"No, that wouldn't give rise to murder. Perhaps he—"

A thread of sound, a faint creak, filtered through the air, and the main door to the library opened.

CHAPTER TWENTY-SEVEN

a click sounded as someone pressed the switch on the wall by the door. The electric sconces that ran along the walls of the ground floor came on, bathing the room in light. In one swift, quiet movement, Jasper and I faded backward into a cleft between two of the bookcases.

Mr. Sprigg strolled down the central aisle between the two rows of shelves and went directly to the travel books. He ran his finger along the row until he came to the red spines of the *Baedeker's*. He selected one, flipped it open, and removed the envelope. In one smooth motion, he put the envelope in his pocket and returned the book to the shelf. Then he reached up to the books lining the highest shelf and took one, seemingly at random. He left the library, snapping off the lights on his way out. Blackness descended, and moonlight again streamed in the windows.

I realized I was holding Jasper's hand in a tight grip. I gave it a little shake. "Mr. Sprigg! I never would have imagined that."

"That's the idea. Of course, I wouldn't have either if I hadn't seen it with my own eyes." Jasper gave my hand a returning squeeze. "Now we have sight of the fox. I'll tell Miss Ravenna in the morning—"

The library door squeaked, a higher pitch as it opened slowly. There was enough light coming in from the lancet windows that I could see Jasper's face, and I mouthed the words, *did he forget something?*

Jasper lifted his shoulder in a shrug. On the ground floor, a torch switched on and a beam of light swept back and forth as someone walked down the central aisle. I couldn't see the face of the man who'd entered, but I could tell from the silhouette that he was too slight to be Mr. Sprigg. The man carried something heavy in his left hand, which caused his shoulders to slope. He went directly to the end of the room and stopped at a table under the tall windows.

The beam from the torch cut upward and sliced wildly along the vaulted ceiling as he heaved something onto a table. He turned and went back to the bookshelves, the spotlight of the torch dancing over the rich shades of the carpet. It was only when he aimed the beam on one of the higher shelves that the light reflected off the man's spectacles.

"Mr. Eggers!" I breathed. The glow of the torch illuminated his face as he scanned the spines.

"And he looks fully recovered too," Jasper said, his volume barely above a whisper.

Mr. Eggers took down a heavy book with a worn cover and a spine several inches thick, his movements careful and precise. He cradled it in the crook of his elbow, then walked across the aisle to another bookshelf with his exact, mincing stride. The spotlight of the torch ran along the spines, then he removed another book, this one smaller and fatter.

Mr. Eggers returned to the table at the end of the library. He switched on a reading lamp, and its hooded glow shined on the object he'd hauled onto the table earlier, a large suitcase. He switched off the torch and dropped it into the pocket of the overcoat he wore.

He set the books down reverently at one end of the table, then unfastened the suitcase and flipped it open. He removed a blanket and smoothed it out on the table. Then he took the larger book and put it in the center of the blanket. The desk lamp glinted on pieces of metal at the edge of the cover. They looked like metal clamps. At one time they had probably been attached to leather straps that had fastened the book closed. I leaned forward, but before I could get a better look, Mr. Eggers wrapped the blanket around the book as if swaddling a baby. He stowed the bundle in the suitcase, then removed another piece of thinner fabric and shook it out.

I put my lips beside Jasper's ear. Mr. Eggers was at the distant end of the library. I was sure he wouldn't hear us if we kept our voices low enough. "He's stealing the books! And he looks like he intends to leave the house right away. Maybe this is why Mr. Eggers killed Bankston? The books must be valuable. What do you think? Can you see what he took from the shelves?"

The skin around Jasper's eyes wrinkled as he squinted over the long distance, then he gave a small shake of his head. "Not well enough to know which books he took. They certainly looked aged. Depending on their rarity, they might be quite valuable."

Mr. Eggers had spread the lighter-weight fabric on the table under the light. I recognized the embroidery on the hem. It was a pillowcase with the initials of Holly Hill Lodge stitched into an intricate pattern of holly. He picked up the smaller book and paused, letting it fall open in his hand. Even from a distance I could see the bright colors inside. Rich red, deep cobalt blue, and sparkling gold glowed from one side of the page. A splash of color filled a small square at the top of the facing one. Dense, dark text marched across the rest of that page.

Jasper sucked in a breath. "An illustrated manuscript—the cad!"

I tensed, afraid that Jasper's words had carried, but Mr. Eggers was absorbed in his study of the book. He adjusted his glasses and looked at a few more pages, which were just as vividly colored. He fingered a tear on the edges and gave a grunt of disappointment. "Well, no matter," he said quietly as he closed the book and wrapped it. "You'll still fetch a nice price." He fit the second bundle into the suitcase. His attention was on tucking it into place, and he missed the sound of a dog's claws as they clicked against hardwood.

But I was aware of it and inched forward. Zeus had already trotted across the short uncarpeted stretch between the door and the large rugs that carpeted the library. He held his red ball in his mouth and moved jauntily down the central aisle. I caught my breath. If he came up the stairs, he might give away the fact that Jasper and I were hiding in the gallery. But Zeus didn't veer from his course. He went directly to Mr. Eggers and sat on his haunches inside the circle of light thrown by the lamp. Mr. Eggers snapped the suitcase closed and waved his hand. "Go! Shoo! Go on!"

Zeus popped up, turned in a circle, then sat again, his tail whipping back and forth. Mr. Eggers jerked the suitcase off the table and shook it in the direction of the Jack Russell. Zeus dropped the ball, whisked to the side, then disappeared into the shadows beyond the lamp's spotlight.

Mr. Eggers buttoned his overcoat and switched off the light before picking up the suitcase. I expected him to turn to the main door of the library, but he moved in the opposite direction. He opened one of the glass doors, set the suitcase outside, and closed the door behind him.

Jasper and I darted to the stairs. As we circled down, I said, "You go after him." Jasper, with his longer legs and tall frame, had a better chance of catching Mr. Eggers than I did. "I'll telephone the village constable. They can stop him in Chipping Bascomb."

Jasper dodged through the tables and armchairs. "Unless he has a motor waiting for him outside the gates."

I hadn't thought of that. I was halfway across the library when Jasper threw open the door and let out an exclamation that caused me to reverse. Cold air coursing through the open door engulfed me. I ran onto the terrace.

Jasper was already down the set of shallow steps and at the first level of the terraced gardens. "Skis!" He shouted over as he plowed through the snow after Mr. Eggers. "He had a pair hidden down here next to the base of the stairs."

The tiered gardens dropped in small increments of a step or two, and with the deep blanket of snow, Mr. Eggers was coasting down the gradual decline. His arms were wrapped around the suitcase, which he held clutched to his midsection as he hunched forward.

The grounds sloped away from the knoll where Holly Hill Lodge was situated. Mr. Eggers could glide all the way from the mansion to the gates or even to the village.

As long as he kept his feet underneath him, the skis gave Mr. Eggers an advantage that Jasper wouldn't be able to overcome. He'd never be able to catch him.

Mr. Eggers had heard Jasper's shout. He flicked a look over his shoulder, then crouched lower and picked up speed. The distance between them widened even as I watched, unable to do anything except telephone the constable. I turned back to the house and nearly fell over Zeus, who was prancing back and forth, leaving little paw prints in the snow, eager to participate in our game.

I darted into the library, then stopped when I saw Zeus's red ball. I snatched it up and raced back into the frigid night. Zeus bounced along at my side as if he were on a spring, jumping up in an attempt to get the ball.

"No, Zeus. This throw isn't for you." I rushed to the edge of the terrace. Snow filtered into my shoes and clumped around my ankles. I heaved the ball at Mr. Eggers as he sailed along the surface of the snow.

I'd aimed for his head. The red ball sailed by his left ear, but he flinched, lost his balance, and fell into the snow with a plop. With his skis in a tangle and the heavy suitcase pinning him to the snow, Jasper was on Mr. Eggers before he could right himself.

Zeus had flown down the steps as soon as I released the ball. He plowed through the snow ahead of me, kicking up little plumes as he made his way toward the men.

I reached them as Jasper bent over Mr. Eggers, whose panicked tones carried through the still night. "Don't hit me! Don't hit me! I'll come quietly."

Jasper picked up a ski that had come off Mr. Eggers' foot. "Glad to hear it. Best decision you've made all day.

And no need to worry. I wouldn't bruise my knuckles by connecting them with your face."

Jasper removed the other ski, then hauled Mr. Eggers to his feet and twisted one of his arms behind him. I wasn't sure the last bit was necessary. Mr. Eggers didn't resist when Jasper turned him in the direction of the house. "Well done, Olive," Jasper said. "You'd do a cricket team proud."

"Thank you. I'll gather up the skis and this suitcase and meet you at the house."

"Jolly good," Jasper said to me, then gave Mr. Eggers a nudge. "Off we go."

I followed them with the skis balanced on my shoulder and the suitcase in the other hand.

Zeus bounded up and circled around us the whole way, the red ball gripped in his teeth.

CHAPTER TWENTY-EIGHT

26 DECEMBER 1923

*L*ater that afternoon, Jasper and I were called to Mr. Searsby's study. We sat on one side of his spacious desk while Chief Inspector Donner of Scotland Yard sat on the other.

Jasper and I had handed over several items to Inspector Donner as we told our story. He'd studied each article, then laid it on the desk blotter. By the time we finished, the desktop was covered in an arrangement that consisted of the note Jasper had taken from Bankston's body, the notebook we'd found in Bankston's sitting room, the *New England Home Companion* magazine, and the vial I'd picked up from the snow.

Mr. Eggers' tripod leaned against the wall nearby. Mr. Eggers' suitcase—the one I'd carried back to the house—rested on a table with his camera equipment. The suitcase was splayed open, one side filled with clothing and Mr.

Eggers' toiletry bag. The other side was empty. The two books he'd removed from the library had been unwrapped and the fabric folded and set aside.

The chief inspector seemed to be a quiet, thoughtful man. He looked to be in his mid-forties and had curly brown hair, a tanned complexion, and an easy manner. He'd greeted us at the study door and motioned us to chairs as if we were joining him for tea, then in his soft Scottish burr had said, "Why don't you tell me all about what happened before you chased down Mr. Eggers in the snow."

Jasper and I had alternated as we told our story, and Donner had let us complete our summary without interrupting. Jasper and I had agreed beforehand that we'd reveal all the information about Bankston but keep the details about the crossword puzzle cipher and Mr. Sprigg to ourselves. Miss Ravenna had agreed with us that Bankston's death was a completely separate issue from what had brought Jasper and Miss Ravenna to Holly Hill Lodge.

So far during our interview, Jasper and I had managed to sidestep any reference to codes, ciphers, hidden documents, and treasonous activities. When we finished, Donner's gaze roved over the items on the desktop as he smoothed down his trim mustache then he fixed his attention on us. "Scotland Yard frowns on amateur investigation."

That was a fact that I knew well, but I could tell Donner had only paused in the middle of his thought, so I stayed quiet.

He drummed his fingers on the desktop. "Nothing but trouble, amateurs. Usually, that is. But in this case, it seems it would be best to overlook your interference." He tapped the desk with his knuckle. "Yes. That's best all around. Especially considering Mr. Eggers has admitted to everything. All that you surmised, Miss Belgrave, is correct."

"He admitted to murdering Bankston?" I knew that Mr. Eggers had been taken away to the police station in the village. On the inspector's arrival in Chipping Bascomb, he'd gone straight to the police station. Laura had brought that news when she arrived with my chocolate that morning, but the fact that Eggers had admitted to murder had not reached the Lodge.

"He did indeed," Donner said. "Mr. Eggers collapsed like a sandcastle when the tide comes in."

"I can't say I'm surprised," Jasper said. "Mr. Eggers was submissive and nervous when we returned to the house."

"Naturally. Ambrose Eggers is the sort of man who can make elaborate and detailed plans and create a Goldbergian murder method such as the one at the belvedere with a bit of string and a carefully balanced rock—as long as he doesn't have to come near murder himself."

"He didn't want to get his hands dirty," Jasper said.

"That's right. He's fine with a distant murder. A cerebral exercise. It's only when the reality of murder—or its consequences—comes near those types that they lose their nerve. He went to pieces as soon as I walked in the room. Admitted everything"—Donner waved a hand at the array of evidence on the desk—"from luring Mr. Bankston to the belvedere to dosing himself with ipecac to divert suspicion."

Since the inspector had given us a mild reproof and currently seemed to hold us in good favor, I asked, "And it was because of the books? That was at the root of the whole thing?"

"Apparently." Donner began gathering the items on the desk together. He tapped the magazine. "Because of the article about the farmer in Vermont, Bankston knew Mr. Eggers wasn't here to study snowflakes. Then Bankston saw Mr. Eggers pack several valuable books into a box, tie it up with string, and label it to go to a bookseller in London. Bankston was smart enough to realize that the books were from the Lodge's library. Once Mr. Eggers sent the books off, Bankston recalculated the amount of money he wanted from Mr. Eggers."

Donner tilted his head toward the table at the side of the room with the suitcase and the antique books. "Mr. Eggers had his eye on those two books. He says they're quite valuable. He'd already lined up buyers when Bankston issued his blackmail demand. Mr. Eggers agreed but said he needed a day to get the funds. Mr. Eggers then arranged the trap at the belvedere. Mr. Eggers admitted to stealing books from three other country homes where he had stayed using the guise of a researcher to gain admittance. Of course we'll have to wait for the experts to find out how valuable the two books are."

"Mr. Rimington is quite a connoisseur of first editions," I said. "Perhaps he should have a look."

Donner said, "By all means. Far be it from a humble Scotland Yard inspector to prevent either of you from adding to our case."

Jasper said, "I'm more of a dabbler than anything else." But he went across the room, removed his spectacles from his pocket, and hooked them over his ears. I joined him as he bent over the smaller book. "Exquisite work," he said.

"I'm afraid I'm not able to help with this one. Illustrated manuscripts aren't one of my interests. Lovely to look at, though." He picked up the larger volume with the metal clasps and gently angled the cover open. He perused a few pages, then his back stiffened. He adjusted his glasses and leaned closer. His voice sounded a bit strangled as he said, "Gracious!" He viewed the page from a distance, then leaned in again. "I'd be extremely careful with this one, Inspector."

The inspector had been busy putting away the evidence in a portfolio. He came to stand at Jasper's other shoulder. "Why's that?"

"Because this, my dear sir, this is an early edition—if not a first edition—of *The Canterbury Tales*."

"What?" Inspector Donner reached for the book and laid it on the table, then stepped back.

"And I bet Mr. Searsby didn't even know it was in the library." I explained how the family had bought Holly Hill Lodge, the building and contents.

"Ah, Mr. Eggers thought he'd fallen into a good thing here, didn't he?" Donner smoothed down his mustache again. "A possible early edition of Chaucer. I imagine that would fetch quite a high price. Any idea what it's worth?"

"I've never dealt with anything like this in my personal experience, but I'd imagine it would be worth many thousands of pounds—if not more."

"Thank you, lad. An excellent motive for murder," Donner said in a satisfied way that made his Scottish burr more pronounced.

When Jasper and I left the study, Miss Ravenna was in the hall, seemingly immersed in examining a display of porcelain in a glass-fronted cabinet. However, as soon as she saw we were alone, she came over to us. She was dressed for a drive in the country in a traveling suit and a Tyrolean hat with a little red feather. "Well?"

Jasper gave a shake of his head. "No need for you to speak to the inspector."

"Excellent. Then I won't have to delay my departure. Walk with me to the Oak Hall?"

We fell into step with her as Jasper asked, "You're going for a drive? The roads are passable?"

"Yes, according to the inspector's men, the roads are much improved. The temperature today is positively balmy—in the low fifties—and the main roads are clear. However, I'm not going for a little jaunt. I'm departing Holly Hill Lodge."

"So soon?" I asked.

"Yes. As much as I'd like to stay, I cannot." We entered the Oak Hall, and she picked up a mink coat, which had been tossed over the back of a chair. She drew on her gloves, then went to a mirror to check the angle of her hat. She caught Jasper's eye. "I'll write to you, of course, and let you know how things go."

Jasper said, "I shall look out for your letter."

"Good." As she turned away from the mirror, Mr. Sprigg came into the hall wearing a bowler hat. A woolen greatcoat with a fur collar flared around his legs as he strode along. He saw us and stopped. "You're ready to leave, Miss Ravenna?"

"Whenever you are."

"Amazing! I've never known a woman to be ready to depart on time. This should be a pleasant journey. Let me check on the motor . . ." He doffed his hat and said goodbye to Jasper and me, then went out the main door, leaving it open behind him.

Miss Ravenna said, "Mr. Sprigg has kindly offered to give me a lift."

"To London?" I asked.

"No. I've had an invitation to stay with some friends in Germany. I'll ring in the New Year with them."

Jasper said, "How auspicious that Mr. Sprigg is traveling the same direction."

"Isn't it?" Miss Ravenna said with a brief flash of a secret smile that only Jasper and I saw. "Well . . ." She held out her hand and shook Jasper's hand first, then mine. "I'm so happy I was finally able to get to know you better, Miss Belgrave. Best of luck to you both. I don't know when I'll be back. I may be in Germany for quite some time."

She was gone in a swirl of a woodsy scent to the Rolls-Royce Silver Ghost. Mr. Sprigg's chauffeur was waiting for her with a mink-lined blanket over his arm. Miss Ravenna climbed in beside Mr. Sprigg. The chauffeur tucked the blanket around her legs, then he took his place behind the wheel. Mr. Sprigg gave the signal, and the motor rolled forward. Miss Ravenna waved to us, then turned her attention to Mr. Sprigg as the motor crunched over the gravel that was wet with pools of melting snow.

"Well," I said. "Mr. Sprigg certainly didn't linger, but I suppose he had very little interaction with Mr. Eggers, and he won't be needed at the inquest."

"And Miss Ravenna kept to her room most of the visit, so she wouldn't have any evidence to give either."

"Is she truly going to Germany for a long time?" I

asked as Jasper closed the door. It was Boxing Day, and the Lodge's servants were having their holiday.

We moved back through the Oak Hall and entered the newer section of the house. "I'm sure she'll stay there as long as she's needed," Jasper said.

"But her work—the theater—is here."

"I only know Miss Ravenna a little, but I'd say she's prepared to make whatever sacrifices are needed."

Blix charged out of the library, nearly running into us. "Oh, I'm sorry. I didn't mean to bowl you down. Bad habit of mine, racing along." She relaxed her stance, settling in for a chat. "Quite a night you two had."

"It was," I agreed, but I probably sounded preoccupied because I was fixated on the small red book she held, a *Baedeker's*. She shifted in her grip, exposing the glittering word *Egypt* on the cover. I nudged Jasper's elbow and directed his gaze to the book.

Jasper gave me a slight shake of his head, which I thought he meant as a warning to not say—or do—anything to get the book out of Blix's hands. But we had to do something—that book was hollowed out. Once she opened it, it would cause questions—questions that I knew Jasper didn't want asked. I drew my gaze away from the book and focused on what Blix was saying.

". . . hearing rather incredible tales. I'm sure you have the real story, and I hope you'll tell me all about it later this evening." She uncrossed her arms and waved the book. "At the moment, I have to finalize some details and send a letter off."

"More travel?" I asked, desperately trying to think of a way to convince her that she didn't need to look at the travel guide.

"Yes. Miss Brinkle has a friend who wants to travel to

Egypt soon and doesn't want to go alone. I volunteered to go with her. I'm going to write out a possible itinerary and send it off. I've found that it's best to get these things settled and make plans as soon as possible."

"Perhaps another travel guide would be better . . . ?" I ventured.

"Oh no. *Baedeker's* is the best. Very thorough, and the maps! So detailed. I'll speak to you later tonight?"

We agreed, and she hurried away, her pace quick.

It took a moment for her to go out of earshot, then I spun to Jasper. "The hollowed-out pages!"

"No need to worry. I convinced Mrs. Pickering to let me into Bankston's room this morning. I slipped in before Donner arrived. It was just as you thought. Bankston kept two copies of the books—one a complete book with all the pages intact, the other one with the pages hollowed out. I was able to retrieve the undamaged *Baedeker's* and put it in the library this morning."

"Where is the hollowed-out version?" I asked.

"Tucked away in my suitcase, along with a few books that he used—mostly tomes of sermons. I'm sure he thought most people wouldn't select a volume of sermons for bedtime reading."

"Thank goodness! I thought—"

Jasper pressed my arm as he spoke over me, "Good afternoon, Mrs. Searsby."

Her brows were lowered into a worried frown. "Good morning, Mr. Rimington. Miss Belgrave. I was coming to see how things went with the inspector." She held several Christmas packages, and the two dogs were on either side of her. Zeus zipped up to me and let me rub his ears, then he darted away, circling over to Jasper, who reached down to pet him. Apollo loped along at a slower pace but also came over to greet both of us.

Jasper bent to pat Apollo's back. "Very well."

"Everything is settled to Inspector Donner's satisfaction," I said.

Mrs. Searsby let out a breath. "That is good news."

One of the packages slipped, and she readjusted her grip on them. Jasper asked, "May I help you with those?"

"Actually, this one is for you, Mr. Rimington. I've been playing Father Christmas. It didn't seem appropriate to have a time of present opening, with the situation around Mr. Eggers. I thought it best to distribute them quietly. Go ahead, do open it."

Jasper removed the paper and took out a leather pocketbook. "This is handsome! I'll get a lot of use out of it. Thank you."

Mrs. Searsby nodded to the drawing-room door. "I hope you'll both join us in the drawing room for tea?"

We agreed, and Jasper took some of the packages from her, then opened the door and stepped back so Mrs. Searsby and I could precede him. "I do so appreciate your help," she said as we passed into the room. "Thank you for seeing that the dreadful situation around Bankston's death was cleared up. One would have never thought that such a priggish little man would have the—"

Miss Brinkle joined us, a cocktail in each hand. "—the consumption to do what he did? Neither did I. Scholarly types! Never trust them and their fancy words. Give me plain English any day. It goes to show some people are too smart for their own good. Thank goodness that nice inspector from Scotland Yard is here and will take care of it all."

Mrs. Searsby shot a look at us as she drew a breath. I

was sure she was about to inform her aunt that it was Jasper and I who were responsible for the case against Mr. Eggers being expedited, but before she could say anything, Miss Brinkle handed one of the cocktail glasses to Mrs. Searsby. "Now you must try this, Julia. It's my own concoction. I call it the Holly Jolly. Would you like one, Miss Belgrave? Mr. Rimington?"

"Of course," I said, and Miss Brinkle darted off. Mrs. Searsby took a sip. She pursed her lips together. "It's actually quite good. Although, if I know my aunt, it's very potent. I would advise only having one glass."

Mr. Searsby came over and shook my hand, then Jasper's. "Thank you for your efforts. Well done. Pity that Scotland Yard had to show up at all, but their man seems to be quite the good sort."

Mrs. Searsby said, "He does. I've invited him to come visit in the spring. He's fond of fishing, and we have excellent fly-fishing nearby."

Mr. Searsby chuckled. "Of course you have, Julia."

Francie brought two of Miss Brinkle's cocktails. She handed them to Jasper and me. "Here's your Holly Jolly. Sip with caution."

I sampled the drink. It was a pleasing mixture of sweet and tart flavors.

Francie said, "Now, Mummy and Daddy, you mustn't monopolize Olive and Jasper. I'm simply bursting to tell them the news."

I was a bit taken aback. The last time we'd spoken, Francie's attitude toward Jasper and me had been distinctly cooler.

Something of my surprise must have shown on my face because she motioned for us to follow her. As soon as we were a few paces away from her parents, she said, "I must apologize for my behavior yesterday. I was so upset about Mr. Eggers' accusations about Theo. Daddy's told me what actually happened—that horrid Mr. Eggers was trying to divert suspicion from himself onto Theo. And he nearly succeeded! But in the end, the whole incident has turned out to be quite a good thing."

"It has?" Jasper asked.

"Yes. Let me show you." She linked her arms through ours and steered us toward a table at the far side of the room, where Theo was bent over several large sheets of paper. "I'm a businesswoman now. I've invested in aeroplane cases." Theo stood as we approached, and she spun the page around so we could see it right side up. "It's a lightweight aeroplane case for ladies."

I bent over the drawing as Francie pointed out the features of the case, then she drew another page over it. "And we'll have a vanity case as well."

I was prepared to murmur polite approval, but the designs were well done with little pockets and sections of exactly the type I would use. Instead, I said, "How clever," and meant it.

"Isn't it?" Theo said, his gaze fixed on Francie, who blushed as he went on, "Francie put it all down for us. She's a wizard at drawing and knows exactly how things should be. They will be aeroplane cases designed by a lady, for ladies."

"Blix helped me refine a few points," Francie said as she stacked the papers. "So at least one good thing has come from the whole ghastly incident with Bankston and Mr. Eggers." She patted the sketches.

Theo came around the table and said, "And that's not all that's happened. I had a long discussion with Mr.

Searsby last evening. I put him wise—to everything, the whole story about my—er—creating a company."

"And Daddy was a brick about it. He said he remembered how difficult it was when he first went into business, and he's forgiven Theo for his little fib. Now that it's all cleared up, Theo and I are forming a joint venture. I'll provide the capital and the unique perspective so that we can appeal to a new market, and Theo will handle the actual manufacturing of the aeroplane cases."

"Sounds like an ideal partnership," I said, and Jasper congratulated them both and shook their hands.

We admired the sketches for a bit longer, and I told Francie to send me a brochure and order form once they were up and running.

As Jasper and I strolled over to the fireplace, Jasper asked, "Do you really want one of their cases?"

"Oh yes. The design is innovative. I think they'll be a success, especially with Francie managing the company."

Tommy and Madge came over to us, holding their obligatory holiday cocktails from Miss Brinkle, and asked Jasper and me to play bridge.

"I don't know if that's a good idea," Jasper said. "You two will probably trounce us."

"Nonsense," Madge said, leaning close. "Besides, it's only an excuse to get you off in a corner and talk to you by ourselves."

"In that case . . ." I led the way to a small table away from the others.

Once we were all seated and Jasper was shuffling the cards, Madge said, "The inspector hasn't asked to see Tommy or me."

"Why would he?" I asked. "There's really no need to

speak to you. You had nothing to do with Bankston's death."

Tommy positioned a pencil and notepad on the table. "Then you didn't mention my—um—visit to Bankston's sitting room to the inspector?"

"No, we didn't," I said. "It would just confuse the issue."

Jasper added, "Inspector Donner has his man. He's not interested in anything . . . shall we say, *tangential* to his case against Mr. Eggers."

The tension left Tommy's shoulders. "You hear that, Madge? We're tangential."

She picked up her cards. "I knew Olive would take care of it for us. Now, let's play."

An hour later Jasper pushed his chair back. "Trounced! Completely trounced, as I predicted."

Madge laughed. "I suppose Tommy and I do have an unfair advantage in that we play together all the time."

Tommy picked up his glass. "I think I'll have one more of those Holly Jolly things. Madge?"

She nodded, and they went back to the group around the fire.

Jasper said, "How about a little fresh air?"

I nodded, and we slipped out of one of the glass doors onto the terrace.

I crossed my arms and breathed in the crisp air that carried a hint of woodsmoke.

"Too cold?"

"No. It's refreshing after the stuffiness of the drawing room."

We stood shoulder to shoulder, taking in the view. Much of the snow had melted. The terrace and the gravel paths of the gardens were clear, but a thin layer of white remained on the grass and the landscaping. Stars were sprinkled across the black sky like diamond chips scattered across a velvet tray. "It's like one of your modern paintings—dramatically monochromatic, all white and black. It's lovely."

"This has been a Christmas like no other."

"It has indeed."

We were silent a moment, then Jasper said, "You know all my secrets now."

I braced my hands on the wet, cold stone of the balustrade. "I have a secret of my own to tell you."

"You're a spy! I knew it!"

I laughed with Jasper, then said, "You're mocking me!"

"Never." His voice had turned softer. "I find it incredibly flattering that you thought I was involved in mysterious doings like espionage."

"But you are."

He waved a hand. "Only a minor cog. Just someone they call on when they need a bit of help sorting out the scrambled letters."

"That's still very important work." I drew a deep breath. Now was the time to confess to my snooping, as awkward as it would be. If I held back, it would be harder to tell him later. "You were joking earlier, but I did try to play the part of a spy—a very bad spy. I followed you around London for several days. It was all such a waste of time. I'm embarrassed now to tell you about it. I think I would have given up then, except you made too many trips to the Gloucester Road tube station."

"Noticed that, did you?"

"It was hard to miss."

"Hmm . . . I can't say—"

"Oh, I know you can't. I'm sure you can't tell me

anything about the man with the mustache who was there each time you were. I'm not asking for details."

Jasper chucked. "It appears there needs to be some variety in my—um—meanderings around London in the future."

"I suppose. I won't be following you anymore. I only wanted to find out what you were hiding from me."

"You knew I was hiding something from you?"

"Of course."

"Yes, you would know, wouldn't you?" His tone was half amused, half chiding—of himself, I thought.

"I knew you were keeping something back, and I was determined to find out what it was. I did visit Gigi at Bascomb Hall, but it was mostly a pretext to be in this area and see if I could spy on you here. I rang up when I got your note, and your charlady told me you'd gone to Holly Hill Lodge. The smashup was exactly that—a smashup. There, now you know everything. Are you angry?"

"Angry?" Jasper laughed. "To have a beautiful woman chase after me? Far from it. I do wonder, though, if you'll stick around now that my intriguing aura of mystery has been cleared up."

"Oh, there's no doubt about that. I'm well and truly stuck."

"Excellent news." He leaned sideways, and we kissed. By the time he pulled back, our arms were wrapped around each other. He straightened the lapels of his jacket, and I realized how cold the air was when I wasn't pressed up against him. "Much as I'd rather stay here alone with you, we should go back inside."

"Yes," I said, but neither of us moved to the door.

"What are your plans?" he asked. "Are you leaving Holly Hill Lodge soon?"

I made an effort to surface from my happy haze. "Well, I need to check on my motorcar. As soon as it's repaired, I intend to drive up to Parkview Hall. I hope to make it there by New Year's Eve. Would you like to come with me?"

"I can think of no better way to ring in nineteen twenty-four than with you, Olive."

EPILOGUE

1 JANUARY 1924

*T*he maid positioned the tray in front of me. "Two letters for you this morning, miss. I brought coffee today, as you asked."

"Thank you." I inhaled the rich, dark aroma and took a few sips. I knew after my late night—actually early morning—celebrations I'd need more than my usual cup of chocolate. Jasper had joined our family New Year's Eve party. We'd rung in the year with a lavish meal, then Violet had insisted we roll up the rug in the drawing room and dance. Aunt Caroline and Uncle Leo had joined us for a few dances as had Lucas' parents, who seemed to be lovely people. Gwen said they'd seemed a bit overawed by the setting of Parkview Hall when they first arrived, but last night they looked comfortable and had even taken a few turns on the dance floor.

Gwen and Lucas had circled the room in each other's arms, completely unaware of anyone else. Violet and

James had twirled around the room with an abandon that meant Jasper had to do some fancy footwork so we didn't collide with them. Even Peter had stayed in the drawing room after dinner. He hadn't danced much, saying he'd rather man the gramophone. He looked well and content, if not almost happy. Gwen said he exchanged letters with someone each week, but he wouldn't tell her who he was writing to. Gwen suspected it was a young woman who'd arrived in Nether Woodsmoor a few months ago for a holiday. She'd stayed at the Old Woodsmoor Inn and rambled the countryside with her sketchbook. Peter was a great one for walking, so it wouldn't be surprising if they'd met while she was in the area.

I examined the names on the envelopes on my breakfast tray. I didn't recognize either one. I hadn't expected one to be from Jasper. He'd received a telephone call late yesterday summoning him to see his father today. He'd planned to set off for Haverhill Hall at first light—that had been hours ago—and we'd said our goodbyes last evening. Both letters had the return address of my new flat in London, South Regent Mansions. I'd asked the porter to forward any post to Parkview Hall.

I put down my coffee cup and opened the first letter, which was from someone named Minerva Blythe.

Dear Miss Belgrave,

I'm Minerva and I live directly across the hall from you. Welcome to South Regent Mansions and our world of little controversies and domestic contretemps, which are made of up riveting questions such as: when Miss Dianna Finch-Ellis returns from the theater with friends in tow in the early hours of the morning, will she remember she must make her omelets quietly so as not to awaken her neighbor, Mrs. Attenborough? Will Mr. Popinjay's cat escape the confines of his flat and dart past Miss Bobbin as she's returning with her shopping, setting off a sneezing fit—she's allergic—and causing her to drop her basket of food? The answer to the last question is definitely yes. *It happens at least twice a fortnight.*

I'm sorry I wasn't able to meet you before the holidays. I'm off on a trip myself, but once I return in February I hope you'll come across the hall for a cup of tea. We can discuss whether or not anyone actually lives in 228. It's let to the Darkwaiths, but no one has ever seen them—at least as far as I can discover. And then there's the new electric panel Management installed in the lift a few days ago. (Controversy!) Mrs. Attenborough declared that it was a sign that things at South Regent Mansions were going sadly downhill. *However, I tend to agree with Mr. Culpepper, who says we're all perfectly capable of punching a button and that there's no need for a lift boy. Of course Mr. Culpepper would say that. He's rather fond of gadgets.*

Until February,
Minerva

A SKETCH of a cat racing along a hallway filled the bottom corner of the letter. Behind the cat's furry tail, boxes and tins rained down. The whole thing was done with an economy of strokes, but it captured the hallway exactly and gave the impression of the cat zipping along. I looked forward to meeting Minerva Blythe.

The next envelope was smaller and contained only a short note.

Dear Miss Belgrave,

I would be pleased if you'd join me for tea on either a Tuesday or Thursday afternoon. I look forward to meeting you.

Your neighbor,
Dolores Mallory

I TUCKED the notes back into their envelopes. It seemed life at South Regent Mansions would be quite interesting. I finished my coffee and threw back the bedclothes. I had packing to do. It was time to return to London.

THE END

~

SIGN UP for Sara's updates at SaraRosett.com/signup to get exclusive content and early looks at the books. I'd love to stay in touch.

THE STORY BEHIND THE STORY

*L*ike Blix, I do love a good murder for Christmas. I hope you enjoyed Olive and Jasper's Christmas mystery. Thanks for spending time with them. Christmas is one of my favorite times of the year, and I loved weaving Christmas traditions into the novel along with Jasper's backstory.

One of the questions I get from readers is how much of a book or series do I know when I begin writing. With Olive and Jasper, I knew from the first book of the series that I wanted their relationship to develop slowly. It was the nineteen twenties and, despite the relaxing of standards, a gently bred upper-class girl like Olive wouldn't rush headlong into a romance, but now at six books into the series—and four months in "book time"—I thought it was time for Olive and Jasper to get a little more serious, which of course meant we needed to learn more about Jasper.

Contrary to all the reader emails I've gotten about Jasper, I knew he wasn't a spy—not in the sense that he was an early James Bond. When I began writing the series,

I had a hazy idea that he worked deciphering messages during the war, and the more I learned about Room 40 during my research, the more I was sure it was a perfect job for Jasper. *Agent M: The Lives and Spies of MI5's Maxwell Knight* by Henry Hemming and *The Secret War Between the Wars: MI5 in the 1920s and 1930s* by Kevin Quinlan provided the background I needed for Jasper's war work.

Until I began researching crossword puzzles, I had no idea that they were created in 1913, and that it was a newspaper typesetter who transposed the words "word-cross" and invented the term "crossword." The puzzles were hard to find in England in 1923, which is why I invented a magazine with a crossword left by an American guest. In 1924, a young publisher with the last name of Simon was searching for content for his publishing house and hit on the idea of republishing some crosswords that had been printed in the *New York World* newspaper. The book was a hit, and crosswords soared in popularity both in the US and around the world. Dictionaries and thesauruses became essential items for crossword puzzle aficionados, and libraries complained crossword enthusiasts were wearing out their dictionaries.

The *New England Home Companion* is a fictional magazine, but there was a man who photographed snowflakes with his camera and a microscope. Wilson Alwyn Bentley was a Vermont farmer who figured out how to take photos of the flakes on a black velvet background. He took the first photograph of a single snowflake in 1885. Before his death in 1932, he captured more than 5,000 snowflakes on film. He maintained that no two snowflakes were alike, a statement that some scientists disagreed with at the time. He donated five hundred of his photographs to the Smithsonian Institution. When I read about Bentley, I knew I absolutely had to include a snowflake scientist in my Christmas novel—how could I not?

It was only when I was about halfway through the book that I realized it would work best for the plot if Mr. Eggers was impersonating the famous scientist, which with the slower methods of communication, would be possible in the 1920s.

Some other interesting research tidbits: Olive and Gigi's visit to Harrods was inspired by my own visit there during a research trip to London. The famous department store's food hall still feels very vintage today after its restoration of the Art Deco tile murals. The real-life lawn tennis champion Suzanne Lenglen inspired the character of Madge. Lenglen shocked the world of sport with her aggressive play. I again turned to the memoirs and biographies of the Bright Young Things for inspiration on possible clues and red herrings, such as the secret wedding kept from the family followed by a lavish society wedding.

I thoroughly enjoyed writing about Olive and Jasper's holiday. I look forward to seeing what happens to them in 1924, and I hope you do too! Sign up for my updates at SaraRosett.com/signup to get exclusive content and early looks at the books. I'd love to stay in touch.

ABOUT THE AUTHOR

USA Today bestselling author Sara Rosett writes light-hearted mysteries for readers who enjoy atmospheric settings, fun characters, and puzzling whodunits. She loves reading Golden Age mysteries, watching Jane Austen adaptions, and travel.

She is the author of the High Society Lady Detective historical mystery series as well as three contemporary cozy series: the Murder on Location series, the On the Run series, and the Ellie Avery series. Sara also teaches an online course, How to Outline A Cozy Mystery, and is the author of *How to Write a Series*.

Publishers Weekly called Sara's books "enchanting," "well-executed," and "sparkling." Sara loves to get new stamps in her passport and considers dark chocolate a daily requirement.

Connect with Sara
www.SaraRosett.com

High Society Lady Detective

Murder at Archly Manor

Murder at Blackburn Hall

The Egyptian Antiquities Murder

Murder in Black Tie

An Old Money Murder in Mayfair

Murder on a Midnight Clear

Murder on Location

Death in the English Countryside

Death in an English Cottage

Death in a Stately Home

Death in an Elegant City

Menace at the Christmas Market (novella)

Death in an English Garden

Death at an English Wedding

On the Run

Elusive

Secretive

Deceptive

Suspicious

Devious

Treacherous

Duplicity

Ellie Avery

Moving is Murder

Staying Home is a Killer

Getting Away is Deadly

Magnolias, Moonlight, and Murder

Mint Juleps, Mayhem, and Murder

Mimosas, Mischief, and Murder

Mistletoe, Merriment and Murder

Milkshakes, Mermaids, and Murder

Marriage, Monsters-in-law, and Murder

Mother's Day, Muffins, and Murder